Love
&
Magick

Mystical Stories of Romance

Judith Ashley

Diana McCollum

Sarah Raplee

Windtree Press
PORTLAND, OREGON

Windtree Press
818 SW 3rd Avenue, #221 - 2218
Portland, OR 97204
http://windtreepress.com
email: WindtreePress@windtreepress.com

Publisher's Note: These are works of fiction. Names, characters, places, and incidents are a product of the authors' imaginations. Locales and public names are sometimes used for atmospheric purposes. Any resemblance to actual people, living or dead, or to businesses, companies, events, institutions, or locales is completely coincidental or with the express approval of the business, company.

Book Layout ©2013 **BookDesignTemplates.com**
Book Cover: Karen Duvall
http://duvalldesign.wordpress.com/book-cover-design/
Editor: Kelly Schaub
http://www.the-efa.org/dir/memberinfo.php?mid=834 5

Ordering Information:
Quantity sales. Special discounts are available on quantity purchases by corporations, associations, and others. For details, contact the "Special Sales Department" at the above address.

Love & Magick by Sarah Raplee, Diana McCollum, Judith Ashley 1st ed.
ISBN 9781940064499

Acknowledgements

We would like to thank our amazing cover designer, Karen Duvall, and our awesome editor, Kelly Schaub, for making this book the best it could possibly be.

We would also like to give special recognition to Maggie Lynch from Windtree Press for going above and beyond the call of duty to mentor us throughout the publishing process. We are in your debt. ~Judith, Diana and Sarah

Curse of the Neahkahnie Treasure

by Sarah Raplee

*This story is lovingly dedicated to my mother
who taught me to believe in true love.*

Acknowledgements

I'm greatly indebted to my fellow anthology authors: my talented sister, Diana McCollum, and my gifted friend, Judith Ashley. Thank for your insightful critiques, your hard work and your friendship.

I also wish to thank my family for their limitless patience and unflagging support. I'm eternally grateful to my wonderful Beta readers for their help: Louise Pelzl, Jen Schwickerath, Andrea McDermed and Echo Reams.

You helped to make this story shine.

Father was dead.

Sorrow as strong and bone-chilling as a Pacific gale snatched Samantha Moore's breath from her lungs. A wave of dizziness threatened to overwhelm her. She forced herself to draw another breath, and then another.

In the weeks since her beloved father had been knifed and robbed in broad daylight, she'd discovered grief lies in wait like a panther, ready to pounce and tear one's heart out without warning. Warm tears trailed down cheeks chilled by the damp spring winds of the northern Oregon coast.

Turning away from the bustle of stevedores unloading wagonloads of supplies onto the dock, she pretended to study a huge sailing ship floating at anchor. One swipe of a dirty cotton shirtsleeve removed the evidence of tears, as well as a good deal of sweat and windblown brine from her face. *Boys are not supposed to cry.* She must take her emotions in hand or she would draw attention to herself. The last thing she needed was to be identified as a young woman.

A sunbeam found its way through the clouds to glint off the rippled water of the mighty Columbia River. Gulls soared on the wind. The odors of fish and pitch mixed with the tang of salt water. Astoria, Oregon, was only seven miles from the Pacific Ocean. Here the river stole salt from the sea tides the way Samantha planned to steal food and coin from the tides of people swarming the docks.

She pressed her lips into a grim line. She had never in her life broken the law, but she hadn't eaten since stowing away on a schooner in San Francisco two days ago. The men who had murdered Father had taken his money as well as his life. She was out of funds and alone in a strange land. And she must honor her father's dying wish.

After glancing around the docks to make sure no one paid undo attention to her, she surreptitiously ascertained the safety of her precious, accursed secret cargo. Placing a hand at the small of her back, she arched as if to stretch out a kink. First her backbone poked her palm through the fabric of her shirt. She explored the hard outline of a small spyglass case with her fingers. She had sewn a secret pocket for the brass cylinder into the rear of the baggy drawstring trousers she wore as part of her disguise.

Her mouth twisted into a grimace. Father had died because of the furled map hidden inside the metal cylinder, a map he'd discovered hidden in the false back cover of a hundred-year-old book. He was conducting research for a historical treatise on Spanish exploration in the Americas when he noticed the back cover of *Las Expediciónes del Pirata Don Carlos Moreno* was much thicker than the front cover. So, being Father, he investigated and found the treasure map. Unfortunately, being a man of science, he had dismissed out-of-hand the inscription on the map that stated the pirate had cursed the gold so "no man may take my treasure."

All things considered, Samantha had come to believe the curse was real.

When they'd begun their quest three months ago in March of 1871, Father had seemed invincible. He was uncommonly tall and strong for a professor of history, possessing a quick wit and a shrewd understanding of the dangers they would face. On top of all that, he was an excellent shot. He carried a pistol in a holster concealed under his coat at all times.

And absolutely no one — or so they had thought — knew of their secret plans.

Father had insisted she disguise herself as a boy. He felt she would be less of a target for outlaws. Truth be told, she'd hacked off her long chestnut braid without hesitation, looking forward to shedding society's expectations for proper feminine behavior. They had set off on what had seemed like a grand adventure. Samantha had dreamed of finding buried Spanish gold, dreamed of living in a big house with her very own library, dreamed of Father growing old in comfort.

Her treacherous stomach growled. Now she dreamed of nothing more than a hot meal and a hot bath.

As Father's lifeblood had soaked into a muddy San Francisco street, he had extracted her promise to complete their quest, to secure her future. Her throat tightened. Without family, hers would be a hollow, lonely future. An accursed future.

She swallowed and squared her shoulders. No matter. A promise to her father was a promise she would keep.

Since sunrise, Harrison Jones had sat at the galley table onboard the *Siren* and mulled over the import of his most recent water temperature readings. The sum total of his findings negated the prevailing theory that the recent small drops in the 1870 and '71 Columbia River spring salmon runs were the result of a temperature fluctuation in the California current.

Might the ocean's or the river's salinity levels have changed from that of past years? He was determined to discover what variable in the environment might be to blame. Many assumed there existed an endless supply of fish for the taking. Harrison, a man of science, knew better. That slight decline could well be an omen of impending disaster for the West Coast fisheries.

Frowning, he removed an unlit cigar from his mouth and threw it onto the polished wooden table. The expensive smoke rolled past his half-empty coffee mug and came to a stop against the raised edge of the table. If the weather weren't so bloody cold and rainy, he'd go for a walk and a smoke to work off his frustration. He'd promised Mother he would never light up on board ship.

His dog's deep barks sounded topside, followed by the heavy thud of Merlin landing on the wooden dock.

Harrison shook his head. The hundred-and-fifty-pound Newfoundland had been a birthday gift from his mother. When she'd saddled him with a black puppy as big as a bear cub, she had insisted he keep the animal aboard the *Siren* in case of an accident. Newfoundlands were legendary water rescue dogs.

Humor me, darling, Mother had said. *Otherwise I'll worry myself to death.* Despite being married to an East Coast shipping magnate, Marie LeBlanc Jones did not trust the sea. Knowing this, Harrison had grudgingly agreed.

Merlin's receding barks climbed up half an octave. The hairs on the backs of Harrison's arms lifted. A Newfoundland-sized splash set his heart racing like a dolphin in a bow wave. He took the gangway ladder two rungs at a time.

Topside, he leaned into the cold southerly wind and shielded his eyes from the rain with his hand. Between the fingers of the quay the water's choppy surface was empty. The docks appeared to be equally devoid of life for as far as he could see through slanting sheets of rain. He listened intently for the bark or splash of a sea lion, but heard nothing. The Newfoundland had learned from painful experience why the sleek swimmers were called *lions*. Surely Merlin was too intelligent to tangle with those sharp pinniped teeth again?

A wide, dark head appeared off the tip of the neighboring dock, jaws clamped onto a protrusion from some large object he had salvaged. Harrison's joints loosened. The rascal was fine. He'd only been off scavenging again. The big dog surged forward with each stroke of his webbed feet. What in God's name had his furry thief brought home this time?

The animal's body partially obstructed Harrison's view. Whatever the dog had found was larger than his usual treasures. He'd never heard of a dog collecting a hoard like a crow, but Merlin brought home all sorts of flotsam and jetsam. Boots with holes in the soles, lengths of frayed rope, the occasional stick, bits of net attached to glass fishing floats, a dead cat — he'd dropped the limp, dripping gray-striped body at Harrison's feet and looked up at him as though he had expected his master to bring the creature back to life like the fictional Dr. Frankenstein.

Merlin rounded the end of the dock and Harrison's thoughts momentarily froze. Bouncing in time with the dog's paddling, what looked like a child's hand dangled from one side of the animal's mouth. The big Newfoundland dragged a small body, face up, beside him through the water.

Harrison jerked off his boots while thanking God Mother had been right about the breed's instincts. The boy's mouth and nose stayed mostly above the windblown wavelets.

Sick with the knowledge the lad might already be dead — his skin was ghostly white and his lips were turning blue — Harrison dove into the icy water. His heart pumped like the tail of a salmon swimming up a waterfall. Merlin swam toward the empty berth at the *Siren's* bow. Meeting them halfway to the dock, Harrison locked an arm around the boy's neck and relieved Merlin of his burden.

When they reached the safety of the dock, Harrison slung the lad over his shoulder and clambered up a short ladder. His dog swam to shore and then ran back down the dock to where Harrison had laid the boy on his side on the damp wooden planks.

The boy lay as still as death. Harrison clenched his jaw and smacked the child repeatedly between bony shoulder blades with the heel of his hand. Finally, the lad coughed up a few mouthfuls of water and resumed breathing on his own.

Harrison swiped a hand down his own wet face and straightened. With luck, the worst of the ordeal was over, although sometimes pneumonia would set in after a near drowning.

Merlin stopped washing the lad's face and shook himself with great enthusiasm, showering Harrison and the boy with water. Harrison smiled. It wasn't as if either of them could get any wetter.

"Good boy, Merlin." He stroked the dog's big, damp head. "I must admit you have proved yourself a worthy sailor."

Merlin's long wet tail waved. Harrison could have sworn the dog smiled up at him with an I-told-you-so gleam in his intelligent brown eyes.

Dismissing the fanciful thought, Harrison scooped up the unconscious boy, slung him over one shoulder and carried him up the gentle incline of the gangplank onto his sailboat. The dog thumped onto the wooden deck behind them. Intent on warming them both up and checking the boy for injuries, Harrison descended the gangway ladder into the shelter of the cabin.

Merlin whined his apparent displeasure at being left behind, but remained on deck. Pleasurable warmth filled Harrison's chest. Today the pup had proved to be the hero Mother had promised.

Harrison laid the dripping boy on the cabin's polished floorboards. Weighing no more than ninety pounds soaking wet, he couldn't be more than twelve or thirteen years of age. A cabin boy? He seemed too frail for hard physical labor. Besides, his hands were not calloused enough for a sailor. A runaway, perhaps?

Carefully, Harrison examined the child's head and neck for injuries. Finding nothing serious, he went on to feel the lad's limbs through his clothes for breaks or dislocations. Although thin, they seemed sound enough.

He would find out how the child had landed in the drink, have Doc Brown check him over, give him a hot meal. His stomach tightened. What if he couldn't send the lad home? He couldn't abide the mistreatment of children or animals. However the last thing he needed was to be responsible for a child.

His shoulders twitched. He was a scientist. Every problem had a solution, and he was very good at finding them.

Fussing like an old nursemaid, Merlin whined and huffed at the top of the gangway. His meaning was clear. *Hurry up!*

The dog was right. Dry clothes and a warm bed were needed to counteract the effects of exposure to the cold northern waters. A sick child would be even more problematic.

Harrison began to unbutton the child's shirt. His fingers encountered an unexpected second layer of wet fabric beneath. He raised his eyebrows and quickly finished the task.

Frowning at a layer of tightly-wrapped bandages around the whole of the lad's skinny chest, he glanced at his delicate features. The smudges of dark lashes and purple, bow-shaped lips against porcelain skin sent a disquieting shiver up his spine. What the deuce had happened to this child?

Trying not to jostle the boy's injured chest, Harrison carefully unwound the soggy dressings. When the last layer came off he stared at a pair of dusky-tipped breasts that seemed to swell with relief at being unbound. He blinked. He'd mistaken a young woman for a boy. His logical mind noted no chest wounds were visible. His body reminded him it had been a very long time since he'd looked upon naked breasts.

Drawing a deep breath, he awkwardly — but ever-so-gently — rolled the young woman onto her side to check for back wounds. He no longer expected to find the bandages had a purpose other than to hide her sex, but he hated to leave a task half-done. Clearly visible from behind, the outlines of her ribs indicated a struggle to survive.

Swearing under his breath, he returned her to her back with care. He stood and strode to his clothes cupboard to find a dry shirt with which to cover her. Pausing, he drew in a deep breath and then blew it out in a near-whistle through pursed lips. He circled his neck on his shoulders like a boxer, reminding himself he could handle the situation in the same clinical and logical manner he employed when examining a dolphin carcass on the shore — although he had to admit finding a half-naked woman in his boat was much more disconcerting than finding a dead animal on the beach.

He returned to the woman's side and dressed her, taking care not to touch her cool, pale skin. The last thing he needed was for her to awaken and scream bloody murder. A scandal would mean returning to Boston with his tail between his legs. He pulled the shirt closed and fumbled with the buttons. His fingers felt like clumsy sausages.

What the devil was the matter with him? He was a grown man. This wasn't the first time he'd seen a woman in the nude.

He buttoned the last button on a sigh of relief. Noticing the darkening hem of the shirt, he bit off a curse. Water was wicking into the fabric from her soaked trousers. He had to remove them. He lifted his gaze toward heaven. *Please tell me she's wearing drawers.*

Mother would swoon if she could see him at this moment. An unexpected smile tugged at his lips. He'd love to see the look on her face when he blamed his compromising situation on the dog *she* gave him. His shoulders twitched. *Might as well hang for a sheep as for a lamb.* He fumbled with the drawstring at the woman's waist.

His thoughts sobered. He needed to hurry but take care not to wake the girl. The last thing he needed was to be accused of attacking a woman on his sailboat. His reputation would be ruined. He'd be shunned from scientific circles, unable to pursue the work he loved. After Mother recovered from the shock, refused responsibility and professed extreme disappointment in him, she would insist he follow the dictates of Society and bind himself in a loveless marriage. Not to mention settle down back East and produce a horde of grandchildren.

Harrison's blood ran cold. Father was a traditionalist. He would back her up.

When he lifted her hips to slide her baggy pants down, something heavy and metallic-sounding scraped the floor. What the devil? Did she carry a hidden knife?

Harrison rolled the young woman onto her side again. He had to force his gaze from the feminine curve of her hip. His physical reaction to the half-starved girl was no doubt the result of having abstained from female company for an extended period. He located a smooth, hard object about the size and shape of a man's cock through the fabric at the back of her trousers.

First things first. He averted his eyes, finished removing her trousers and pulled down the shirt. The damp hem nearly reached her knees.

Tearing his gaze from her slender legs, he reached over to tug a scratchy wool blanket off the forward bunk. When he had her wrapped up, he hoisted her in his arms and carried her to the aft bunk, where he pulled back the colorful patchwork quilt and tucked her in, blanket and all.

She whimpered and squirmed like Merlin had when he was a pup. He stroked short, wet bangs off her cool forehead. A halo of dark curls dampened his pillow. He'd never imagined a woman could appear feminine with her hair cut short. When her skin began to pink up and her breathing settled into the rhythm of restful sleep, he moved her wet clothes from the floor to the galley table. The metal cylinder in her secret pocket made a hollow clunk.

He poured himself a shot of whiskey while debating the wisdom of delving into her secrets. Throwing back the shot, he gave up the pretense. *No doubt my curiosity will be the death of me.* That or the chains of chivalry his mother had manacled him with from an early age.

Picking up the woman's soggy trousers by the waist, he unbuttoned her cleverly-designed inner pocket. He'd only just removed what looked like a brass spyglass case when a gun barrel nosed the base of his spine.

"Hand me the cylinder," the woman rasped behind him.

He froze long enough for a string of logic to play itself out in his brain. She could not possibly hold a firearm; he'd just inspected every inch of her and she had no way of knowing his rifle was stowed in the broom closet.

In a lightning-fast move, he reached back with his free hand, grabbed her wrist and swung her about. Ignoring her squeal of dismay and the clank of the brass tube on the galley bench, he heaved her onto the table in front of him in a whirl of flailing arms and bare legs.

Merlin set to barking his head off topside.

He had her trapped on the table in the galley nook, but the sparks in her cloud-gray eyes indicated she wasn't convinced an escape attempt would be futile. His gaze landed on the last of his cigars clamped in the girl's fist. He snatched the ruined smoke from her.

"How dare you rifle my coat pockets?" he growled.

It was imperative that he maintain the upper hand to discourage her from trying to bolt, at least until he knew what kind of trouble she'd gotten herself into. She must have been desperate to disguise herself as a boy. He placed his palms on the table on either side of her ribcage and scowled in what he hoped was a suitably menacing fashion.

Color rose in her cheeks. She raised her chin and lightning flashed in her eyes. "How dare you rifle my person!"

The memory of discovering her *person* was female left him speechless for a moment. "You nearly drowned," he pointed out. "My dog saved you. I had to get you warm and dry immediately."

Beneath the graceful wings of her brows her eyes narrowed. Apparently saving her from death was not a good enough excuse for undressing her. He had an uneasy feeling his mother might agree.

"That doesn't explain why you stole my — my — " She seemed intriguingly at a loss for words. "My inheritance!"

His first reaction was relief she was not going to pursue the issue of her dishabille. Next, it occurred to him she was being cagey about the contents of the brass cylinder. *Intelligent as well as attractive.*

His gaze popped to lips that had gone from pinched and purple to full and soft and pink. Desire rushed through his veins like a storm surge. Even finding the girl dressed as a cabin boy, how had he mistaken her for anything other than a slender, nubile young woman?

A foghorn sounded a warning in the distance, reminding him of the old sailor's superstition that women aboard ship were bad luck. This one certainly could prove problematic if she learned he was heir to a fortune. Most of the women he had encountered back East had been gold diggers interested in his money and social standing. Just because this one thought he was after what little she owned of value — questionable value, at that — didn't mean she was any different than the rest. He had to ensure she didn't learn his secret.

He reached down to locate the brass cylinder where it had fallen onto the galley bench. Standing upright, he proffered it to her. "Is this the item to which you refer?"

Relief and sorrow seemed to meld in her eyes. Moving as stiffly as an old woman, she levered herself into a sitting position. Her face paled.

His chest tightened. She must feel like bloody hell.

She reached out and plucked the mysterious item from his grip. Turning the cylinder in her fingers, she frowned. "I may have misconstrued the situation."

A logical woman? How very refreshing. He offered a cautious nod. "My Newfoundland, Merlin, pulled you to the dock. After you coughed up half of Young's Bay, I carried you aboard to warm you. People die of cold in minutes in these waters, miss."

Swaying, she blinked at him owlishly from her perch on the table. Her lips turned up in a lovely, wistful smile. "My knight in shining armor."

His heart lurched sideways like a ship smacked by a sneaker wave.

Then her eyes lost focus and rolled back. The intriguing metal cylinder slipped from limp fingers and clanked onto the cabin floor.

Harrison caught the fainting girl in his arms. He carried her back to her bunk.

"Wake up, miss," said a deep male voice Samantha tried to ignore. "You need nourishment to get your strength back."

The heavenly smell of a spicy fish stew dragged her back to consciousness. Her stomach was so empty it cramped in response to the delicious odor.

She rolled over and blinked up into eyes the color of summer sky. Intelligent eyes. Kind eyes. The black-bearded stranger who had saved her from drowning stood next to the bunk. He seemed much less intimidating with a smile on his face.

A dog woofed somewhere above them. She glanced toward the ladder that led to the deck. Gray daylight shone through the open hatch. "How long have I been asleep?"

"You fainted an hour ago. Exhaustion must have taken over." His smile faded. "Is that how you ended up in the water? You fainted?"

She shook her muzzy, aching head. "I don't remember." Had she fainted and fallen into the harbor? Or had her ruthless pursuers caught up with her? She pushed up onto her elbows with fear clawing her chest. *Where is Father's map?*

"Your inheritance is on the table," he said. "Dinner will be served shortly." He turned his back, apparently busy cooking on a one-burner alcohol stove.

Her face grew warm. Were her thoughts so easy to read?

She pulled a blanket around her shoulders for modesty's sake and for warmth. Swinging her legs off the side of the bunk, she braced a hand against the wall and wobbled to her feet. A cool plank floor rose and fell slightly beneath her bare feet. She made her way to the galley table. The map cylinder rested against the raised bar that edged the table. Other than the days she'd spent stowed away in the cargo hold of a schooner, she'd never been on a boat before. Who knew they had a clever invention to prevent meals from sliding off tables in rough weather?

She would not insult her rescuer by looking inside the cylinder for the map. This stranger had saved her life and treated her kindly. He wouldn't steal from her.

"Please sit down before you faint again," the man said.

She slid onto the bench.

He crossed the floor in one stride and set a crockery bowl of thick, meaty stew on each side of the table. "Harrison Jones, at your service." He held up a silver soup spoon, his smile asking a question.

She returned the smile and accepted the ornate spoon. "Samantha Moore."

Mr. Jones set another spoon by his bowl. Next he brought two slabs of bread slathered with butter. Sliding onto the bench opposite her, he gestured at the mouth-watering feast in front of her. "Eat, Miss Samantha Moore. Slowly, though, or your empty stomach will rebel. We can get to know each other over coffee."

The dog whined behind her. She peered over her shoulder and spotted the big black animal staring through the open hatch.

"Ignore him," Mr. Jones said. "He gets the leftovers."

As if he understood English perfectly, the dog heaved a dramatic sigh.

"I can't ignore him," Samantha said. "He's a hero." She frowned. "Did you tell me his name?"

"Merlin."

"Merlin deserves a reward." Although her stomach felt like her throat had been cut, she tore her bread in two. Before she could rise to offer one half to the heroic animal, Mr. Jones snatched the bread from her hand and tossed the treat up to Merlin. His jaws snapped and he gulped it down.

"It's not wise to stand below him when he's eating," Mr. Jones said. He quirked an eyebrow at her and gestured toward the hatch.

When she looked up the dog met her gaze. He'd braced his front paws on the top rung of the ladder. His panting mouth was open in a silly dog grin. Streams of drool hung from his jowls. A mucus glob broke off and plopped onto the floor.

She grinned. "Thank you for rescuing me, Merlin. Good boy!"

Merlin wagged his tail.

She turned back to the dog's master. "And thank you, Mr. Jones. I apologize for my suspicious behavior earlier."

"My pleasure," he said. "Please, call me Harrison." He dug into his stew.

Samantha hesitated. Everything considered, it seemed silly to stand on formality. "All right, Harrison."

She forced herself to eat slowly. The last thing she needed was to be sick. The hollow ache in her middle began to ease. The simple act of chewing half a slice of bread taxed her strength so she had to pause to catch her breath. When she felt ready, she spooned stew into her mouth. The rich mixture of salmon, vegetables and broth melted on her tongue. She closed her eyes on a moan of pleasure.

"I had no idea a woman could experience rapture while enjoying my cooking," Harrison said drily.

Samantha's eyes flew open at the inappropriate remark. She swallowed and rushed to explain her unladylike behavior. "I — I haven't eaten in days."

Beneath long, dark lashes, dusky blue eyes full of a different kind of hunger brought heat to her cheeks. Low in her belly, something responded in kind. Perhaps she should have held fast to propriety after all. She wished she had more experience interacting with men. Until a few months ago she'd led a sheltered life.

In an effort to discourage further conversation, she kept her eyes firmly fixed on her bowl and enjoyed her stew in silence.

After they finished eating, Harrison made coffee. He studied a journal of what he called his "notes on the salmon run." She was surprised he hadn't pressed her for information about her strange plight. She peeked at his strong, intelligent features through her lashes. Perhaps she could enlist his aid. Would it be wise to share her story with this kind stranger?

Her heartbeat quickened. She could offer Harrison a cut of the treasure if he would sail her to Nehalem Bay and help her dig up the gold on the mountain labeled *Nicarni* on the Spaniard's map, Neahkahnie on Father's modern map. That is, assuming they could find the Spanish treasure.

Samantha took inventory of the wood-paneled cabin. Every inch of space had a purpose, and though the room had few inches to spare, it was nicer than she would have expected to find on a fishing boat. The wood had a lovely luster and the brass fittings gleamed. There were two bunks instead of hammocks for sleeping.

Still, she didn't think fishermen made a lot of money. A partnership might be good for both of them.

But what about the curse?

Father had scoffed at the idea a pirate's curse recorded on a treasure map could hold any power other than that of suggestion. But Father had been murdered for the map. The murderers might well catch up to her and Harrison before they left the mountain with the gold. Or the ship could sink.

She glanced at the man across from her who had first saved her life and then shown her only kindness. Goosebumps puckered her skin. She couldn't risk it. She didn't want Harrison Jones's death on her conscience. Although her task was daunting, she had to find the treasure on her own — or die trying.

As if sensing her gaze upon him, Harrison looked up and closed his ledger. "Are you feeling well enough to tell me why you were so desperate as to disguise yourself as a cabin boy?"

She nodded, trying to decide how much to tell him.

On deck, Merlin barked a warning. Samantha flinched. The dog continued to growl and bark.

"Stay here," Harrison said. His tone raised the hairs on the back of her neck. He rose and opened a tall cupboard. Pulling a rifle from behind a mop and broom, he took the weapon with up the ladder onto the deck.

At Harrison's command, Merlin quieted.

Samantha searched the small cabin for her clothes, but they were nowhere to be found. She grabbed the map cylinder, dropped her blanket and then hurried halfway up the ladder to hear what was happening. The cold, damp air on her bare legs made her shiver.

Someone hailed the *Siren* from the dock. "We're looking for a boy, works for me," the man said. "Name's Sammy."

Samantha's insides turned to water. That gravelly voice was branded on her brain. It belonged to one of Father's killers. The two men who had murdered her father for the map had finally caught up with her.

She forced herself to breathe. Would Harrison convince them to leave? She had no doubt he would try. She drew comfort from the knowledge she had an ally. Even so she feared this encounter would end badly. Was the curse working against her?

"A couple of boys passed by this morning," Harrison said. "What does he look like?"

"A scrawny-assed kid with curly brown hair, about chest high on a big man like you. He ran off with my poker winnings last night. We followed him down to the docks. He's probably tryin' to buy passage out of Astoria with my money."

"I'll keep an eye out for him. Where you staying, mister?"

A deeper voice spoke. "He's lying, boss. Those are Sammy's clothes hanging on the rail."

Samantha heard the *snick-snack* of rifles cocking and squeezed her eyes shut, her breath coming in short, sharp puffs.

The dog growled. "Merlin, down!" Harrison said.

Her fingers tightened on the brass map cylinder. She could remove the map, give them the cylinder, and hope they didn't notice for a while. But the curse meant that plan was unlikely to be successful. She forced her eyes open. She could not live with herself if Harrison Jones or Merlin died trying to protect her and her inheritance. Surely Father would have understood her decision. She would survive somehow without the gold.

"I got no beef with you or your dog, mister. I only want what's rightfully mine."

The bald-faced lie gave her the strength to do what she had to do. She crept up a few rungs to peek outside.

"Tell you what," Harrison said. "Why don't you send your friend for the sheriff? I'll be more than happy to let him sort it out."

Before things could escalate any further, Samantha climbed until her head and shoulders cleared the hatch. She put her fingers to her teeth and let out a shrill whistle to get their attention. Four pairs of eyes riveted on her. Then she held up the brass cylinder so it gleamed in the sun.

Samantha took a deep breath and called out. "You are welcome to the map. The treasure is cursed. You murdered my father. The curse will avenge his death for me."

She hurled the brass cylinder in a gleaming arc toward the dock by the stern. For a second, time seemed to stand still. Then all hell broke loose.

The two men thundered down the dock toward the *Siren's* stern. Merlin surged over the rail after the map cylinder, landing on the dock with a heavy thump. Forgetting her lack of adequate clothing, Samantha flew to Harrison's side. The brass cylinder clanked and rolled on the dock. Sighting along his rifle barrel, Harrison followed the outlaws' progress down the dock after the treasure map.

The taller man tripped in his haste and fell into the water. His companion snatched up the brass cylinder with his free hand just in time to prevent the tube from dropping over the far edge and falling into the marina the way Samantha had intended. Unfortunately for him, he straightened too late to stop Merlin plowing into him like a steam locomotive.

The man's pistol boomed as they spun heads-over-heels-and-paws into the water. Samantha's heart stuttered. Had the dog been shot?

When Merlin's head broke the surface, a golden tube clamped between his jaws, she let out the breath she'd been holding.

"Hands behind your head," Harrison hollered at the first man to fall into the water. The outlaw had managed to climb up onto the dock. The big man complied, at the same time craning his neck to stare at Samantha's unclothed legs.

"Eyes down," Harrison ordered. His gaze flowed over her body like a caress. The corner of his mouth lifted. "Can't say I blame him, though. You are a sight to behold, Miss Moore."

The desire in his eyes spread warmth throughout her body. Cheeks flaming, she mustered what dignity she could, crossed the gangplank and hurried up the dock to meet Merlin.

Merlin dropped the map cylinder at her feet. The big dog gazed up at her, wagging his wet tail.

"Good boy, Merlin. You are my hero." Holding her shirt-tail down with one hand for modesty's sake, she scratched behind his wet ears. Merlin turned his head toward the water.

The second outlaw's body had surfaced in a pool of red. Half his head had been blown away. Samantha's stomach turned over at the awful sight. Fearing she might lose her first meal in days, averted her gaze. *Another victim of the curse.*

"You on the dock," Harrison called out. "I'm keeping you in my sights. Go pull your friend out of the water before the tide turns."

She watched the big man jump into the clearing water. Grabbing the dead man's arm, he swam to the dock ladder, pulling the body behind him. He flung the corpse over his shoulder and climbed the short ladder, pausing on each rung. Reaching the top, he laid his partner in crime on the dock. He collapsed onto the wooden planks beside the dead man. Streaks of red marred his light-colored shirt.

To avoid looking at the body, Samantha picked up the map case and unscrewed the cap. The rolled yellowed sheet inside was dry. She sighed. Father's last request weighed on her spirit like an anchor. *I have faith in you, Samantha. Have faith in yourself. Do this so I can rest easy, knowing you'll be all right.*

Samantha capped the case. She might never be right again.

Merlin growled.

"Give me the map, *señorita*," a strange man shouted from the shore. She spun about and stared into the black Cyclops eye of a rifle barrel aimed at her middle. A black-haired man with a dapper mustache and a bowler hat sighted down the barrel from the corner of a shed. Her heart thudded against her ribs.

The stranger cocked an eyebrow and glanced over her head in Harrison's direction, as if his words were meant to warn them both. "I do not wish to kill a helpless woman or a loyal animal. Cooperate, and you will not be harmed."

His English was quite good, other than a telltale lisp. *Not a Mexican, then. A Spaniard, like the pirates who buried the gold and drew the map. Interesting.* She was middling fluent in Spanish.

"Walk to me," the Spaniard said. He pinned her with a dark gaze that showed no hint of emotion. It was easy to believe the Spaniard served the map's curse.

"Stay where you are, Samantha!" Harrison said. "His hired gun can take the map to him. There's no need for you to put yourself within his reach."

One side of the Spaniard's mouth lifted in a half-smile. He nodded his acceptance of the arrangement.

A scuffling noise was followed by the approach of heavy footsteps. Samantha squared her shoulders. Merlin growled a warning.

"Merlin, down!" Harrison said. "I have his boss in my sights. He won't try anything."

She wasn't sure if his last words were for her or the dog. Rumbling his displeasure, Merlin lowered his head to his paws. Samantha turned her back on the rifle-wielding Spaniard to grab the dog's collar.

The hired gun eyed the Newfoundland with apparent trepidation. "Yer a good dog," he said in a silly, high-pitched warble. "Ain't you, boy?"

Hackles raised, Merlin stared at the man and grumbled his disagreement.

The outlaw peered past Samantha and raised his voice. "You never said nothin' about no devil dog or no curse. It was bad enough that the professor was armed. We never meant to kill no one. Now Duarte's dead and I'm wanted for murder. I want a raise, Don Moreno. A big one."

Samantha's blood chilled as though she had been touched by a ghost. The Spanish pirate who had buried and cursed the treasure had signed his map El Moreno, The Dark One. She doubted the appearance of another Spaniard named Moreno hunting the treasure was a coincidence. More likely, he was a descendant of the original blackguard. Apparently he had inherited his ancestor's evil, greedy disposition. He'd paid the two ruffians to steal the map.

"I'll raise your pay a hundred dollars," the Spaniard said to his hired man. "And you'll help me give Duarte a decent burial."

"Fair enough," the big man said. He sauntered back to the dead man, picked him up and flung him over his shoulder. Then he strode toward her and Merlin.

She reached over Merlin's head to proffer the map case to the outlaw. Never once taking his eyes off the unfriendly animal, the man took the brass cylinder from her fingers. He continued up the dock at a faster pace. She wrapped her arms around the dog's neck and buried her face in his damp fur. The outlaw's footsteps receded.

The logical course of action was for the Spaniard and his henchman to depart with the map, leaving Samantha and Harrison unharmed. Don Moreno had what he needed to find the treasure. Since she had no proof the Spaniard had her father murdered in San Francisco, the Sheriff had no compelling reason to pursue the outlaws. Killing Samantha or Harrison would give him one.

Besides, Harrison had Moreno in his sights.

Even so, Samantha couldn't stop shaking. If the curse was real and she its target, logic would not protect her. She kept her head down and inhaled the comforting odor of wet dog and dirty salt water for what seemed like hours.

"They've gone," Harrison finally called out.

She lifted her head and pushed to her feet. Her knees wobbled. Her gaze found his. Darkness crept in from the edges of her vision.

"Oh, bother!" she said.

Then everything went black.

Harrison lifted Samantha's head and shoulders from the bunk and poured whiskey into her mouth in hopes of reviving her quickly. He wished he could allow her to rest, however if they were going to beat Don Moreno to the treasure, they must act with due haste. Without the gold she faced a life of poverty and ruin. No wonder she called the map her "inheritance."

Samantha sputtered on the spirits. She shoved away his shot glass and sat up, coughing. "Are you trying to kill me?"

"Quite the contrary. I had to revive you. You fainted again." He handed her his handkerchief and waited for her to wipe her streaming eyes and blow her nose.

"I have a confession to make," Harrison said. "The first time you fainted, I looked in the cylinder. I couldn't protect you if I didn't know what you were up against."

Her eyes were full of a profound sadness that tugged at his heart. "I wanted to tell you about the map and the Spanish gold, but I didn't want to put you in danger. The treasure is cursed."

"So you planned to bolt," he said. Why did the knowledge bother him so much?

"Are you listening to me? The gold is cursed." Her voice dropped to a whisper. *"Any man who seeks my treasure shall die."* At least two men have already died. Don Moreno had my father killed in San Francisco for the map. Now one of his men is dead, too. The curse written on the map is real. It has power."

He forced himself to his feet. "I do not believe in curses, Miss Samantha Moore." He cleared his throat. "Please accept my condolences for the death of your father."

She gave him a little nod.

"Do you have any means of support?" he said.

She shook her head.

"So it is obvious that without that gold, you face a life of poverty and ruin. There is only one acceptable course of action. We are going to Neahkahnie Mountain to find El Moreno's treasure. I'll explain my plan after you dress." Grabbing her dry clothes from the foot of the bunk, he tossed them into her lap.

Her eyes widened. "Knights in shining armor are more valuable than gold. I couldn't live with myself if you died because of me." Tears glistened in her eyes.

His face warmed. No one had ever called him a hero before. And Miss Samantha Moore cared about him, apparently more than she cared about finding the gold.

How very disconcerting.

He scrubbed his face with his hands. In a few weeks' time Samantha had suffered the loss of her father, pursuit by ruthless outlaws, starvation and near-drowning. Her propensity for fainting indicated she was physically fragile. Emotional fragility would explain her belief in the curse. Until she regained her physical and emotional stamina, he must humor her.

He reached into his shirt and pulled out the gold cross he always wore. He doubted Mother firmly believed the talisman would protect him from harm, however she definitely believed in hedging her bets. "This was a gift from my mother," he told Samantha, "to keep me safe in God's hands. Mother had it blessed. If the curse is real, I am safe."

Was that a glimmer of hope in her eyes? He pressed the advantage. "I'm going, with you or without you, Samantha. I have made my decision."

She stared into his eyes for a moment, seeming to read his soul. Then she squared her shoulders. "If we are successful, which seems unlikely given we've lost the map, half the treasure is yours. Now please turn around so I can dress."

He did so, keeping his grin out of sight.

Once she was dressed, he insisted she drink coffee and eat a slice of buttered bread while he laid out his plan. "You must rebuild your strength. Our quest shall be physically taxing."

He waited until she took a bite before proceeding. "I have a fisherman friend who will help us. I've only to ask him. He'll move the *Siren* up Young's River tonight. With luck, Don Moreno will believe we've sailed to Portland, that we've given up."

Samantha swallowed. She raised an eyebrow at him. "You have a different plan?" She raised her coffee mug to her lips.

Harrison cradled his steaming mug in his hands, enjoying the warmth while he shared his ruse. "We will obtain horses from the stable in town. The Indian trail will take us south toward the mountain. Near Seaside, we'll camp with friends of mine."

She eyed him over the rim of her mug. "How do you propose to locate the treasure without the map?"

He couldn't help grinning. "When you fainted I did more than examine the map. I drew a copy for insurance."

Her eyes widened. "How could you?"

He wasn't sure if she was aghast at his presumptuousness or amazed at his accomplishment. He chose to assume he had once again impressed her. "I'm a fair cartographer and quick with a pen. You were out for an hour. It seemed like a good use of my time."

A slow smile brightened her features. "Perhaps you are immune to the curse after all, Harrison Jones."

He grinned. "Indeed."

Although she had napped for a couple of hours that afternoon and eaten a hearty dinner, by the time they reached Elk Creek on horseback around midnight, Samantha could barely keep her eyes open.

Harrison had gone into town while she slept to meet with the friend who would move the *Siren*. Afterwards he had procured horses and purchased a warm coat, boots and oilskin slicker for her to wear on the journey. At the general store he heard Don Moreno had hired a bar pilot to guide his vessel over the famed Columbia River Bar. Many a ship had run aground in the shifting channels and unpredictable currents where the great river met the sea. Harrison assured Samantha they would reach the mountain first the pilot would insist on daylight and a favorable tide before setting out.

On the trail Samantha's good spirits had been quashed by the grueling ride through the forest. They arrived at Elk Creek in darkness. The camp consisted of a small fire surrounded by a few tents. When she dismounted, her legs gave out. She would have fallen if she hadn't grabbed hold of the stirrup and leaned her forehead against her patient mount. The treasure seemed like a mirage in the desert, farther away than ever.

She sensed people moving in the darkness, but no longer had the strength to lift her head. Two men conversed in hushed tones. When she recognized Harrison's approaching footsteps, her heart somehow found the energy to skip a beat.

"My legs are not cooperating," she told him, her voice muffled by horsehide.

"I'll help you to bed." Strong arms lifted her and she clung to his neck. She caught glimpses of men wearing conical hats as Harrison carried her to a small tent.

"Who are these people?" she asked.

Inside, Harrison knelt to lay her on a bedroll. "They are miners. Chinamen. And they are my friends." He pulled off one of her boots.

"How do you know them?" she asked. She was too exhausted to give a hoot about propriety. She offered him her other foot.

He grabbed her boot heel and tugged the footwear off. "Last year I helped Mr. Wang, his two sons, and his nephews out of a tight spot. They'd been claim-jumped in the Cascade Mountains." Harrison set her boots beside the tent wall. "I had sailed to Portland to purchase supplies. The Chinamen had come to the city because Mr. Wang needed a doctor. Unfortunately, the recent fire that burned much of downtown Portland was blamed on a Chinese laundry. A lynch mob targeted the Wangs, even though they had only just arrived in town."

"How awful!" She smiled because Harrison had helped them to escape. He was such a good man. "You helped them the way you're helping me."

"They did nothing wrong. I couldn't let Innocent men hang."

He pulled a blanket over her. Reaching up, she found his bearded jaw by instinct alone. He stilled beneath the stroke of her fingertips. "You have an amazing mind and a huge heart, Harrison Jones."

His head turned. Warm lips pressed a kiss to her palm. She discovered the poets had the truth of things. Even a chaste kiss from the right man could burn a woman's skin like a brand.

When Harrison tucked her hand under the blanket, she folded her fingers into a fist, holding tight to the memory of his kiss. He gave a low whistle. A moment later, Merlin shoved his way inside. The dog's panting filled the small tent.

Harrison ordered the dog to lie down beside her and to stay. "He'll protect you." He paused, seeming to search for words. Her heart beat a little faster. The silence stretched until he finally said only, "Get some rest, Samantha. Tomorrow will be another demanding day. I'll bed down next to the fire."

With that, he left her alone with Merlin and her jumbled emotions. The Newfoundland whined. She threw an arm around the dog's big, furry neck. "I want him to stay as well," she whispered. In unison, they sighed.

The next morning after they'd broken their fast on pemmican and hard tack, Harrison took Samantha aside to speak to her privately. He explained he'd hired the miners, their wagon and their digging tools to help recover and transport the treasure.

"You should have discussed hiring the Chinamen with me first," she hissed. She glanced over her shoulder at the men already packing for the journey.

Harrison felt as though she'd slapped him. She'd wanted him to take charge yesterday. Why in God's name was she angry with him this morning?

"You didn't object to leaving the arrangements to me yesterday, Miss Moore. Without help, we cannot possibly find and transport the gold to a bank before Don Moreno arrives."

She lifted her chin and glared at him. "That's not the point."

His chest tightened. He'd believed she trusted him, trusted his judgment. He narrowed his eyes at her. "Are you worried about losing another cut of the gold? Or do the Chinamen make you uncomfortable?"

Her face paled. She crossed her arms over her chest. "How can you be so obtuse?"

The realization he'd missed the mark eased the tightness in his chest. He took a deep breath, let it out slowly. "This was my logic. We must locate the treasure, dig it up and transport it to a secure place quickly or we'll have a battle with the Spaniard and his men on our hands. The Wangs need the work. What would you have me do?"

"Remember the curse? Who are we to risk five more lives?"

Heaven help him, he'd forgotten about the curse this morning. At least he'd remembered to play along last night when he spoke to the Wangs. "I explained the curse to each of them. Each in turn made his own decision with full knowledge of the risks."

The anger in her eyes shifted to uncertainty.

He pressed her further. "They are not children, Samantha. They are aware of all the risks our endeavor entails and have weighed those against the possible benefits. You are not responsible for their choices, any more than they are responsible for yours."

Her brows formed two perfect arches above the gray pools of her eyes. "They are willing to gamble their lives that the curse is not real?"

He grinned. "Mr. Wang shares my assessment that the odds are in our favor."

The second night they reached a small clearing on Neahkahnie Mountain where the wagon ruts they'd been following disappeared at the edge of the primeval forest. Samantha wanted nothing more than a meal and a good night's sleep. They pitched their tents side-by-side around a fire ring that indicated they were not the first to camp in this spot. One of Mr. Wang's sons soon located a nearby freshwater spring. He refilled their canteens.

Dinner consisted of more hard tack, smoked salmon and an earthy green tea Mr. Wang brewed. Although it tasted nothing like English tea, the hot drink warmed her insides just as well.

They ate in near-silence. Everyone looked as bone-tired as she felt.

"According to the map," Harrison said when they had finished their meal, "we are only a half-mile from the treasure."

The younger Chinamen cheered. Samantha dredged up a smile, but misgivings rumbled in her belly. The closer they had gotten to the gold, the more certain she had become that the curse was not finished with them yet.

The sleeping arrangements were identical to those at the miners' camp. Harrison and two of the young Chinamen laid on bedrolls by the fire. Mr. Wang and his sons would occupy one tent, while Samantha and Merlin would sleep in the other. After the meal she called Merlin and they turned in. Crickets chirping and the faint, rhythmic rumble of breakers crashing against the base of the mountain lulled her into a dream.

A giant, bearded black man dressed in rags entered their encampment. Speaking in lisping Spanish, he ordered their little band to go. His voice boomed like thunder. Hombres! Marchanse!

"He says we must go," she told the others.

Despite the giant looming over them, the men stood their ground, rifles at the ready. "Tell him the treasure does not belong to him or anyone else," Harrison said.

Samantha translated his words.

The black giant scowled. Hombres! Marchanse! *He lunged at one of Mr. Wang's sons and knocked the wiry youth to the ground with one blow from a melon-sized fist. Shots rang out from multiple firearms. Incredibly, they all seemed to miss the target. The big man did not slow down.*

"Run," Harrison shouted. He continued to fire his rifle.

Samantha's feet became cannonballs. She tried to turn away. A big, wet maple leaf fell from the sky and plastered itself to her cheek. Before she managed to take another step the air was thick with falling, blood-red leaves. Despite her efforts to slap them aside, they stuck to her ear, her hair, her nose, threatened to smother her in a warm, damp second skin —

And then Samantha lay in darkness, slapping at a furry head that smelled of dog breath. *Merlin.* The dog had been licking her face with his big, wet tongue. Heart pounding, she shoved him aside and sat up, listening. The crickets had stopped chirping. Horses snorted and stomped from the direction of the wagon they were bedded behind. Something had spooked them.

The small hairs rose on the back of her neck. Had Moreno followed them? Was he even now approaching, intent on murder? Were all the men asleep?

Somewhere nearby, leaves rustled and a twig snapped. Merlin moved to the front of the tent and gave a low whine. Thankful she had remained in disguise in trousers and a shirt, she crawled to the foot of her bedroll to reach the tent flap. She endeavored not to make a sound. The dog waited at her elbow, shouldering his way past her when she lifted the canvas to peer outside. He moved toward Harrison's bedroll without making a sound, like a black ghost outlined against the glow of the fire's embers.

Beyond the fire circle at the edge of the trees she sensed movement. A finger of dully-glowing, dense fog crawled out of the forest, inching its coils along the ground at the height of a man's boot top like a ghostly snake. The noisome odor of decay filled the clearing. Samantha heard the men murmur around the fire circle. Blanket's rustled as they rose.

She released the breath she hadn't realized she'd been holding. They would not be caught unaware.

Instinct told her that something unspeakable would happen if the unnatural mist reached a sleeping man — and that something even worse lurked in the shadows under the ancient trees. The sounds of a stealthy approach through the mist-shrouded woods continued: the swish of leaves, a soft footfall, the skittering of disturbed gravel.

Samantha forced herself to move. She crawled out of the tent her breath coming in frightened gasps she made a great effort to control. *Slow, deep breaths.* She must not faint. Their lives might depend on her warning the Wangs of this eerie attack.

Halfway to their tent the unsettling *snick-snack* of a rifle being cocked brought her up short with her heart in her throat. Peering back over her shoulder, she spotted a rifle barrel silhouetted against the glowing coals. Whether the firearm belonged to Harrison or to one of the Wangs, she could not tell. Nor did it matter. On this side of the fire, the weapon belonged to one of their small party. She swallowed her heart back down into her chest.

Before she could resume crawling, one of the Chinamen near the fire shouted in Chinese. He pointed toward the shadowed forest beyond him. More of the unnatural fog tendrils advanced from the forest. A figure darker than the shadows moved amongst the trees.

She blinked. It must have been a trick of the dim light. How could one shadow be blacker than another?

Then what sounded like a large rock thudded to the ground on the near side of the fire ring. She heard the object bounce and roll. Merlin chased after whatever-it-was, grabbed the thing in his jaws and then took it to Harrison.

The eerie echo of a man's laughter boomed out of the woods and set Samantha's teeth on edge. She scrambled to the near front corner of Mr. Wang's tent. Another projectile smacked the ground on the near side of the fire pit, sending dirt skittering. The thing rolled across the ground, stopping in front of the Wangs' tent flap.

Had Mr. Wang and his sons awakened? She must warn them they were under attack.

Merlin ran over to nose the object. His breath fogged the air. When had the temperature dropped so precipitously?

She glanced at the eerie fog tendrils and gauged they had advanced a couple of feet. Crawling as fast as she could, she reached the tent flap.

Merlin whined and scampered away. Someone muttered inside the Wang's tent.

"Mr. Wang?" she whispered, scratching at the oiled canvas.

From inside the Wangs' tent came the distinctive sound of a rifle being cocked. Samantha's heart skipped a beat. "Don't shoot! It's Miss Moore."

The tent flap lifted, revealing Mr. Wang's long white beard. "Come inside," he said. "You okay?"

"Yes." She banged her hand on something heavy and stifled a cry. Exploring the curved surface with her fingers, she was wracked by a chill that reached into her bones. "This is what hit your tent."

She grabbed Mr. Wang's hand and placed it on the cold metallic surface. He stilled, then uttered what she guessed was a swear word in Chinese. "Old cannonball," he said. "Now come inside."

She'd just gotten into the tent and discovered Mr. Wang's sons were awake when Mr. Wang shouted what sounded like, *"One-jay-boo-foo!"* and opened the tent flap wide. He pointed across the clearing. "Look!"

The young men crowded in close to peer out. They smelled of horse and man-sweat. Their breath fogged the air, making it hard to see past them. Samantha shivered. She edged closer to the opening and spotted what Mr. Wang had seen. A shadow, blacker than the others and at least seven feet tall, loomed at the edge of the trees.

She heard the men outside speaking in low, urgent tones. Harrison swore under his breath. They must have seen the apparition, too. The sight of the giant shadowy figure had lent the scene an otherworldly quality like nothing she'd ever before experienced. All of her short hairs stood on end.

She touched Mr. Wang's shoulder. "Do you have a spare gun?"

"No, miss. So sorry," he said.

Across the clearing, the shadow man spoke. *"Hombres! Marchanse!"*

Samantha lost her breath. His was the ominous voice of the huge black man from her nightmare, and his words were identical. *Men! Go!*

How was that possible?

A guttural moan emanated from the shadow man. *"La maldición, la maldición…Dios mio, quiero la libertad, por favor, por favor…"*

She heard what sounded like the clanking of chains. Samantha gasped. Their attacker was moaning about the curse, begging for freedom —

One of the men by the fire shouted and pointed at a glowing tendril of fog that had nearly reached his feet. Harrison grabbed the pail of water they kept handy next to the fire pit and threw the liquid on the unspeakable thing. Water droplets punched holes through the glowing mist and fell to the ground as ice pellets. The remnants of the damaged section dissipated. All the glowing tentacles withdrew to the shelter of the trees, hissing like angry serpents.

The air was rent by a sickening sound like that of a meat mallet finding its target. One of the Chinamen outside fell back onto the hot coals in the fire ring. He screamed in agony.

"Stay here, miss," Mr. Wang said. He and his sons ran out of the tent to help. By the time they reached the fire pit, Harrison and the other man had already grabbed the burning man's flailing arms and dragged him out of the fire. Mr. Wang grabbed a blanket from one of the bedrolls to smother the orange flames that licked up the man's sides.

The odor of burnt flesh made Samantha retch. She covered her mouth with her hand and swallowed. The injured man made a low keening sound that was somehow worse than his screams.

She peered across the clearing and found the ghost had disappeared from view. She must warn the others of the inhuman nature of their attacker and tell Harrison about the cannonball. Keeping low, she dashed across the open ground to where everyone else huddled around the injured man.

That was when she realized Harrison had also disappeared. Her lungs compressed. "Where is Mr. Jones?"

Mr. Wang gestured toward the nearest trees. Peering along the edge of the forest, she detected movement inside the tree line about twenty yards closer to where the spirit man lurked. Metal glinted dully for a brief moment. Harrison's rifle barrel?

He must have decided to circle around through the woods to get close enough to hit his target in the dark. She must catch up to him in time to warn him their attacker was not a large angry man armed only with stones. Instead, he was a spirit with magical powers cursed to guard the treasure until the pirate returned. No matter that El Moreno was long dead; the apparition and the curse were still very much a reality.

The Wangs were busy moving the injured man to the tent. Samantha made a dash for the forest's edge. Ignoring a warning shout from behind her as well as the quaking of her heart, she worked her way into the dark shadows beneath the ancient trees.

The air was heavy and cold and smelled faintly of cedar. Rough tree bark scratched her palms as she slipped from giant tree to giant tree. She heard something move through the woods behind her and prayed the noxious fog would not find her. When she heard panting and a warm, furry body pressed against her legs, her muscles went weak with relief. She patted Merlin's head and he licked her hand.

She sighed. There was nothing for it but to keep the dog with her and try to catch up to Harrison. Merlin was disinclined to move with stealth, so Samantha gave up trying. Together they sounded like a floundering buffalo. Surely when he heard them Harrison would stop to find out who or what was following him.

Samantha considered what might happen if Harrison confronted the shadow man. Her skin puckered. Harrison would try to shoot the ghost from a short distance, putting himself in harm's way to protect his friends.

She no longer cared about finding the treasure, or even about fulfilling her father's dying wish. The only thing she wanted was for them all to escape with their lives. For that, she would have to find a way to free the ghost from the curse.

For a big man, Harrison could move with great stealth when he so desired. He credited his childhood fascination with Indian lore and spy craft. With their attacker distracted by the events around the campfire, he'd had the opportunity to slip, hopefully unnoticed, into the trees. He must sneak around the clearing to capture or, if necessary, kill the enemy. Shooting a man armed only with stones seemed rather unsportsmanlike. The giant must be one of Don Moreno's men, although Harrison didn't understand why he didn't just shoot them.

Perhaps Don Moreno had instructed him to distract Harrison's party while the Spaniard and the rest of his crew crept closer. His jaw clenched. One more thing to worry about.

Harrison peered back across the dark clearing at the Wangs' tent. Mr. Wang and his nephew were manhandling the injured man through the entry. He scanned the rest of the clearing and determined that Samantha must have taken shelter in a tent. He became aware of the sounds something large moving through the forest behind him. Turning, he peered into the shadows. Might it be Merlin?

Leaves rustled behind him. The hard metal of a gun barrel poked into his spine. Harrison froze, heart racing. He raised his hands high, still grasping his rifle.

"Drop your weapon, *señor*." Moreno's breath warmed the back of his neck.

If he could distract the Spaniard, he might get the drop on him. He spoke softly. "Did you really believe your big man over there would convince us he's a ghost? Scare us off the mountain? Such an amateurish ploy seems beneath you."

Something clunked against the side of the wagon. The horses whinnied. Moreno's gun barrel slid a tiny bit sideways as the man shifted his weight.

"I have come to offer a mutually-beneficial agreement. Your life for a quarter of the gold. A truce between us." Moreno took a step back.

Harrison lowered his rifle and turned to face him. "How do you explain your sudden change of heart?"

"You will think me a fool," Moreno said. "It is the curse."

Harrison's jaw dropped. "You believe in the curse?"

"My ship caught fire and sank. My men drowned. What are the odds it was a coincidence?"

Harrison narrowed his eyes at the Spaniard. Was Samantha right to fear the curse? He tilted his head toward the giant. "If your men are all dead, how do you explain his presence?"

The giant picked that moment to yell at the Chinamen again in Spanish.

Don Moreno kept his pistol aimed at Harrison's chest. "To my family's great shame, the Pirate El Moreno practiced Black Magic. That is why he came to be known as The Dark One. He murdered his slave, Fernando, and bound the man's spirit to the task of guarding the gold from any man who sought to claim it before his master returned."

Moreno had to be lying. There was no such thing as magic. Was there?

"He is telling the truth," Samantha said from behind Harrison. His gut clenched. It must have been her, not Merlin, who'd followed him into the woods. She moved to his side. Merlin followed, panting. "That is why our bullets have no effect on the giant, Harrison. He is a cursed spirit, already dead, chained to this place. He moans about the curse and begs for his freedom. You must believe me!"

Harrison shook his head. "We simply missed our target in the darkness. He is Moreno's man, playing a role."

Moreno laughed without humor. "You men of science are all stubborn fools when faced with things you cannot explain, be it a curse or a woman's beauty."

He flipped his pistol, catching it by the barrel, and turned to Samantha. "I would not have shot you on the dock, señorita," he said. "I was bluffing. I'm no murderer."

He handed her the weapon before facing Harrison once more. "Do you believe me now, señor?"

Harrison watched Samantha check to see if the weapon was loaded. "Moreno has ammunition. If the giant is his man, why surrender to us?"

Merlin growled a warning. The answer struck him like a bolt from the blue. Why, indeed, other than to distract them?

"Cover Moreno," he said, spinning on his heel and raising his rifle to his shoulder. The giant had closed the distance between them to a few yards. Harrison fired.

The giant didn't even flinch. Knowing he could not have missed his mark over such a short distance, he nevertheless emptied his rifle into the man, to no effect.

"Run," Harrison yelled. He lifted his weapon with both hands like a club. Perhaps by some miracle he could delay the specter long enough for Samantha to escape.

Her small figure darted past him directly toward the giant with Merlin on her heels. Harrison lost his breath.

"Reclamo el tesoro y liberarte de la maldición," Samantha shouted. *"No soy un hombre. Soy una mujer!"*

The giant figure halted not three feet from her and the dog, seeming to consider her words.

Harrison was torn between terror for Samantha's safety and admiration for her bravery.

"The *señorita* says she will claim the treasure and free him from the curse," Moreno said. "She is not a man. She is a woman. And what a woman she is! By the saints, she may have found the way to break the curse."

The undisguised admiration in the Spaniard's voice made Harrison wish he'd shot the brigand when he'd had the chance.

Samantha made a sweeping gesture with her arm that included Harrison, Moreno and the Chinamen. *"Estos hombres son mis amigos."*

"The *señorita* says we men are her friends," Moreno continued. "For the record, if she breaks the curse I will be honored to call you both friends."

"Don't count on it," Harrison said.

The fearsome specter dropped to his knees at Samantha's feet with a rattle of chains. Still towering above the girl, the giant bowed his head. *"Gracias a Dios,"* he rumbled. *"Eres el ángel a quien he orado. Quiero descansar en paz."*

Moreno cleared his throat. "He told her she is the angel for whom he has prayed. He wants to rest in peace."

He clapped a hand on Harrison's shoulder. "The stars are fading, my new friend. It promises to be a beautiful day."

Harrison shrugged off Moreno's hand. He shook his head. "I'll be damned."

"No," Moreno said. "However you nearly were." He nodded toward Samantha. "The *señorita* saved us all."

A week later, Samantha again stood on the Astoria docks while stevedores loaded her luggage onto a ship bound for Portland. From there, a train would transport her to the East Coast within the week, although she had no good reason to return. She only knew she could not remain in Oregon.

Dressed once more as a lady, albeit a much wealthier lady than she had been back East, she pretended to study a huge sailing ship that floated at anchor. Tears stung her eyes. She blinked them back. She must take her emotions in hand before Harrison arrived to see her off.

She had done everything possible these past few days to ensure he saw she was an attractive young woman. Seemingly unaffected by her efforts, he had left her in Mr. Wang's company most of the time. In fact, he had gone out of his way to avoid her. Clearly, Harrison Jones did not love her. But she loved him with every beat of her silly, aching heart.

A sunbeam found its way through the clouds to glint off the rippled water. She forced a smile. At least she had a full stomach and was not faced with a moral dilemma. And she had honored her father's dying wish.

When she thought of Father now, she remembered the good times. Completing their grand adventure had given her a measure of peace. She had found the buried Spanish gold, broken the curse and given a wronged man's bones a Christian burial so he could rest in peace. She was wealthy enough to purchase a big house with her very own library and grow old in comfort the way she had dreamed.

Alone.

She pressed her lips together. It seemed the curse had ruined her life after all. Without family, hers would be a hollow, lonely future. An accursed future. A tear trailed down her cheek.

She sniffled and blotted her eyes on her lace handkerchief. Straightening, she squared her shoulders. No matter. She would — she would —

A dog barked nearby.

That's what she would do. She would get a dog. Merlin was certainly good company, and he had loved her from the moment he rescued her, unlike —

Familiar footsteps approached from behind. She fought the urge to turn while she blinked back tears. Soon Harrison Jones would be nothing more than a memory. Saying goodbye was going to break her heart.

Big hands grasped her shoulders. "Marry me, Samantha," Harrison said into her ear. He spun her around and gave her a tiny shake. "Please. I know I shouldn't ask."

Samantha could not believe what she was hearing. He had ignored her for days and now he wanted to marry her? She took in his haggard, unshaven face and her heart melted. None of that mattered. The tears overflowed.

"Yes," she said softly.

He seemed not to hear her. "I tried to convince myself I could be happy with you on my estate back East," he said, speaking over her. "We'd produce a horde of grandchildren for Mother to spoil." One corner of his mouth lifted in a half-smile. "Not that I wouldn't enjoy making babes, however the truth of the matter is I love my work nearly as much as I love you."

Harrison released her and began to pace. "I know the situation is terribly unfair to you, but there it is."

Had she heard him correctly? "You love me?"

He shook his head. She felt Fate close the book on the joyous future she'd momentarily envisioned. She must have misunderstood him. Her heart twisted. Still, if they married perhaps in time he would come to love her. Love had come to other couples after marriage. Perhaps she could love enough for them both.

Harrison had continued to speak. Samantha's dazed brain only caught the end of his message. " — leave you behind." He paused as if awaiting her response to a question.

"No!" They must remain together. Otherwise she would never have the chance to win his love.

He dropped his gaze to the tips of his boots where it remained for what felt like an eternity. With a great effort, he cleared his throat. "I see." He swallowed, looking anywhere but at Samantha.

"Harrison, look at me." When he complied, his eyes were the dark blue of the sky at sundown — or at dawn. "You may not love me yet the way I love you, however if we are to marry, I must insist we stay together to give love a chance to grow."

He blinked.

"I love you, Harrison. Of course I will marry you, but I am curious. Why do you want to marry me, if not for love? You no longer need money." Whatever the reason, she would marry him anyway. However she needed to understand his motives and expectations.

He surprised her by pulling her into his arms and squeezing her as if he would never let her go. She found comfort in the masculine scents of shaving cream and leather and tobacco. He set her away a little. "It was never about the money, Samantha. I was born with a silver spoon in my mouth."

Her gaze lingered on the aforesaid mouth until the import of his words reached her brain. She frowned up at him. "You're not a fisherman?"

Grinning, he shook his head. "You haven't heard half of what I've said, have you?"

He lowered his head and kissed her on the lips, and nothing else mattered. She rose up on tiptoes, wrapped her arms around his neck and poured all her love into that kiss. He groaned and his arms tightened around her. A plethora of pleasant sensations coursed through her body.

When Harrison broke the kiss, he was breathing like a runner at the finish line. So was she. Surely he'd enjoyed the experience?

His smile was reassuring. He traced her sensitive lower lip with the ball of his thumb. The delicious sensation sparked a response deep in her belly. "I love you, Samantha Moore."

"Say it again, please," she said. "Enunciate clearly this time."

"I. Love. You."

How had she missed that?

Harrison laughed. "I have loved you ever since you had the unmitigated gall to hold me up on my own boat with my own cigar. That is why I want you to marry me."

She pretended to frown. "Because I held you up with a cigar?" He lifted her chin. Would he kiss her again?

"No," he said, leaning so close his breath warmed her lips. "I want to marry you because I will love you until the end of time."

Against all odds, the second kiss was even more thrilling than the first. To her disappointment, Harrison again broke it off. "As for our second misunderstanding," he said, "I take full responsibility. I led you to believe I was a fisherman when in fact I am a gentleman scientist. My father owns Fairweather Shipping and my mother was the belle of New Orleans society until she eloped with a Yankee."

"Why did you mislead me?"

"I feared you might break my heart. I've had a number of unfortunate encounters with female gold diggers."

And there I was, literally hunting for gold. No wonder he had been cautious. "I forgive you."

Love seemed to light up his eyes. "Did I mention that I find you a most refreshing woman?"

She wiggled her eyebrows at him. He laughed and kissed her on the tip of her nose.

His expression grew serious. "My current research will benefit Oregon's fisheries. Unfortunately this research that I love, although not as much as I love you, requires me to spend a lot of time at sea. I know it's unfair to ask you to cope with the isolation of life aboard the *Siren*. However leaving you ashore would be unthinkable."

The thought of helping him in his scientific research the way she had Father warmed her heart. She had no doubt she belonged at his side.

Harrison drew a deep breath. "Forgive me. Asking you to marry me is the most selfish thing I have ever done. But living without you would be like living without the very air we breathe. Impossible."

The expression in his eyes made her heart take flight. "You missed half of what I said as well, my love," she told him. "Immediately after you said *marry me*, I said *yes*."

THE END

ENCHANTED PROTECTOR

by Sarah Raplee

This story is dedicated to my husband, who is the inspiration for all my heroes.

Acknowledgements

I'm greatly indebted to my fellow anthology authors: my talented sister, Diana McCollum, and my gifted friend, Judith Ashley. Thank for your insightful critiques, your hard work and your friendship.

I also wish to thank my family for their patience and unflagging support, and my awesome Beta readers for helping me to make this story shine: Lily McDermed, Louise Pelzl, Jen Schwickerath, Andrea McDermed and Echo Reams.

The frigid, rising wind promised snow, but Ruby gauged she had time to complete her dreaded task before the storm reached Helmsdale. A flash of red made her pause to watch a male redbird and his drab brown mate peck for seeds on the hard ground. Mated for life, the pair seemed ever cheerful, even in the depths of winter. Today they failed to brighten her spirits.

Squaring her shoulders, Ruby set off at a determined pace from her tiny farm cottage down the short dirt path to the village proper. With each step, a thumbscrew pinched her heart tighter. Having to sell Father's ring was a hard blow. He had been so proud of the ring, a gift from the Dragon Horn King himself for service to the crown, and a symbol of the king's protection. Ruby sighed. Not even the king had been able to protect Father from the Wasting Sickness.

A gust of wind cut through Ruby's patchwork cloak like an icy sword. She pulled her knit shawl tight around her ears and draped one end across her face, leaving only a tiny slit for peering out. The warm wool made her chin itch. Tucking her left hand into her apron pocket, she fisted her right in the fabric of her cloak to protect her bare fingers. The last thing she needed was chilblains on her one good hand.

The weight of Father's ring in her other pocket lay heavy on Ruby's spirit. Since he had been taken from them two years past, her small sister, Star, had found comfort in holding his golden ring whenever she missed him. Going to the goldsmith to sell the talisman was a betrayal of both her little sister and her beloved father. However, as the mistress of the family, she had no choice.

Being orphans, the girls had barely managed to survive on Father's soldier's pension and his meager savings. Then nine months ago, the king had been forced to eliminate soldier's pensions after blackguards had robbed the Royal Treasury. It was rumored Prince Rolf was somehow involved in the theft, as the king's wastrel son had disappeared afterward. The thieves had never been caught. With the country bankrupt, the Dragon Horn King had been left with no choice but to cut spending and raise taxes many could ill afford to pay.

Now Father's savings had run out. Starvation lurked like a wolf at their door.

Ruby paused at the top of a rise to catch her breath. Her fingers and toes stung from the cold. Through a copse of bare alders, she caught a glimpse of Helmsdale below. She drew a deep breath and trudged onward.

Not far now.

If only she could earn enough money to support herself and Star by reading letters to her neighbors. Most people in the area were illiterate farmers. Father, a former scribe, had taught Ruby to read. But missives from outside the village were few and far between, and the stone hard truth was that, for other work, no one wanted to hire a girl with one good hand — no matter how dependable and hard-working she was.

Ruby had gotten herself and Star through the fall selling root vegetables from the garden and mushrooms they gathered in the forest, as well as milk and cheese. With winter at the door, she had run out of options. She must sell Father's ring, even if doing so broke Star's heart.

Having reached the bottom of the hill, Ruby entered the walled village though an arched gate. Two-story, thatched buildings built during more prosperous times lined the cobbled street. The heavenly smell of meat pies made her mouth water. Storm coming or no, Third Day was market day on the village square.

Ruby's stomach ached with hunger as badly as her toes in Father's old boots ached from the cold. Of late she had been giving Star portions of her meals. The child was in the midst of a growing spurt and needed nourishment more than she.

When Ruby passed into the market near the pasty stall, she averted her eyes for fear her hunger would drive her to snatch a meat pie and dash away. Lowering clouds spit ice pellets that stung her eyes. Dry grass crunched underfoot as she made her way around the village green to the tavern at the corner of Potter's Alley. A wooden sign above the doorway sported a red, horned dragon breathing fire.

Ruby turned into the cobbled alley and a strong headwind. The goldsmith's shop awaited two doors down behind an unmarked door. The smith was a wise man who placed his trust in word of mouth. It would be foolish to make his shop a target for thieves.

Ruby pushed into the wind with her head down. She had seen no one in the alley, but a moment later her feet tangled with some small creature that screeched in outrage. She windmilled her arms and then fell on her bum. The unforgiving stones jolted her spine to the top of her head. For a moment, her eyes would not focus.

After a few seconds, a wizened little face with a white beard and bushy white brows floated into view. A frown of apparent concern scrunched the little man's face. "So sorry, miss," he said. "My fault entirely. Let me help you up."

Hands the size of a small child's tugged on her arm with surprising strength. Ruby wobbled to her feet and blinked down at the small Fae man. He straightened her apron and brushed dirt off her skirt. Her head began to throb and her heart began to pound.

He finished and peered up at her. "That's better, wot? Right as rain you are, I trust."

Ruby drew her brows together. The word *trust* did not belong in the mouth of a gnome. Or was he an elf? Both were small in stature, with pointy ears and an odd way of speaking. Ruby had trouble telling the two Fae races apart. It was said that elves were merely mischievous, whereas gnomes would steal the shirt off a man's back while he drowned.

The little man smiled, and it became obvious what was what and who was who. Whilst an elf's teeth were small to match the size of his mouth, in shape and number they appeared human. This gnome had what looked like a hundred narrow, pointed teeth.

Ruby lost her voice. The enduring memory of Mam sewing up her mangled left hand when she was small caused her to sway in the face of all those needle-like teeth.

The gnome lifted his face skyward as if he were a dog scenting the air. His smoke-colored eyes widened and then he twirled in place, scanning the square. He backed away from Ruby. "We must be off, with snow coming, wot? Carry on, miss. Carry on."

He scurried down the alley, mumbling to himself as he disappeared into the shadows. Lightning cracked overhead and snowflakes poured like eerie white rain from the storm-tossed clouds.

Prince Rolf of Helmsgaard, heir to the Dragon Horn Throne, lowered his muzzle to gnome height and followed Thumble-no-skin's sour scent into the village. The strong odors of unwashed humans, wood smoke and cooking meat layered with the Fae creature's scent trail. Not to mention the smell of sewage, which he luckily minded less than he had when he had been fully human. Since the devious little gnome had cast the enchantment that had transformed him into a wolf, Rolf had learned to use his heightened senses to his advantage.

The gnome's scent trail was fresh, the sour odor of his evil magic strong. Rolf's heart lifted. Thumble-no-skin could only have arrived recently or Rolf would have caught his scent sooner. Perhaps he could finally catch the Fae man without a bolt-hole nearby.

He trotted down the cobblestoned street the villagers had deserted in favor of the market. The bustle of the crowd reached his ears. He caught the sweet feminine perfume of a maiden, as if the girl had passed this way only minutes before him. One of his frequent waves of melancholy threatened. Lying with women was one more thing denied him since the treacherous gnome and his gang of thieves had played him for a fool.

He picked up a trace of tangy gold attached to the maiden's scent and awakened from his reverie. The hackles on the back of the prince's furred neck lifted. The girl's small treasure would be as irresistible to the gnome as a shiny buckle to a crow. Few of the villagers possessed so much a farthing.

Hot on the scents, Rolf darted into the crowded market. A woman screamed and scooped up her small child when he passed her stall. The fact that the market was crowded worked in his favor. He was gone from the frightened woman's sight in the blink of an eye. Nevertheless, he must remain vigilant. He had no desire to end up as a rug in some peasant's hovel.

This was a rare opportunity for the prince to ambush his gnome nemesis. The spell that had transformed him into an animal would only be broken when the gnome who had cast the enchantment died.

A growl rumbled in his chest. Rolf bared his teeth. This time he would triumph.

Making his way around the market, he darted beneath carts and dodged behind stalls. Soon the sting of spirits in his nostrils told him he neared the tavern. The maiden's feminine scent grew stronger, layered beneath the alcohol and above the golden tang of whatever she carried.

Gold-struck, Thumble-no-skin would be completely focused on the girl and unaware of Rolf's presence until wolf jaws crushed his throat. There would be no chance for escape.

Drool flooded Rolf's mouth. Memories of the satisfying crunch of bones in his jaws and the warm, coppery taste of fresh blood flooded his mind. His stomach simultaneously tried to growl and heave, resulting in him emitting a noise disconcertingly close to the honk of a goose.

He must never forget he was a man, not a wolf! Despite the humans all around him, the prince halted and shook himself as if he could shake out the animal urges and instincts that remained in the body of the wolf. He prayed he would never lose control of the bloodlust that at times threatened to overwhelm him. Humans were not his prey, nor were the Fae folk.

Killing Thumble-no-skin was a necessary evil. Eating the gnome was unthinkable.

The mouth-watering scent of the girl tangled with the metallic scents of a smithy and the sour odor of Fae magic. An uneasy yawn stretched his jaws wide. What if the sharp-toothed gnome hurt the innocent maid before Rolf had the chance to kill him?

He broke into a reckless, ground-gobbling lope, ignoring the screams and shouts that marked his passage. The prince had watched from the shadows as his people struggled against poverty and famine over the nine months since Thumble-no-skin had stolen the king's Treasury. The knowledge that he was partly responsible for their anguish made his heart ache. He couldn't let another innocent suffer at the hands of the gnome.

The scent trail led him around the corner into an alley where cobblestones slowed him to a cautious trot. The smithy would be too well guarded for the gnome to gain entry, but Thumble-no-skin no doubt waited nearby. Rolf raised his nose to scan the alley's scents even. He peered into the shadows. Gnomes avoided face-to-face fights whenever possible, preferring stealth to achieve their goals. If Thumble-no-skin did not have a secret tunnel near the smithy in which to disappear in a flash, he would draw his poison-tipped knife for defense.

Even a wolf might be bested by poison.

The only person in the alley was a cloaked woman who kept her head down against the wind and plodded along well to the left of the sewage-filled gutter that ran down the center. This was no doubt his sweet-scented maiden.

Rolf peered past her down the alley. He saw no place for Thumble-no-skin to hide. He raised his head to scan the walls and the edges of the roof two stories above, and again found no sign of the gnome other than his fading scent.

The maiden knocked on the third door down, turning her head toward him as if to shelter her eyes from the wind. Her shawl hid most of the girl's face, but he had no trouble hearing her scream when she caught sight of the wolf following her.

Whilst continuing to cry out for help, she alternately pounded the smith's door with one fist and tried to force the portal open, all to no avail. The scent of her terror pierced his all-too-human heart.

With the alarm raised and the gnome gone, he must make his escape. To ease the maiden's fear, he leapt over the gutter and bounded past her on the far side of the street. From behind came the deep notes of men's agitated voices and the girl's heart-wrenching sobs.

As he left the village behind, Rolf's melancholy returned. The maiden would be safe from Thumble-no-skin — and safe from the perceived threat of the wolf who was in fact the missing Prince Rolf of Helmsgaard, heir to the Dragon Horn Throne.

Rolf searched the fields and forests around the village for hours. He found no trace of Thumble-no-skin. The exercise and his weather-resistant fur coat kept him comfortable in the inclement weather. At dusk he caught a stoat for his dinner, savaging the animal more ferociously than was strictly necessary when one considered the first snap of his wolf jaws had broken its neck. The warm, bloody meat tasted delicious, however his lack of control added to his melancholy.

Did the wolf in him grow stronger? Would his human soul eventually lose control and disappear? Worse yet, would his spirit be driven out of this body and be doomed to wander the world as a specter?

Not even the Wise Woman of Mountainfall knew the answers to these questions. Some things remained beyond the ken of mere mortals.

With meticulous care, he licked himself as clean as one of his father's courtiers. *Human is as human does.* At least he hoped so.

His next breath drew in the scents of distant wood smoke and porridge. The comforting scents filled his head with thoughts of hearth and home. Needing the company of his own kind, he set off to follow the scent to ground. Mayhap human contact would help him to remain a man on the inside.

Rolf's wolf nose led him to a small cottage. The smell of cow dung layered with the sharp odors of mouse urine and feline musk emanated from a weathered barn that tilted to one side like a drunkard. The ammonia-laced scent of poultry droppings — Helms chuks, if he wasn't mistaken, barn-cat-sized local birds domesticated for their eggs — added to the scent cloud that surrounded the leaning building.

However it was the scent of the maiden from the alley in Helmsdale that inspired him to find a hiding place from which to observe the occupants' comings and goings. He smelled the recent trace of only one other person, a female child.

Rolf hid himself beneath an evergreen. He lay on a bed of aromatic pine needles with his head resting on his front paws. His breath blew away a snowflake falling past his muzzle. How he longed for the comfort of a home fire and a loving greeting — things he had held in disdain prior to being enchanted. Father had always told him that suffering builds character. If having character meant knowing what is important in life, then Father was right. In nine short months he had gained a lifetime of wisdom.

He turned his morose thoughts to his pursuit of the gnome. Like many afternoons before, this one had ended in disappointment. How many cursed bolt-holes could one small Fae man dig? Thumble-no-skin had disappeared once more.

At least the gnome had not molested the girl in the alley. Something about the maiden triggered his protective instincts.

His sensitive ears pricked at the murmur of a woman's voice inside the cabin. The high-pitched notes of a child's protest followed. Drawn to listen to their human conversation, Rolf stealthily crossed the open ground to sit in front of the wood-plank door.

He scented the maiden from the alleyway. His pulse began to race. He strained to hear her response to the child.

"I wish it had not been necessary to go to the smithy, but we must eat." Her patient tones were as sweet as her scent. "We are truly blessed that God moved the smith to help us, Star. I thought all was lost when I discovered the gnome had stolen our father's ring from my pocket."

Rolf's lips drew back. He managed to suppress a snarl. He had believed the gnome left the maiden unscathed. Thumble-no-skin had even more to answer for now. Not even the King's Treasury itself had been enough to satisfy his lust for gold.

The young woman continued. "I saved the best news for last, little sister. The smith gave me a reference for employment as a scribe for the tax collector. We shall have a steady income once more."

"But Ruby..."

The tension that had settled in Rolf's chest when he'd frightened the maiden eased a little. *Ruby. Her name is Ruby.*

"What shall I do without you all day, Ruby?" the little girl said, sounding lost.

Rolf controlled a strong urge to whine in sympathy. The child sounded much too young to be left on her own all day.

"You'll keep busy," Ruby said in a voice as bright as a sunny day. "You're a big girl of nearly eight years now, Star. Even in winter, there are eggs to gather, a cow and chuks to feed, stalls to muck out..." Her voice trailed off. Had she realized how much work she was piling on her sister's small shoulders?

Rolf heard her begin to pace.

"No, *I'll* milk the cow and muck out her stall. And I'll teach you to make farmer's cheese from the extra milk. Why, I wager you'll have supper waiting for me most nights as well. You do love to cook." Ruby's voice wavered slightly.

"I already know how to bake bread," the little girl ventured.

"Yes!" Ruby said, apparently regaining her confidence. "And you have your embroidery to keep your hands busy."

"But I will be lonely without you, sister." Star's tone held a plaintive note.

Fabric swished on the far side of the door. Rolf heard what sounded like the scrape of a chair leg. Mayhap Ruby had taken the child onto her lap?

"I know, Star," Ruby said softly. "I will miss you as well, my sweet."

Other than the crackle of the fire and the sighing of the wind, all was quiet for the space of a drumbeat.

"I have a wonderful idea," Ruby said. "You may have one of Maizy's kittens for company — the orange tabby from last spring's litter. He's quite large, but very docile. Mind, he must sleep in the barn at night."

"Really?" Star said breathlessly. "When I asked you before, you told me God created cats to keep the rats and mice out of the barn."

"That's true, but a cat can be a good friend when a person must spend a lot of time alone. Remember when Goodwife Rondsen was sick and we cared for her? She told us her tabby was fine company. Besides, cats do most of their hunting at night."

Silence prevailed. Perhaps Star was considering the coming changes to her life. After a few minutes, he heard the little girl yawn.

"I should like a kitten for a friend," Star said. "I would rather things be like before, when we had the soldier's pension for Father's service to the king. I would much rather you stayed home with me."

Guilt twisted Rolf's stomach. The king must have been forced to cut the Soldier's Pensions, even those meant for widows and orphans. Ruby and Star were in dire straits because of him. It was his fault the Treasury had been sacked.

"If wishes were horses, beggars would ride," Ruby said, quoting an old saying. "Now, time for bed."

Rolf skulked back to his hiding place under the pine tree. A bitter taste filled his mouth. His arrogance had led to the maids' suffering — and to that of countless others. He had believed he could maintain the upper hand with elves and gnomes, however he had been grievously mistaken. Playing at cards with tricksters and thieves had been a fool's game.

The Fae had plied him with wine and let him win until his recklessness had been his undoing. Thumble-no-skin cleaned him out and then accepted his promissory notes until, even deep in his cups, Rolf finally recognized his own foolishness. The gnome had played him. There was nothing for it but to confess his peccadillo to his father and ask to be bailed out — or so he had believed until the gnome offered to cancel his debt. The price? Naught but a peek at the king's Treasury.

In his drunken state, Prince Rolf saw no harm in granting the little man's wish if doing so would mean he did not have to further disappoint his father. The Treasury was well-guarded and the gnome diminutive. What harm would possibly come of it?

And for a few months afterward, no harm had occurred.

Rolf had stopped his reckless drinking. He had never again gambled except when fully sober. He had allowed himself to lose only what he could afford. In spite of his efforts to reform, someone had bashed him over the head and he'd awakened in Thumble-no-skin's presence in the body of a wolf.

You, Wolf Prince, are the ace up my sleeve, Thumble-no-skin had told Rolf when he awoke, weak and confused. *If something goes wrong with my plan to rob the king's Treasury, to which you so kindly allowed me entry, I will regain my freedom by offering to lead him to you.*

The thieves had picked the king's Treasury clean and gotten away without discovery. Although his father stood up for his good name, most of the citizens of Helmsgaard believed missing Prince Rolf was to blame for the robbery. He'd always been a wastrel. Why else had he disappeared?

Rolf heaved a sigh. In a way, they were right.

Ruby and Star's plight burned his conscience like a hot poker. Nine months ago his attitude had been that of a spoiled child. The hardships he'd since endured had forged him into a man, albeit a man in the body of a wolf. His own sorry fate paled in comparison to the suffering he had brought upon his people and the vulnerable position in which he'd left the kingdom. It was high time he accepted the responsibility to which he had been born. He must not only regain his human form, but also find out where Thumble-no-skin had buried his hoard. In this way, he would clear his good name as Prince of Helmsgaard and, more importantly, put things right for his people.

Perhaps clues to gnomes' hoarding habits lay amongst the meager information he had gleaned from the one person who had recognized him since his enchantment, the Wise Woman of Mountainfall. The kindly crone had Second Sight and perceived his true nature. She had diligently searched for answers to his plight in her ancient Book of Magick.

The Wise Woman had warned him of gnomes' affection for poison-tipped knives. She had broken the news that there existed only two ways to reverse his enchantment. The gnome must volunteer to do so (which rarely happened), or the gnome must die. He had been hunting Thumble-no-skin ever since.

Rolf began to pant.

What was that rhyme she'd insisted he memorize? Rolf was certain he remembered the inclusion of the word *hoard*. Committing the riddle to memory had not seemed important at the time, since ways to kill gnomes were not even mentioned.

The Wise Woman had counseled him one never knew what might be of value in future dealings with the Fae people.

At last the words came to him in the manner the crone had intoned them.

Guardians of the Hoard, Earth,
Wind, and Fire.
Elements of Gnomish funeral pyres.
Watersong, the Hoard Hunter's guide.
Cleverness, his triumphant pride.

His tail stilled.
What in God's name do the words mean?

At dawn the next morning Rolf returned to what he had deemed his place after a satisfying breakfast of freshly-killed pheasant. He found the scent of pine oil that emanated from the deep cushion of pine needles under the low-hanging ever-green boughs comforting. The sharp odor reminded him of cleaning days at home in his father's castle.

His ears pricked to the scrape of a wooden bar. The cottage door opened.

This morning Ruby's shawl was draped loosely about her head and shoulders despite her breath fogging the air. She stepped out into the cold sunlight holding a wooden milk pail in her right hand. For the first time, Rolf was able to view her countenance.

His heart thudded against his ribs. Every hair on his pelt stood on end. She had the face of an angel, from her porcelain skin to her bow-shaped mouth.

When she spotted his wolf tracks in the light snow her rose-petal lips parted on a sharp indrawn breath. Slowly, she turned her head to peer all about the edges of the forest with wide sapphire eyes.

Rolf willed himself to remain as still as the surrounding trees.

A small girl peeked around Ruby's skirt and then pulled the door shut. She carried a pail that his nose told him was filled with eggshells for the chuks.

Where Ruby's hair was as black as the finest nightwood, Star's braids glinted like gold beneath the winter sun. Looking even younger than her almost-eight years, she was as pretty as a pixie.

Finding he had started to pant, Rolf closed his jaws. Through the drooping pine boughs the little girl's pale blue gaze locked on his. She glanced up at her sister and then back at him, lifting a finger of caution to her pink lips.

His pulse pounded in his ears. Her gaze seemed to pierce his wolfish façade and touch the human soul at the heart of him. Then she did the most extraordinary thing.

She made a curtsy, feed pail and all, giving him a beatific smile before turning to her sister. His heart stumbled.

Was it possible the child possessed the power of Second Sight? He found it unsettling to consider that the Wise Woman had once been a child not unlike this one.

Star had pulled Ruby's free hand out of her apron pocket and was tugging her sister forward. "Please hurry. I'm cold." She gave a dramatic shiver.

Ruby sighed and set her pail down. She reached across and pulled Star's shawl up onto her head. "Silly goose." She tweaked the girl's nose and smiled at her fondly before retrieving her milk pail.

He remembered how the maiden had pounded on the smith's door yesterday with only her right hand and how she seemed to be in the habit of keeping her left hand in her pocket. Something was wrong with the way that hand now lay in Star's grasp.

His chest tightened. Had there been an accident? Had someone mistreated her? A growl tried to rumble in his chest. Not wanting to frighten the girls, he cut it off.

The sisters hurried to the barn. Star set down her pail and released Ruby's hand in order to remove the bar locking the barn doors.

Rolf's wolf vision made out ridged scars twisting the maiden's flesh at the edges of what had once been a horrific wound. His body tensed and his hair lifted. Her two outer fingers and nearly half her palm were missing. He had seen enough soldiers' wounds to know this was the work of a beast, not a man.

The wolf in him tried to throw back his head to howl. However the last thing he wanted was to frighten her again. Instead, he watched her shove her misshapen hand back into her apron pocket. The sisters disappeared into the barn amidst the peeping of excited chuks.

Rolf remained in his place under the pine trees, thinking. Ruby had told Star securing a position with the tax collector would be a Godsend, but he was not so sure. The villagers might shun her for helping the tax man take from their meager earnings. The idea did not set well with him, but there was nothing he could do but redouble his efforts to locate the gnome's hoard.

Longing to lay eyes on the sisters again, he awaited their return. When at last they emerged from the barn, Star carried a half-grown orange tabby who seemed content to let the little girl hold him. Not even Rolf's scent seemed to disturb the placid feline. Ruby hauled a steaming pail of milk. Both girls' breaths made smoke in the air.

Nearing the cottage, Ruby gestured at the muddle of wolf tracks in front. "Some large beast visited our cottage last night. When I leave for work, you must stay indoors until I come home. The beast may return. Promise me, Star."

"I promise," the little girl said, her face solemn. "I will keep Mouser safe as well."

Ruby smiled. She turned toward the cottage door.

Star gave a little wave with one of Mouser's front paws at Rolf's hiding place. "Stay, Prince Rolf," she said in an urgent whisper. "Please, sir. We must speak."

When her little sister opened the door to her that night, an exhausted Ruby was greeted by the delicious aroma of baking potatoes and roasting poultry. Star pulled her inside and barred the door. Ruby blinked at the dressed game bird sizzling on the spit over the fire. The rest of the room was in shadow. They could not afford to waste money on candles.

Surely this had to be a dream?

"Dinner is nearly ready," Star said. She beamed up at Ruby. "Mouser and I wanted to surprise you. And we have another surprise, too. He caught a mouse in the roof thatch, so he really is a mouser!"

The cat was stropping against Ruby's tired legs.

"That's wonderful," Ruby said, furrowing her brow.

She hung her shawl on a hook by the door and then sank into one of the three willow chairs Father had made for them. Star had set their small wooden table for dinner. Ruby focused on the impossible bird in the fireplace. "How did you come by a pheasant?"

When her gaze found Star's, the younger girl's slid away. "I found it on our doorstep." She brightened. "A gift, perhaps from the smith?"

Ruby's heart quaked at the obvious untruth. Had the child snuck out to beg food from the smith? Had she let someone into the cottage to trade for the bird? What did they have that any man would want?

When she could speak with a calm she did not feel, she patted her lap. "Come sit, my sweet."

Star's shoulders drooped as she complied. She sat sideways and leaned her head against Ruby's shoulder. Ruby kissed the top of the child's head. "Tell me the truth, my sweet. Everyone makes mistakes. Did you go outside after promising to stay indoors?"

Star shook her head. "When Prince Rolf scratched at the door, I only opened it a tiny crack to see what he had brought. I didn't want to be rude."

Ruby held Star away from her so she could peer into the child's eyes. "And what would the heir to the Dragon Horn Throne be wanting with the likes of us, missy?"

Star bit her lower lip.

"Tell me the truth, Star. I promise I will not be angry."

The little girl clasped Ruby's face between her palms and held her gaze as if searching her thoughts. With a sigh, she released her. "You will not believe the truth, but here it is. Prince Rolf is under an enchantment. His spirit now dwells in the body of a wolf."

Ruby's doubt must have shown in her eyes. "This is not one of my stories," Star said. "This is the truth."

Ruby chose her words with care. "Even if this is true, how can you know such a thing?"

Star lifted her thin shoulders. "I know. That is all. Just as I knew the mayor's wife carried twins, a boy and a girl; and I knew Father had died whilst we were doing chores in the barn; and I know your hand the dog mauled aches when you use it."

Ruby swallowed her words of denial. She did not believe Prince Rolf, in the guise of a wolf, had brought them a pheasant for dinner. Still, Star had demonstrated uncanny knowledge once or twice in the past. There was a small possibility God had gifted her with Second Sight, like the Wise Woman of Mountainfall. No doubt a child would have difficulty distinguishing her fantasies from knowledge gifted to her. To express disbelief would serve no good purpose.

She shifted Star's weight. Perhaps Star's wolf was a symbol for a man. Perhaps he had told the child the story and she only repeated what he had said. The thought brought her no comfort.

"No one came inside?" she said finally. "Not even the wolf?"

Star shook her head.

Ruby sighed. "Promise me you will never, *ever* open the door to man nor beast whilst I am at work, my sweet — not even to the king himself. Otherwise I shall worry myself to death."

Star nodded. Her thumb had found its way into her mouth. She pulled the comforting appendage out. "I promise."

Ruby prayed the promise was enough to keep Star safe.

Having learned what had transpired between the sisters over the pheasant, Rolf concluded he must win Ruby's trust. Given that a dog had mauled her hand and wolves had a well-deserved reputation amongst the populace, the odds were stacked against him. However he could not turn his back on the sisters. They were the only humans, other than the Wise Woman, with whom he had connected since becoming a wolf. Until a few days ago, he had been overcome with melancholy. Already the human contact had restored his spirits and strengthened his resolve.

For the next three days, he presented Ruby with a freshly-killed rabbit or game bird each morning as she left the cottage for work. The first time her gaze fell upon him, she screamed and ran back to pound on her door. Whether by accident or design, Star took a long time opening the portal. Apparently needing to keep track of his movements, Ruby had turned to face him with her back pressed against the wood. Seeing him amble away from the cottage must have calmed her, because the screaming had stopped.

Each day, he went a little closer to the cottage before dropping his gift. By the third day, Ruby did not bother to scream. Instead, she stared at him with something akin to wonder in her eyes. He considered her change in behavior a promising development.

Whilst Ruby was at work each day, Rolf searched the countryside for Thumble-no-skin's scent. Each time he discovered the gnome's trail, the wily Fae sensed he was being followed and escaped down a bolt-hole. The underground passages were much too small for humans or, in his case a wolf, to follow. It was the gnome way to crisscross a chosen hunting ground with ever-growing mazes of underground tunnels having numerous hidden entrances. Each night, Rolf had a strong urge to howl his frustration to the moon.

Rolf chose to look on the bright side of the current situation. Thumble-no-skin's growing warren indicated the gnome planned to winter over in the Helmsdale area.

There was an old saying amongst men. Where goeth a gnome, so goeth his hoard. How the wee men moved their massive fortunes remained a mystery, but move and re-bury them near each new hunting ground they did.

All Rolf had to do to restore the king's Treasury was solve the riddle of the Wise Woman's rhyme and somehow convey the hoard's location to the king.

If only he were clever at riddles.

With Ruby forced to walk home after dark as the days shortened, Rolf made it his business to follow her every evening at a discreet distance.-Well before moonrise on the night of the full moon, she was halfway home when he smelled a stranger hidden even from his wolf sight in the dark forest ahead. The man reeked of mating lust.

A rage stronger than any he had known to exist sent Rolf streaking past Ruby. He knew only that he must tear the challenger's throat out. *Ruby belongs only with me.*

The stranger caught sight of Rolf at the last moment. He threw up an arm to guard his throat just before the force of the wolf's attack carried them both to the ground. A dagger flashed in the moonlight. Rolf's shoulder burned as if it had caught fire.

The agony of his wound banked the fire of his rage. He rolled off the man to assess the damage and avoid further injury. He scrambled to his paws, choking on the smell of his

own blood. Standing on his three good legs, he snarled a fe-
rocious warning that belied his weakened condition.

The skulking coward ran like a rabbit.

He caught Ruby's scent before he heard the crunch of
her running footsteps. Turning with care, he watched her slide
to a stop not six feet away. He began to pant.

Slowly, she approached him.

Unbelievable thirst forced him to his belly to moisten
his tongue with snow. Dimly, he remembered this to be a sign
of great blood loss. Gentle hands urged him onto his side.

"I must stop the bleeding," Ruby told him. Cloth ripped
and then she pressed hard against his wound. He moaned,
but it came out as a whine.

A gentle, maimed hand stroked his head. "I'm sorry,
Rolf," she said. He smelled the salt of tears. "For your own
good, I fear I must add to your pain."

With quick, sure movements she removed her shawl,
folded it in half lengthwise and then wrapped the cloth around
his shoulder. When she moved his leg, he hoped he would
faint, however he was not so lucky. Blackness did not over-
take him until she looped the ends of the shawl into a knot and
cinched it tight against his wound.

Rolf awakened to warmth and the overwhelming
scents of pine needles and wood smoke. His wounded shoulder burned. He lay in a soft place — his place? He was so
very tired. Had he crawled to his place under the pine tree to
die? Wasn't that what a wolf would do when mortally wounded?

Perhaps, however a man must fight until the end. If he had the strength, he would open his eyes, but he was already fading from this place…

The next time he awakened, pine needles pricked his muzzle. A small hand stroked the fur between his ears. Star's little-girl scent made his tail attempt a welcoming wag.

"Good morrow, Prince Rolf."

He groaned and forced his bleary eyes open. A thatched ceiling framed Star's sober little face and burnished braids. A fire crackled in the fireplace. They had somehow brought him to the cottage. His tail thumped the floor once.

"I brought you something to drink," Star said with a sweet smile.

A large crockery bowl thudded to the floor beside Rolf's muzzle. He lifted his head and sniffed the silted liquid that swirled inside. The bitter scent made him sneeze, which in turn made him dizzy. He dropped his head to the floor and closed his eyes.

Just let me die in peace.

The little girl's tone became stern. "The bad smell is medicine to make you better. You must be brave and drink it, for your own good."

He moaned. The wolf in him would rather drink mud. He had no strength left to fight the beast. He was done for.

Star lifted his muzzle between her palms. He forced his eyelids open.

The little girl's blue eyes flashed. "*Ruby* made this tea for you. She says you suffered a grievous wound while pro-tecting her from the bad man. She says you *must* recover. She *says* you are her hero. If you can't drink this for me, then you must drink it for Ruby!"

Rolf blinked. A wavelet of energy surged through his veins, then another. He was Ruby's hero. He licked Star's chin with his big wolf tongue. She squealed and let go of his muzzle.

Against all odds, Ruby cared about him. She believed him a hero. He held the knowledge of Ruby's affection for him safe in his heart as he lapped up the bitter brew.

When he had finished, Star set the bowl aside. "I thought you would like to be Ruby's hero," she said. "You're sweet on my sister, are you not?"

His tail thumped the floor like a drumstick on a drum. He could not seem to control the unruly appendage.

"Well, then," Star said in a stern tone. "You must finish your quest and return to your human form. Otherwise, how will you marry?" She began to stroke his side with her gentle little hand.

It touched him that Star trusted his intentions toward Ruby to be honorable. However when he closed his eyes, he found himself speculating about the possible mechanics of a wolf-human mating. He forced his heavy lids open. He could not risk the innocent child reading those thoughts.

To distract himself, he concentrated on solving the riddle of the Hoard.

> Guardians of the Hoard, Earth,
> Wind, and Fire,
> Elements of Gnomish funeral pyres.

At first these two lines had seemed rather forthright. He had soon learned better. Gnomes believed their hoard would accompany them into the afterlife, thus the funeral pyre reference was easily explained. The hoard would be buried in the gnome's current hunting ground in a windy place. That narrowed his search to all of Helmsdale and the surrounding countryside.

Rolf heaved a sigh. Fire must be the key, but what did it mean in the context of the riddle?

He had already examined every forge, potters kiln and burned ruin to no avail. What was left? A fireplace? A candle?

He yawned. All this thinking was making him tired. Or perhaps it was the medicine. The pain from his wound had settled to a dull throb.

He found the next line of verse similarly confusing.

Watersong, the Hunter's guide.

What did the made-up word *watersong* denote? He was to use whatever-it-was for a guide. The babble of a brook? If so, he would be stymied until spring. All the brooks were frozen solid.

The last line seemed to indicate a hunter must be extremely clever to have a chance of finding the hoard.

Cleverness is the Hunter's pride.

He groaned. Once again, he'd come full circle. He was not good at solving riddles.

His jaws parted in a wide yawn.

Star's hand stilled on his side. "Ruby is very clever, you know," she said. "Father even taught her to read, and now she is teaching me. Ruby says I may be as clever as she, but I doubt that is true. Perhaps when she comes home this evening she will help you with your quest. For now, you must rest."

With that, she gave his side a pat and left him with the certainty she was already wise beyond her years. It had never occurred to him Ruby might be educated. He shook his head at his own foolishness. The tools to demonstrate his humanity to her had always been in his possession. She would be forced to accept her little sister's story as the truth. Her wolf was, indeed, the Heir to the Dragon Horn Throne.

That night before darkfall, Rolf struggled to his feet and scratched at the door. Star donned her wool cloak and then followed him out, urging him to take care with his injured leg. Mouser streaked past on his way to the barn for the night.

Apparently having deduced his intentions, Star led him around the cottage to an open, snow-covered expanse that was no doubt their fallow garden. She pulled up the end stake from a row of bean poles and presented the stout stick to him with a flourish.

"Ruby says the written word is the most powerful tool of all. Use it well, my prince."

As the sun sank below the horizon and the night star appeared, Rolf dropped his makeshift stylus and studied his work. He was panting from exhaustion and pain, but his efforts had been well worthwhile. The letters scratched into the crusty snow were legible. He'd stirred up the dirt beneath and Star had sprinkled pine needles in the grooves in hopes of making them easier to see.

An incredible lightness filled him. His heart skipped a beat. Tonight at moonrise Ruby would recognize him as a man.

Star knelt beside him, shivering. "We must go inside now. It is written."

Although he was uncertain whether she referred to his missive or a prophecy, he needed to rest until moonrise, when with luck something magical would occur.

At the scrape of the door bar, Ruby looked up from cleaning blood out of Rolf's fur. Uneasiness slithered up her spine. This was the third time since supper Star had peeked outside to look for the moon's silver orb. "Why do you care when the moon rises, Star?"

After shutting and barring the heavy door, her sister clasped her hands in front of her, smiled and bounced on her toes. "I have something important to show you in the garden, but until now it was too dark for you to see. The moon has risen."

Ruby's heart stumbled. "You went outside while I was at work?"

Star's face fell. Her lower lip protruded. Defiance sparked in her eyes. "Rolf needed to go out. He would not let anyone harm me, Ruby. You know that to be true."

The wolf's tail thumped as if in agreement. He rose and limped over to stand by the door.

Ruby's stomach tightened. "Did someone visit you today, Star? Did Rolf have to protect you?"

Star shook her head. "No, no. Only Rolf, Mouser and I went out." She wrinkled her nose. "Mouser ran into the barn. He did not help."

Ruby shook her head in exasperation. Tired as she was, there was nothing for it but to investigate. Otherwise Star would pester her to death. "All right. However after you show me your surprise, it will be time for bed."

She rose and donned her cloak, checking to make sure Star was warmly dressed.

Star slid the bar aside and peered up at her with shining eyes. "This is a good surprise, Ruby. I promise. You've no need to worry."

They entered a world of sparkling silver and white. A thousand stars glittered in the sky. Rolf led the way around the cottage. If danger had lurked, she was confident the wolf would have warned them.

Star pointed to a broad disturbed swath of snow. "Rolf wrote you a message in the snow, Ruby. He needs your help to solve this riddle. It is the key to finding the gnome's hoard. We will have Father's ring back."

Ruby chewed her bottom lip. Could a child with Second Sight lose her mind? Or might Star be telling a truth only she could see?

Using coal on the hearthstone, Ruby had begun to teach Star her alphabet, but the child could barely write her own name. Her small sister had obviously made a great effort. The markings were evenly spaced, with extra width between groupings.

Moving closer, Ruby studied the slashes and squiggles drawn along the nearest row. They had been darkened with dirt and what looked like pine needles. She made out the letters *t* and *r*, letters from Star's name.

Then her eyes fell on the word *the*. Her throat went dry.

Where had Star learned to write an entire word?

She tried to maintain the appearance of calm, although her insides were in turmoil. She retraced her steps. This time, she studied each cluster of markings intently. Slowly, she walked down the garden row. One by one, she read aloud the words Star could not possibly have written. *"Cleverness is the Hunter's pride."*

Star spoke so quickly in her excitement Ruby could hardly understand her. "The words are a riddle that tells where to look for a gnome's hoard. Rolf must find the hoard of a gnome named Thumble-no-skin. It is he and his gang that robbed the king's Treasury, Thumble-no-skin cast the spell that turned Prince Rolf into a wolf. Finding the hoard will restore the king's wealth."

Ruby caught the wolf's gaze. He jumped to his feet and yipped, then limped to the far edge of the message. Ruby felt compelled to follow.

"Read all the words to me, Ruby," Star said. "We must help solve the riddle." She dropped her voice to a whisper. "Rolf thinks he is not clever enough to solve the puzzle alone."

Ruby did not know what to believe. It was true that Rolf did not behave like a wolf most of the time. She had thought perhaps he was raised by humans. Could the truth be stranger still?

Reaching what must be the beginning of the missive, Ruby began to decipher the words. Star slipped her hand into Ruby's maimed one. They paced the rows together as the wolf watched and listened.

Guardians of the Hoard,
Earth, Wind, and Fire,
Elements of Gnomish funeral pyres.
Watersong, the Hoard Hunter's guide.
Cleverness, his triumphant pride.

"How did you write this?" Ruby said, staring at the wolf. Rolf limped over to where the sisters stood and dropped a beanpole at her feet.

By the next afternoon Rolf barely noticed the pain in his wounded shoulder. His wolf body was quick to heal. All traces of the melancholy that had dogged him for so long had vanished. Today was the day he would be redeemed. Ruby and Star's future would be secure. He had yet to kill Thumble-no-skin and reverse the enchantment, but his time would come soon. Today was a good day to be alive, as man or wolf.

While he waited for Ruby and Star to finish their mid-day meal, he lay on the hearth and remembered how Ruby had helped solve the riddle the night before. Once she had put her mind to the puzzle, she'd been quick to understand the solution must be unique to each hunting ground. Gnomes never stole from one another, so sharing guidelines made sense.

They had warmed themselves by the fire whilst Ruby studied the clues in the rhyme for some time. He inhaled deeply of the already-familiar and comforting odors of the cottage and the sweet scents of the maids. A feeling of drowsy contentment overcame him.

Eventually Ruby offered up a possibility. "An abandoned tin mine, a tunnel in the earth, lies not a mile from this cottage," Ruby told them. "From the mine, in summer, you can hear a nearby waterfall. Perhaps that is the *watersong*? A ring of blackened earth marks the spot where the miners had their cook fire." She sighed. "For the element of Wind, there is only our blustery Helmsgaard weather. Nothing else comes to mind."

Star leapt to her feet and grabbed Ruby's hand. "No matter. The mine is where Thumble-no-skin buried his hoard."

Ruby had arched an ebony brow. "Are you certain, Wise Sister?"

Star had laughed. "As certain as I am that the moon will rise tonight!"

With that she pulled Ruby down to sit beside Rolf, so close the heat of her body warmed him. He gave in to an impulse and licked her soft cheek. She tasted sweet and salty, and she did not pull away.

Star begged to accompany him and Ruby to the mine on the morrow, but Ruby would not give her permission. She told the little girl she had an important job to do by staying home. She and Rolf had only to walk to the mine, where Rolf would smell the hoard even though it was buried. They would immediately return home. If they did not arrive back at the cottage within two hours' time, Star must go to the kindly smith for help. She was to tell him where Ruby had gone and why.

The scrape of the door bar startled Rolf out of his musing. He leapt to all fours and his shoulder protested.

"Are you ready?" Ruby said. She must have donned her cape and shawl while he was lost in thought. She made them look elegant.

"Rolf?" Ruby said.

He stopped staring at her like a besotted youth and trotted to the door in reply. Her easy smile made his heart beat faster.

"Shall I bring Father's sword?" she asked him.

The weapon would be heavy and he doubted she had any training. Besides, gnomes could smell metal a mile away. Rolf shook his head to indicate his answer was *no*.

At her side, Star looked every inch the worried little girl. Ruby bent down to kiss her sister. They exchanged a fierce hug.

"Why can't I foretell what will happen?" Star said. "I've tried and tried."

Ruby tweaked her button nose. "You have already worked miracles, my sweet. Second Sight can be capricious."

When the child hugged him, Rolf licked her face until she giggled. Then he hurried outside. Mouser streaked into the cottage just before Ruby closed the door. He was glad Star would have the cat's company while she waited.

They listened for the bar to slide home before they set off for the mine.

They made good time. At the outset Ruby told him she would not speak in case the gnome was in the area. He admired her caution.

When they reached the little clearing where the mine's entrance yawned like a great square mouth, Rolf searched until he found a heavy stick, a tree branch really, that ended in a thick knob. He dragged the makeshift weapon over to Ruby and dropped it at her feet. He could not leave her defenseless while he explored the mine.

"Thank you," she said. She heaved the cudgel onto her shoulder. Satisfied, Rolf picked up a short, straight stick in his jaws to scratch a single word in the snow. *Stay.*

Ruby nodded. "Take care."

He raised his muzzle to scent the outdoors one last time and found no unseen danger lurking. Turning, he strode into the mine's gaping maw.

A few yards in he stopped to let his vision adjust to the darkness. His wolf eyes soon adapted to the dim lighting. At first he scented neither gnome nor treasure in the dusty air. Then he caught a whiff of old, sour magic.

His heart beat faster as he moved deeper into the tunnel. One of the Fae had passed through weeks before. He spied the entrances to several narrow tunnels along the way that were just big enough for a gnome to pass through. Bolt holes, no doubt, but not used recently.

Soon the main passage split. Rolf nosed the mouths of both tunnels and inhaled a mote of gold dust on the left. He veered that way and within a few feet the scent of gold grew stronger. He panted with excitement. Thumble-no-skin's hoard lay deeper in the mine.

Rolf hurried to retrace his steps. His paws felt light, as if they barely touched the ground. They must send word for the Royal Guards to come recover the stolen treasure immediately. He would make amends.

He stepped out of the cave into warm sunlight.

"Good news?" Ruby asked with a smile that warmed his heart.

He wagged his tail and trotted toward her.

Ruby glanced upward and her eyes widened. "Behind you!"

Rolf whirled just in time to dodge the swing of Thumble-no-skin's lethal knife. The gnome must have had another bolt hole connecting to the hillside above the cave. Snarling, the wolf danced back and then darted in to snap at the little man's legs. The Gnome screeched and launched himself into the air over Rolf's head. The wolf crouched to avoid the thrust of the gnome's weapon.

The Fae man somersaulted in the snow, springing to his feet between Rolf and Ruby. He flashed a wicked smile and ran straight for the maiden. Fury powered Rolf's gigantic leap. He'd snap the Fae man's neck in his jaws before Ruby came to harm.

The treacherous gnome spun and raised his hand to throw his poisoned knife.

Ruby's scream echoed in Rolf's head as the gnome went sideways and everything went black.

Ruby's cudgel connected with the back of the Gnome's head and split his skull like a ripe melon. Blood and brains splattered both her and the snow as if they were juice and seeds. The cudgel's swing pulled her sideways and she fell into the snow. Rolf tumbled past in a blur.

Ruby sat up and stared at Thumble-no-skin's limp form. The metallic smell of blood brought bile to her throat. She swallowed and wiped her wet cheek with the hem of her shawl, then stared at the smear of red blood on the wool. Her pulse roared in her ears.

"Ruby, are you injured?" rasped a deep male voice from behind her.

She peered over her shoulder at a darkly handsome stranger who wore naught but a wolf pelt around his loins. She noticed fresh blood seeping from the partially-healed wound that marred his muscled shoulder. His gaze caught hers and for a moment, his golden eyes seemed to glow.

Her heart leapt. *Wolf eyes.*

With one hand grasping the wolf pelt, he climbed to his feet and approached. He gave her a tentative smile and offered his hand. At a loss for words to fit the strange situation, she silently allowed him to pull her to her feet. She tried to ignore the heat that flowed up her arm from their clasped hands.

He released her, then caressed her cheek where she'd smeared away most of the gnome's blood. The concern in his golden eyes set her pulse pounding. "Did the creature mark you with his knife?"

She glanced at the bloody cudgel and shivered. "The blood is Thumble-no-skin's."

The man helped her to her feet. Ruby's gaze followed the disturbed snow where Rolf had tumbled past and slid to a stop behind her. The only tracks that led from the spot were a barefoot man's, and that trail ended where the stranger with wolf eyes stood beside her.

"Ruby," he said. "When the gnome died, the enchantment ended. You saved my life and my humanity. With all my heart, I thank you. It is a debt I can never repay."

She found her voice. "Rolf, you saved my life first. In fact, you have saved all of us. You have saved Helmsgaard."

Prince Rolf of Helmsgaard, Heir to the Dragon Horn Throne, smiled at her. He pulled her to him with the hand not holding the wolf pelt around his loins and kissed the top of her head. His muscled chest warmed her cheek. He smelled of wolf fur and man sweat. For a moment she forgot that a peasant girl with one good hand could never have him.

"It is you who saved me, Ruby. You and Star." He set her away and lifted her chin. His sensuous lips were only inches from hers, his golden eyes luminous. "When the two of you came into my life I had nearly lost myself in the beast. You grabbed onto my human heart and wouldn't let go. You helped me find the gnome's hoard so I can put things right in the kingdom. And you saved me from a torturous death at Thumble-no-skin's hand."

Her gaze slid away from his. She stepped back and shoved her hands in her pockets in hopes of hiding their tremble. Rolf-the-Wolf had been hers and Star's enchanted protector, their friend, perhaps more. However, Rolf-the-man must leave them. He belonged in Helmsgaard Castle. He had a kingdom to provide for and to protect.

"I will miss you," she said. "Will you bid Star farewell before you return to the castle?"

"No."

She blinked up at Prince Rolf. He stepped closer and gently pulled her maimed hand from her pocket. Then he uncurled her thumb and two fingers and raised each to his lips in turn.

"I would rather live as a wolf in your cottage than leave you behind," he said sternly. "Star knows my intentions toward you have always been honorable."

Ruby lost her breath. *Intentions?* He felt more than gratitude toward her, then. And her disfigurement did not offend him.

Rolf's golden eyes darkened. "You must stop looking at me like that, or we shall be late returning and Star will needlessly send the smith and his sons to save you."

She lowered her lashes. Heat rose in her cheeks.

Rolf took her arm. "I'm beginning to feel the cold. The walk — "

A high-pitched giggle interrupted him. "Beginning to feel cold, my foot," Star said, stepping out from behind a tree.

Ruby felt her jaw drop.

"You'll be glad I brought you some of Father's clothes, sir," Star said to Rolf, holding out a shawl-wrapped bundle. "You must be half-frozen by this time. Shortly after you left, I finally had a vision of Ruby killing the gnome and you landing naked in the snow. I thought you must be freezing, so I fetched Father's army uniform from our trunk and followed you."

Her gaze switched to Ruby. "Please don't scold me. I knew Prince Rolf needed my help. I couldn't let him freeze to death. I couldn't!"

Tears filled Ruby's eyes. Star had shown great courage and resourcefulness. Ruby opened her arms and the little girl ran into her embrace. "You were so brave to come after us, not knowing when the gnome would die."

"I hid in the woods and watched," Star told her. "I didn't come out until I knew it was safe."

"An intelligent strategy," Rolf said. "You are wise beyond your years, little one."

Smiling shyly, Star offered him the bundle of clothing. "I brought some rags to bind your feet. Ruby sold Father's boots." She gave her an apologetic glance. "We needed the money."

Rolf seemed to be struggling to maintain his solemn expression. "Thank you, Star." His gaze found Ruby's. "Please excuse me for a moment whilst I dress."

With that, he marched into the woods. Ruby could not pull her gaze away from his muscled back and shoulders until he disappeared behind a large evergreen tree. With a small sigh, she came to her senses and caught Star grinning at her. Her cheeks warmed under the child's scrutiny.

"He told you the truth," Star said. "His intentions are honorable. He loves you, Ruby."

Ruby raised her brows. "And what do you know of love, little sister?"

"You would be surprised," Star replied. She immediately dropped her gaze and seemed to become absorbed in digging a hole in the snow with the toe of her boot.

Ruby frowned. What had Star read in Rolf's thoughts? Or in her own, for that matter? When she'd watched the prince walk into the woods just now, her thoughts had been far from pure. Remembering, she felt a delicious flutter low in her belly.

"You love him, too, Ruby," Star said. She paused in her excavations to pin Ruby with a knowing look.

"Whether I care for him or not isn't what matters," Ruby said.

"On the contrary, it is all that matters," Rolf called from behind the tree.

The sisters each clapped a hand over her own mouth. They stared at each other with wide eyes.

Rolf walked out of the woods in their father's too-small uniform with the wolf pelt slung over his shoulder. The blue wool jacket's sleeves ended well above his wrists and the jacket hung open. He'd managed to fasten Father's trousers, but the legs left a good six inches of skin exposed above his bare feet.

"I was speaking of my intentions," he told them. He sat on a fallen log and began to wrap the rags Star had brought around one foot. "After the Treasury and the Soldiers Pensions are restored, with luck both my father the king and our people will find it in their hearts to forgive my past mistakes."

"Surely they must!" Ruby said. How could they fail to recognize the honorable man he had become?

One corner of his mouth lifted in a half-smile. "It is my fervent hope."

He finished the job and switched to the other foot. "If not, I will continue to work to earn their respect and for-giveness."

He remained silent until his second foot was wrapped. Rising, he caught Star's hand and they approached Ruby. He clasped her good hand in his free one and smiled. "Once I have been reinstated I intend to ask you to be my bride."

He glanced down at Star. "Your sister has given me her permission." His gaze found hers and warmed her to her core.

"I love you, Ruby. I want you and Star to be my family."

Unaccustomed joy swelled her chest. Was this how the drab redbird hen felt when the gorgeous male danced for her, offering her everything he was, everything he could be, for the rest of their lives?

"I love you, too, Rolf. Whether or not you regain your throne, I will be honored to marry you."

He pulled her and Star into an embrace. Ruby rose up on tiptoes to warm him with a kiss.

THE END

Thank you *for reading my stories. I hope you enjoyed them! I'd love for you to visit my website a* **www.SarahRaplee.com** .

The Crystal Witch

BY DIANA MCCOLLUM

Dedication
For Loyd and my children, for all their love, encourage-
ment and support.

Acknowledgements

To my critique partners Sarah McDermed and Louise Pelzl thank you for your generous and honest critiques.

To my Beta readers thank you for taking the time to read this story, because of you it is polished. Beta readers: Lisa Pino, Lisa Daniels, Katie Llamas, Sarah McDermed, Judith Ashley, Louise Pelzl, and Andrea McDermed.

And a huge shout-out to my Bend lunch bunch, writers who didn't mind answering all my questions: Marie Harte, Karen Duvall, Linda Berry, Ruth Colter, Paty Jager, Mary Pax, & Vella Munn.

October 15, 2012

The right mixture of violet and blue evening sky laced with bolts of scarlet bouncing off the clouds always brought to mind the evening of her death, or what would have been Hettie's death had she not escaped.

Even after ten years in the small coastal town of Waxing, Massachusetts, a death-sky inspired panic deep in her chest. She took several calming breaths, repeating her time-worn mantra.

"'Tis a frivolous fear, for naught dangerous be near. Bless this house, bless this store, bless me ever more." Hettie intoned the mantra three times.

She put a match to bundled sage twigs and walked the boundary of her small gift shop, the Crystal Witch. Climbing the stairs to her apartment, at the door she murmured an opening charm and crossed the threshold then proceeded to walk the length of every wall, in every room. The blessed smoke from the stems both cleansed and protected the space. She stopped by the front window. Pulling the lace curtain aside, she looked out at the sky, almost dark now. The shadow of a figure merged with the dark of the woods across the street. Did she see a lonely soul out for an evening walk, or something more sinister? Her stomach clenched; it could be time to pay her debt.

Samhain was approaching. The time of year when the veil between worlds was easily accessible, when good or evil could pass through with barely a ripple in the curtain. Hettie was uneasy this time of year, and with good reason; if Declan came for her, it would be during this preternatural time.

He'd have to find her first. He didn't know where Shaman Adahy had sent her. If Declan knew where she was, he would have come for her. This she knew without a doubt. One didn't make a deal with the devil unless one was willing to pay the price.

After taking the small ceramic pots of spearmint and peppermint off the window sill and placing them on the counter, Hettie closed the curtain. Gathering a wooden spoon, small pan and mesh strainer she set about brewing a calming tea. The ritual of making tea at the end of a busy day comforted her. She gently removed leaves from the plants, washed them, and put the sprigs in the pot sitting on the stove. In the pantry she took a jar of dried chamomile off the shelf. A teaspoon of chamomile went in the pan.

She took the wooden spoon, pressing the leaves against the side of the pot, bruising the herbs. She closed her eyes and breathed in the released aroma. She added two cups of water and turned the stove on.

Hettie stirred until the pot bubbled briskly, and then removed the wooden spoon. Holding her hands over the steam she spoke.

With plants of earth I make this tea,
Charged with magick to its task;

May the Goddess in me,
Help me relax,
So mote it be.

Hettie gently settled the lid on the pot, turned the fire down for the required half hour of steeping.

She changed into her favorite silk pajamas, and pulled on her fleece bathrobe to fend off the evening chill. Taking a mug out of the cupboard she poured the steaming tea into the cup. She sat in the maple rocking chair, her favorite one, the rocker that reminded her of Mama's. She sipped the hot brew and closed her eyes.

October 30, 1692

The day in the village of Waxing began as a quiet fall morning, with a break in the rain that had plummeted from the sky for the past several days. Henrietta took the pail off the hook by the hearth and left to fetch the morning water. She was sixteen years now and considered a woman. Papa had died in a hunting accident last year and Gram shortly after. Now there was just her and Mama. The depression that had plagued Mama since Papa's death was consuming her, and Henrietta helplessly watched Mama shrink a little more each day.

Henrietta had prayed to the goddess asking for help in the matter of her mother's illness. The Goddess had come to Henrietta in a dream last night, and told her to go into the woods on the full moon, to the sacred circle, and Mama would be cured. Tonight was a full moon and Henrietta was deter-mined to follow the instructions from her vision.

She worked the squeaky crank on the well, pulling up a fresh bucket of water, lifted it over the edge and dumped it into her own pail.

"Ho, Henrietta, I'll carry your bucket," said Waya. He picked up her pail, his arm muscles bulging under the weight. "Have you time for a lesson?"

Waya, the Cherokee shaman's son, was a few years older than her. She had been instructing Waya in his letters for several months now. In return, he brought venison, birds and grains for her and Mama. If it weren't for Waya, they might have starved. He was a great hunter just like his namesake, the wolf.

"Of course, I have time for you. Mama needs her morning meal first. Come along and you can join us." His nearness sent a shiver up her spine. They had grown close over the past few months and the bond went both ways. She felt good in his company, safe; yes, she felt safe. He'd kissed her a few times. She would welcome more. She glanced sideways at him.

They were careful with their friendship, since personal association with anyone from the tribe was frowned upon by the community elders.

Waya had kissed her yesterday. Not the quick kiss, friendly thank you type of kiss, but a passionate kiss. She had daydreamed of being crushed in his embrace; their clandestine relationship was the most thrilling thing to ever happen to her. Thinking about the kiss sent butterflies fluttering in her stomach.

Yesterday she would have made flummery save for the lack of sea moss and milk, two key ingredients. Then she could have served the pudding to Waya this morning.

They reached the picket fence and Waya set the pail of water down.

"Do you have chores, Henrietta? I can help today." He scrunched up his forehead, searching for the right words. "I have no teachings today from Adahy. I am free as the — ," he said turning his hand in the air, fluttering his fingers, "bird." He smiled and his eyes twinkled; he looked quite pleased for finding the proper words.

"Henrietta!" Declan Blackthorn called out, his tone disapproving.

"Yes?" She turned to see the preacher's son barreling down on them.

"What are you doing with this heathen?" Declan looked Waya up and down. "He's barely dressed! Cover yourself, man. Henrietta is a decent God fearing woman and you dare to seek out her company?" Hands on hips and long black coat flapping around his legs, he was an imposing sight at six foot and five inches. He was older than Henrietta by five years.

"I'm helping him with his handwriting and reading proficiencies. Declan, he is good to Mama and me. He brings us venison and other food. Otherwise we would have starved after father perished!" Such a fury boiled inside her, it churned in her stomach and rose up to her heart, increasing the rhythm of the beat till she thought her heart could surely be heard by both men. She must keep her fury restrained; she summoned her will power and tried again. "Declan, sir, step away from us, begone."

"Get out of here, heathen, and don't come back." Declan flung his arm wide and pointed toward the woods.

Waya seemed to grow taller in front of her eyes. He was majestic with his long black braids, muscular chest and snapping black eyes.

"Ho, Henrietta, I wish to cause you no trouble. The tree we talked of...." Waya touched the carved bone moon that hung on a beaded cord around his neck. He tipped his head slightly in acknowledgment, turned and walked toward the woods.

I'll be there tonight, at the full moon, Waya's voice whispered in her head.

Henrietta, stunned to have heard Waya's silent words, could only stare at his retreating back. She turned back to Declan so fast her long skirts flared out. "What is wrong with you? He is human like us, and he is very nice. You have no reason to treat him so."

"He is the shaman's son. There is devil magick there and you'd best watch what magick you want to be associated with." Declan walked around her looking her up and down, measuring her like one of his prize horses. His boot landed in a puddle and sprayed the edge of her dress with muddied water.

"And what would you know of magick, Declan? Aren't you the preacher's son? Isn't magick the devil's tool?" Her hands balled up, her arms shook in a desperate attempt to control the building rage.

His green eyes flashing, he leaned in close to her till their noses almost touched, so close in fact she counted three small hairs growing out of the mole on his left cheek.

"I know of magick. I know of magick in your family, Henrietta. Watch your back," he spat out. He turned and took his leave.

The fury rolled out of her extended hands, scooping up the muddy puddle and slamming it against Declan's back with the intensity of an Atlantic Ocean wave, sending him hurling to the ground.

"What... who... did that?" Sputtered Declan. He wiped his muddied hands on his wet coat.

Henrietta grabbed the still full pail of well water, passed through the gate, and hurried through the door. She set the pail on the floor and leaned against the wooden door.

This was the year when her magickal abilities would reach full force. Gram had told her what to expect. Mama didn't know. The powers were passed down to the firstborn girl on her father's side of the family. The magick had been show-ing up in bits and pieces. Was the fury that coursed through her part of the magick? And how could she hear what Waya whispered in her head?

One thing was clear; Henrietta would be at the hem-lock tree tonight, right after she visited the sacred circle.

Mama was standing in the middle of the room, a va-cant expression on her face. Henrietta hastened over and took hold of her arm. "Come, Mama, sit in the rocker. I'll fix you some porridge."

The afternoon was spent practicing spells. She could conjure fire, heal a cut and mend a slash with nothing but an incantation and her will. Gram had given her the family Tome of Magick. Gram said to memorize as many spells, curses and hexes as possible. Once she knew how they worked, Henriet-ta could create her own as needed.

She sat now in her mother's rocker thumbing through the tome. This morning's demonstration of her awakening power gave her hope she could work a spell to relieve her mother's great grief.

She sighed. Nothing. There was nothing she could do, no quick magick spell that would fix her mama.

She tried to send out several thoughts to Waya. No response. That would be an area she would need to work on.

Henrietta reached the sacred circle at the apex of the full moon. She set her candles on the four points of the directions of the wind, east, west, north and south. She slipped out of her clothes and let the moonlight bathe her. She chanted the welcoming song to the Goddess. Dancing and swaying in the moonlight, bringing power from the circle, she sang an incantation, and then put forth her request for Mama's recovery. She ended her invocation, bared to the moon, arms outstretched, when she saw Waya standing beneath the hemlock at the edge of the circle. She was not embarrassed; it was as it should be, and she welcomed him into the circle.

He discarded the deer hide breech clout and leggings. The moon totem on a leather thong around his neck, the only thing he wore as he stepped into the sacred circle. He brushed her long hair from her breasts and laid it over her shoulders to hang down her back.

His hands moved magickly over her breasts; she was shocked by her own eager response to his touch. The touch of his lips on hers sent a shockwave of passion through her body that pooled in her woman parts. He eased her down to the grass. "Henrietta, I have desired you since I first saw you. Is this joining what you wish too?"

Heat of the craving they shared warmed her. She nodded, too delirious with passion to speak. She surrendered herself to his seduction and together they burned with desire.

Later they lay naked and still, moist from their lovemaking, too tired to move. She wanted to stay here forever with her lover.

"Little one, I've had a vision. You are leaving." He raised her hand to his lips.

"No. I'm not going anywhere."

"Evil is coming." He stood and gave her a hand up. "You must leave this place. No matter — I will find you. Wherever you are, I will find you. Don't fear. Be brave, little one. You have the magick in you and it will keep you safe." His eyes were hooded like those of a hawk. "We have mated. I am yours, you are mine."

"I want to be with you forever, Waya. Surely Mama and I could dwell with you. I could be with you, and we could live with the tribe?" Her eyes threatened to spill tears down her cheeks.

"No. Evil has already visited your home this night. Get your things and meet me by the Hemlock tree. We will find a way to protect you." He settled her dress over her shoulders. "My totem." He took off the bone moon necklace and placed the cord around her neck. "Wear this always, and if we are parted, I will find you." His kiss sent new waves of ecstasy through her.

She ran through the woods toward home. The autumn air was cool on skin still hot from loving Waya.

The loud, frightening voices of zealous townsmen halted her on the edge of the woods. A parade of torches marched from her house toward the town square. What was going on?

Henrietta ran after them, her hair flying. She grabbed the arm of her neighbor, Amy Scotts. "Why were they at my home? Where is everyone going?"

"Henrietta, you were gone. The men came and took your mama to jail. She was called a hag and charged with witchcraft." Henrietta's stomach churned with fright at the panic in Amy's voice.

The fools didn't understand the great grief that had struck Mama and said instead her soul had been claimed by the devil and she was his servant now.

"Amy, you know mama is struck by melancholy right now. You know, Amy!"

"Let go of me, lest I scream for assistance." Amy wrenched her arm away. "We know the mind is the feeblest when downheartedness strikes. I'm sorry your mama succumbed to the devil. Declan said today she threw muddied water with such force it knocked him down."

"Declan lies!" Tears burned a trail down Henrietta's cheeks.

"Watch yourself! To call the preacher's son a liar is blasphemous." Amy spun away and hurried after the townspeople.

Henrietta stood in the middle of the street. Waya had been right. Evil had visited her home tonight. There had to be a way to save her mother. The elders spurred by Declan had accused many and hung some declared to be witches. Her heart beat a rapid tattoo. She couldn't let this happen to her mama.

Inside her house, she grabbed the Tome of Magick and wrapped it in her shawl. She crept out of the house. The shouting of the angry villagers faded away, and only then did Hettie venture past her gate. She snuck past the dwellings of the townspeople, quiet now, all snug in their homes. She stayed out of the moonlight instead seeking out the shadows till she reached the window of the jail cell where Mama was being held.

"*Psst. Psst.* Mama!" Henrietta grasped the metal bar and pulled herself up to peer inside.

"Henrietta, dear child, I don't understand, why have they taken me? Where am I?" Mama asked, her face a mixture of uncertainty and awareness.

"Mama, you're better. My prayers have been answered." Henrietta choked out. To have her mother healthy only to be hung at the gallows on the morrow was more than she could bear. The witch trials were short and punishment by hanging swiftly executed. She had to do something to save her mama.

"Better? Was I ill?" She grasped the metal bars wrapping her hands over Henrietta's

"Papa died and you've been suffering terrible ever since," Henrietta said.

"But why have they put me in jail?" The moonlight shone through the window on Mama's face, her brow creased with worry.

"They are accusing you of being a witch, having sold your soul to the devil. Mama, I have to get you out of there." She jerked on the metal bars in frustration.

Henrietta felt his presence before his arm came around her waist, pulling her up against him. His hand over her mouth, Declan said in a rasping voice, "I can save your mother. But in return you have to give me something I want. Something I need."

She nodded yes, anything, she'd do anything to save her mother from the hangman's noose.

"If I remove my hand from your mouth, do you promise not to yell?" His whispered words were hot in her ear.

She nodded yes. Tears welled in her eyes, spilling over. He removed his hand and readjusted his arm around her waist, pulling her even tighter against him. With his free hand, he brushed her hair away from her neckline and ran his tongue up and down her neck. "What I want from you" — he nipped at her neck with his teeth — "is your magick power."

Henrietta drew deep inside herself for calm; to show fear in the face of evil would give him more power. This was not the Declan she knew. Since Gram had introduced her to the world of magick, she had been aware there were things in this world she knew nothing of — things of both joy and evil. Gram had said *evil walks among us.*

"I have no magick power." She closed her eyes and breathed deep. She must remain calm to help Mama.

"Ah-h, but you do. The first daughter of each generation of your father's family has power, and that my dear, would be you." Another nip of his teeth sent pain searing through her skin.

"Even if I had such power, magick, I'd not know how to give it to you." Her heart beat so loud and fast she was sure he could hear it, but she kept her voice steady.

"Do you want to save your mother from hanging in the gallows tomorrow?" He shook her.

"Yes." His grip sent shock waves through her.

"Do you want your mother to live?"

"Yes!"

He turned her around and holding her shoulders, lifted her with strength not of this world until her feet swung like a rag doll. His eyes blazed like green glass, the only color in the gray, moonlit landscape. "Henrietta Anne Wynn, do you pledge to come to me of your own free will when your mother is safe from further persecution?"

"Yes!" With this final 'yes' she had made her deal with Declan. The power of three would be next to impossible to break.

Declan let loose of her and she dropped to the ground in a heap. The structure holding the cell dissolved in a cloud of dust and smoke. Mama sat on the ground beside her, and wrapped Henrietta in a comforting embrace.

Declan stood with one arm outstretched towards the destroyed building. He chanted in a tongue unfamiliar to Henrietta.

Mama gasped as the rubble rose up into the air and rebuilt the jail.

"I have wiped the memories of the events of this night from the fair citizen's minds." Declan turned on his heel and disappeared in a cloud of fog.

"Mama?" The tears spilled over and she looked into Mama's eyes, no longer vacant but full of concern.

"It's all right. He's gone. Let's go home." She smoothed Henrietta's hair.

How could Declan destroy the building that held Mama? What had he said to her? *Do you pledge to come to me of your own free will?* She needed to get Mama home and go meet Waya. His father, Adahy, was the Shaman. He would know what to do. She fingered the moon totem. She would need all the help she could get to break the curse of giving herself to Declan.

Sun broke over the treetops, painting the trees with a profusion of autumn colors. Henrietta pulled on her cloak. Pine needles and fallen autumn leaves crushed underfoot sent a pungent smell into the air. The Hemlock tree was not far from the path. She sat on an old stump near the meeting site. The forest was quiet now, and she watched the morning unfold.

Birds began their morning chirping and flying to and fro. Fall had come late this year and many trees had not yet lost their vibrant leaves. The forest was waking up. Her eyes closed, she concentrated on all the life currents around her. A rustle in the fallen leaves, the babbling brook, and the hum of insects not yet taken by the frost; she had all the elements she would need. Magick was part will, part tokens and conjuring. A leaf here, a twig there, her crystal wand and the right spell. All different incantations took the assistance of different bits and pieces.

Tonight was Samhain. According to Gran's book, this was the strongest night for magick. This was a night the veil was thin between the mortal and magickal realms. Perfect. Tonight she'd somehow escape Declan and her pledge.

She heard a footstep on the path and opened her eyes.

"Waya!" She ran to him and into his waiting embrace. "Something terrible has happened. The townspeople called Mama a witch and were going to hang her. Declan has an evil power in him and made me promise to come to him, and in exchange he would save Mama."

"What did you answer, little one?" He gently rubbed her back.

"I'm sorry, Waya, I had to answer *yes*. I had to save Mama."

A muscle quivered in his jaw. "Declan is a powerful dark witch. He spouts his dark magick. He is trying to become a force to be reckoned with. The witches who were accused by Declan and the elders, and hung, he inherited their life forces. He is stronger for it."

"He's the preacher's son! How can this be?"

"Declan is no longer the preacher's son. When I looked into his eyes yesterday, it was not Declan who stared back but pure evil. Another entity has taken over his soul." Waya set her away from him. "We must devise a way to save you until you are strong enough, powerful enough, and clever enough to oppose him."

"He said he wants me to come to him of my own free will. Mama is safe. That cannot be changed, can it?" Her heart skipped a beat, and a chill raced up her spine at the thought of Mama sinking back into her depression. Her recovery was due to the Goddess and could not be undone by Declan.

Shaman Adahy walked towards them from the woods. "Henrietta, you know the power of three. Declan asked you three times and you answered three times. The magick he performed saving your mother is sealed for eternity. Your pact with the witch Declan is not sealed. To give him control of your magick you must do so willingly. There are consequences if you don't follow through. But the outcome can be altered."

The old Shaman leaned heavily on his medicine staff. Adahy waved one hand around the expanse of the clearing. "There is powerful magick here. I was favored by your Grand-mother. We had a bond of harmony and worked together on many enchantments. She performed much of her magick in this space, as did I. Because of her and what came before this time, we will make great magick on this hallowed ground." He lifted his staff overhead. The feathers bound by leather thongs danced in the light fall breeze. He turned in a full circle, chant-ing in his native tongue.

Henrietta was mesmerized by the Shaman's dance. Waya laid a hand on her shoulder and they both watched. "Father is asking the great spirit to show us humble beings a way to fight this evil."

Adahy thumped his medicine staff against the forest floor three times. He stood head bowed for a moment, then lifted his head.

His sage face fairly creased with wisdom. "It has been shown to me, Henrietta, you are a powerful witch, like your Grandmother. Waya too, a mighty warrior and seeker of justice, has great magick to fight this evil. The struggle comes tonight and will take all three of us if you are to survive." He walked toward the cover of the woods.

"What are we to do?" She was sure the men could hear the rapid beat of her heart.

Adahy stopped and looked over his shoulder. "Before the day is done, while the sun makes the journey into night, we will meet here at your sacred circle. There all will be decided. Go now, prepare for the meeting. Declan will have no choice but to be there, this my vision has shown." He disappeared into the thick woods.

"Henrietta." Waya cupped her chin. His expression stilled as he leaned in and kissed her. "Be brave, little one. I have much to do before we meet tonight. Stay in your house till then. Declan can only come in if you ask him to."

"I will. And, Waya?"

"Yes?"

"Thank you for telling Adahy and asking for his help."

"I didn't. He knew from his visions. Come, I'll walk you back."

Tonight's ritual would take all the power Henrietta could summon. She practiced protection spells, chants and charms while Mama, with the help of a relaxing tea, slept the day away. In the middle of learning how to summon the power that dwelled deep inside of her, there was a rap on the door.

She drew in a calming breath, and spoke through the door, "Who's there?"

"Henrietta, it's me, Declan, open up." His voice was young again, not the harsh rasp of last night.

"No, Mama is ill. She's sleeping." She crossed her fingers against the lie, that it might not wreak mayhem with her magick. "Declan, do you remember last night? What happened between us?"

"I didn't see you last night I was in bed before dark. Come out, walk with me," he pleaded. "Tell me Waya is not in there. You shouldn't be seen in his company."

"No, Waya is not here, and no, I'll not walk with you. Go away." Convinced the evil spirit lingered inside him, she wasn't going to take any chances.

She waited by the door until his footsteps on the graveled path faded. The candle on the table flamed to life with a flick of her hand. Another hour and she'd leave for the sacred circle. She had studied the book, memorized what she could, and tried spells she could do inside. She would pen a letter to Mama that she was going away for a while. With Mama's health restored by the Goddess, Declan having wiped the witchcraft charge out of the villager's minds, Hettie knew her Mother would be fine.

Picking up a quill, Henrietta penned a missive telling her Mama not to worry, she needed to go away for her own safety.

She charmed a totem with a protection spell, and wrote that her Mama should wear it always. They had discussed Declan, witches and all that had transpired the night before.

She moved the candle to the hearth and spread her shawl on the trestle table. Gathering the Tome of Magick, candles, crystal wand, and sacred rocks, she placed them on her shawl and bound it up tight. Dressed in her black wool dress, her unruly hair in a tight bun with various tendrils escaping even now, she slipped her cape over her shoulders, pulled the hood up, picked up her bundle and tiptoed out the door.

The evening sky was fantastically full of color. Just the right mixture of violet and blue laced with bolts of scarlet bouncing off the clouds. It was a crimson sky only with deeper more passionate colors. She stopped at the edge of the woods to admire the sunset and breathe in the scent of the pines. She shifted her bundle on her shoulder and entered the woods. She found it dark and hard to see in the forest. It didn't matter, she knew where to go. She'd been there a hundred times since Gram had given her the spell book. She missed Gran; her passing came soon after Papa's and had left an empty space in her heart.

Waya and Adahy were at the circle and had built a fire.

"We will guard the circle and you." Waya took her cape from her, folding it and placing it in the circle.

"I must prepare the sacred space without you. The circle must be consecrated for the goddess to attend." She felt blessed they had come.

"We know this. Rest assured we will protect you. I have spread the essential herbs around the edge of the ring. The fire will ward off animals and all spirits that have an aversion to flame."

Adahy began his chant and dance around the circle for protection. Waya carried her bundle to the circle. His ebony eyes sparkled with the reflection of the firelight. "Father has worked a ritual that will see you safe in another place until Declan can be dealt with. I'll find you." He lifted the totem that hung around her neck. "Rub it when you need extra power." He pressed the bone moon against her chest and stepped back away out of the circle.

The fire crackled and popped, sending a spray of sparks skyward.

Waya's bronze skin glistened in the firelight, giving the impression he was made of gold. A black tattoo of a wolf decorated his arm and the eyes seemed alive in the light from the blaze. He was magnificent and he was hers. She believed with all her heart they would be together one day.

"What are you doing?" roared Declan, as he lumbered from the woods. His long black coat flapped with each stride. "Come out of the circle, Henrietta. You owe me!" He prowled around the circle ranting on until he came face to face with Waya.

Henrietta began chanting, with her arms lifted towards the stars. She turned with her eyes closed visualized a safe place, a place not unlike Waxing, where she lived now. A place without Declan, a place where she could live and be safe.

She opened her eyes to see Waya push Declan to the ground and advance on him. Declan jumped up, hand outstretched and sent a bolt of light energy knocking Waya down. In a matter of seconds Declan spun around stalking the shaman.

Adahy's fevered singing reached a high pitch, almost a screech.

Waya yelled, "No! Father!"

She turned in the circle, still chanting, reaching the end of her spell. Adahy pointed his staff at her and a bolt of energy swept over her, knocking her down. The last thing she saw before the engulfing darkness was Adahy crumbling to the ground with Declan's knife sticking out of his chest.

October 16, 2012

Hettie woke with a start. She glanced at the clock on the wall. It was well past midnight, two in the morning to be exact. A whiff of smoke and pine assaulted her nose. She checked her sage wand where it lay spent on the iron, leaf-shaped plate. Could the smells be remnants of her dream?

Waya — what had become of him? Did Adahy die from the blade Declan stuck in him? She would give anything to know, but the chances of her ever knowing were slim to none. She fingered the moon talisman; she wore it always.

Setting her cup in the sink, she looked out the window at the sliver of moon. It would be full by Samhain. She wanted to try a new spell when magick was the strongest, a seeing spell. Instead of the future, she wanted to see into the past.

In her bedroom, she flicked her hand and the drapes closed. The Tiffany lamp flickered on and soft melodious music filled the air. This was her sanctuary. She had arranged her altar against the wall in front of a small octagonal window facing the arc of the moon; the light shining in now made her crystal wand glow. It had never been a straight wand, always a bit bent on the end, and the shaft had four smooth sides instead of being round. The wand had traveled from England on a schooner with Gram to the new world, to Waxing.

The rod of crystal had been Gram's and Gram's mother's before her, and passed down through the ages till Gram had placed the wand in Hettie's hands along with the Tome of Magick.

Moonlight empowered the wand, and it grew stronger each passing cycle. She rarely used it. Once in a while she would visit the sacred circle in the woods, always alone, the same one she had used all those centuries ago. The ancient hemlock tree was still alive; it appeared healthy and strong, and she was sure great magick dwelled in it. Waya and Adahy had used the tree in many of their supernatural invocations. She hadn't witnessed this, but Waya had told her many stories of the great tree and how it was a significant part of their rituals. Even Adahy and Gram had shared their rituals and magick beneath the great branches.

The forest was alive, and she knew where every berry bush, mushroom and toad lived. They were her woods. Thanks to the Historic Landscape Preservation Program the woods were safe from loggers and the encroachment of towns. Waxing, being a small community, focused on the fishing industry. Not many people wandered the forest paths. The woods were her sanctuary. That's where she would go on Samhain.

She snuggled down in her bed, appreciating the pillow top mattress. She pulled the dark blue comforter up. Picking up *Techniques for Dating Mr. Right*, she opened it to the bookmark. Relationships had eluded her in this new world. She dated a few different guys over the years, but none had clicked. Her fault, she guessed.

Hettie had led an isolated life since she arrived here. The less anyone knew about her the better. She wasn't a good liar, so she kept her life simple and safe. She longed for love, comfort and connection. Who wouldn't? After ten years in the new world, who was she kidding? Unless he fell in her lap, she'd probably never meet Mr. Right.

Determined to make a change in her love life, she began reading.

"Try something new. Take up jogging, it's healthy and you never know who you will run into. Are you a TV buff? Go out to a movie instead, and stop at the local coffee shop for a late night latte. Learn a new skill. Golf, bowling, archery or ballroom dancing are great ways to meet singles." She slammed the book shut.

Kitty chose that moment to jump up on the bed. The big orange cat purred and kneaded the blankets. Kitty was another lost soul Aunt Bea had taken in not long before she'd found Hettie wandering, lost and confused, in the woods nearby. She'd opened her heart and home to Hettie when no family could be found. Aunt Bea had called Hettie's condition *amnesia,* and Hettie had been relieved when the old lady stopped asking her questions about her past.

Hettie could picture Aunt Bea with her silver hair, shaking her finger and saying, "I have no family. Now I have you. We are family, us and Kitty." Then she'd embrace Hettie in a warm loveable hug.

Aunt Bea had left the shop, apartment and a small inheritance to her. Hettie was eternally grateful for Aunt Bea's generosity, and missed her every day.

"Kitty, you're my good boy." Petting him was soothing. "You miss her too, don't you?" The tension eased out of her shoulders. Her eyes began to droop and she felt sleep coming on.

Halloween would be here soon. Hettie worked on decorating her shop. She enjoyed Halloween and the costumed children, the cute little witches, vampires and superheroes; it didn't matter to her, she loved them all. This year she had ordered an extra special treat for the children, miniature crystal witches holding a crystal wand and a broom. She would bless each one to protect the children on Samhain. This would be a happy day and a dangerous one.

She longed for a child of her own. Deep in her heart, she knew she'd never have a family. Unless she would put herself out in the, what did the book call it? The dating game.

She plugged in the purple twinkle lights that hung around the storefront window and stepped back to admire her work. Yes, she liked it. Kitty, curled up sleeping in his cat bed in the store window, added to the overall theme. The public would expect a black cat. Orange would have to do. Besides, he complimented the Jack-O-Lantern. She waved her hand and set light to the spice candles she had bought from Ella, her friend, and occasional employee.

Hettie would have to order more candles from her friend. The wonderful smelling and long lasting harvest candles were flying off the shelf. She wrote on her list of things to do *call Ella*. Maybe Ella would have the candles ready by Saturday when the coven was scheduled to meet.

The delivery door buzzer rang. Hettie opened the door to a tall man, easy smile, dark hair, and warm cinnamon skin. Not old Mr. Tuttle, her usual delivery man.

"Where's Mr. Tuttle?"

"He's been assigned a desk job. Hurt his back last week."

"I have a couple of boxes you'll need to sign for." He handed her the electronic signature board.

She signed the board as he carried the boxes in one by one and stacked them in her small storeroom.

The last box was not squarely on top. Kitty chose that moment to meander over and leap on the top box, causing it to tip over, and crash to the floor. Emitting a loud '*meow*' he scampered off.

"Sounds like something broke. Let me open it up and we'll do a damage assessment." He pulled out a box knife.

"No! Everything is fine." Hettie leaned over and mumbled an incantation, placing her hands on the center of the damaged box, repairing the broken goods.

"Look, lady, it's my job. I heard something break. We need to assess the damage."

"Okay." She glanced at his name tag. "Mr. Wolf."

"Evan."

"Evan, then," she liked the sound of his name.

He opened the box and a look of wonder crossed his face. His brows puckered together. "Looks like all the little... witches are intact. Sure sounded like they all broke. Shattered."

He looked at Hettie, really looked at her. His look seemed to appreciate her as a woman. Her heart missed a beat. His obsidian eyes crinkled at the corners. His mouth was full and his cheekbones high. A ruggedly handsome face, not the face of youth, but a mature looking man, and for a moment she thought this would be how Waya would have matured.

Take a chance, said a little voice in her head. "Would you have time for a cup of coffee or tea while I pack up a few items I need to return?" The words had flown from her mouth, and now she couldn't take them back.

He took a quick look at his watch. "Sure, coffee would be great."

Evan Wolf followed her through the hallway to her office area. She poured coffee into a mug bearing the words *Witches are people too.*

His fingers touched hers and she had the wildest urge to jump back. Maybe this was a mistake, inviting him in. She put a box on the desk, started wrapping bubble wrap around a music box. "I'm Hettie, I own this shop, the Crystal Witch." She smiled and secured the package with the mailing tape, then handed it to him.

Evan held the box. Had she felt that jolt of electricity when he accidentally touched her fingers? She had the most intense blue eyes, set off by wild, long, curly black hair. Nothing tame about this woman.

"Would you be free for lunch or dinner tomorrow?" He was curious how she'd respond after seeing the look of puzzlement on her face when he asked the question.

"I...."

It was too soon; he should never have asked her out. What was wrong with him? He just met the woman. "I'm sorry I put you on the spot. Maybe another time?" What a fool he was.

"No, it's all right. I would like to have dinner with you. Tomorrow night will work for me. Ella Stone looks after the shop on Tuesday evenings." She smiled and the glow warmed him.

"Small world. Ella is a friend of my cousin, Darla Blackfeather. Do you know her?"

"Yes, I do. Darla is wonderful person. She never mentioned you to me. I only say that because she's always trying to fix me up with a date."

He chuckled. "That sounds like Darla. I finished my tour with the Marines a couple weeks ago. Just got back in to town and my old job."

"What time should I pick you up?" He couldn't stop staring at her mouth, especially when her pink tongue darted out to wet those full lips. He shook his head; what the hell? She oozed sexuality.

"I can leave at six o'clock when Ella gets here." Her high-heeled red boots clicked on the tile floor behind him as she followed him to the door.

"See you then," he looked over his shoulder at a picture of perfection. She was the whole package, curly black hair, tight black dress and killer red boots, and he had a date with her.

Evan was prompt. He hadn't had a date in a very long time. He parked his car and hit the security lock. Around the corner and two doors down from the Crystal Witch shop, cinnamon and cloves tickled his nose. The bell over the door sang out when he entered. The purple lights in the window cast a festive luminous light into the shop. The crystal witches he'd delivered yesterday were standing in neat rows by the Jack-O-Lantern in the front window. There must have been a couple of hundred of the three inch glass witches. He couldn't imagine Hettie selling that many in the next couple of weeks.

"May I help you?" Ella finished cleaning her eye glasses and put them on. "Evan Wolf! Are you Hettie's date?"

"That would be me, the date. I'm here to take Hettie to dinner." He held out his hand.

She placed her dainty hand in his big one, and then pulled him close for a hug, "You be good to my friend. Don't go breaking her heart you gorgeous man, you." She squeezed his hand before letting go.

"Ella, are you trying to scare my date away?" Hettie said, with a laugh as she emerged from the office at the back of the store.

He couldn't take his eyes off of her. She'd been in his dream last night. He had tasted those sweet lips and tangled his hands in her hair. And all she wore was the red high heeled boots she wore yesterday and she sported now. A tight, mid-calf autumn green dress accentuated her smooth curves, and a black beaded shawl was the icing on the cake. Her hair was pulled back in some kind of twist and secured on her head with an ornamental clip which sparkled when she turned to hand Ella a slip of paper.

"My candle order, I can't keep the harvest ones on the shelf."

That clip would have to come out, he decided. She had a slim, wild, unearthly beauty with her black curly hair trying to escape from the clasp, cobalt eyes and skin like bone china.

"You look beautiful." He crooked his arm and she slipped her hand through. Even through the layers of clothes, he felt a jolt of electricity. Was it just him, or did she feel it too? "Thought we'd have Italian, if it's okay with you?"

"Love Italian!" She squeezed his arm, sending another shock through him.

"There's a really good restaurant a short walk from here. You game?" He winked when he caught her eye.

She laughed. "I'm game."

By Saturday Hettie was on cloud nine. She'd been out of her comfort zone and out on a date every night this past week with Evan. He didn't mind waiting for her to close up the shop. They laughed and had such a good time together. Tonight was the coven meeting. She had a date with Evan on Sunday, but she didn't know if she could wait that long. Since she met him, her body seemed to be supercharged. Ella told her she needed to get laid. Maybe that was it. All she knew was the mere thought of Evan sent her heart racing, and her nether region tingling almost inducing a self-inflicted orgasm.

Sunday was a long twenty-four hours away. Her longing for Evan was outside the norm. She knew this, but didn't have a logical explanation for this feeling. She feared she would explode if they didn't make love soon.

Tonight she'd be with the coven, her friends. She still practiced her craft. She had learned to control her power. The local coven of five witches had welcomed her among them. Hettie practiced as a gray witch. *Do no harm* was her creed. However, she would defend herself and those she cared about with whatever means available to her. Luckily, nothing had happened in Waxing to force her to try out the fighting spells she'd learned. She joined the coven and attended the monthly meetings, mostly for the companionship.

She picked up the feather duster and made her way around the shop. She selected one of Mae's handmade soaps off the display table.

Mae, the first coven witch she'd met, made wonderful healing soaps. Hettie held the cheerfully wrapped bar to her nose and breathed in the calming lavender essence. Ella, her good friend and sister witch, created the most amazing aroma therapy candles, and Hettie had a hard time keeping up with the demand.

She ran the duster over the few candles left on the shelf, then continued to the teas nestled in the bookcase display stand. The tea blends made by Ivy, the youngest member of the coven, were medicinal and in high demand as the teas worked exceptionally well. Often Hettie would take special orders for teas to treat different afflictions.

Kitty rubbed up against her legs and "Meowed".

"I know, you're ready for some dinner and comfy time. I'm almost done tidying up."

Kitty gave a final "Meow" and headed upstairs to wait for his mistress.

She gathered the papers on her desk, mostly spell and incantation notes, and put them in her red briefcase.

The door buzzer rang, announcing a customer. Dang, she had meant to lock up five minutes ago. A cool breeze swirled around her legs and sent shivers racing up her spine until the small hairs on her neck stood up as if electrified.

The customer turned and headed toward her, his long coat flapping around his legs, his hands stuffed into deep pockets.

"Sorry, I'm closed. I forgot to lock the door."

He looked at her from under the hood to his coat. His face shadowed.

He took a step closer. There was something familiar about his stance.

"You'll have to come back tomorrow. The shop is closed for today." She grabbed the keys out of her pocket and marched toward him.

He threw back his hood. "Hello, Henrietta." His mouth curved up in a deadly grin. His green eyes, sharp as emeralds bore into her.

She had dreaded the day she would hear that voice again. Declan! She tried to move around him, but he grabbed her and threw her up against the wall. Her stomach churned. She had to get away.

"It's your turn to fulfill our little bargain. It wasn't nice to leave as you did. I had to kill that old Indian. He finished his invocation before he died, useless old man." His voice was inflamed and belligerent, his breath hot on her face even from the two feet that separated them.

She ran for the back of the store; he was there before her. All that stood between them was an oak table full of handmade soaps. She mumbled a quick spell and the soap dissolved into hot liquid. The melted liquid ran down on to Declan's shoes and a hissing noise rose as the molten soap burned holes in his shoes, scorching his feet.

Declan screamed in agony, hopping about, trying to get away from the hexed soap.

Hettie grabbed her briefcase and cell then ran out the back door. In her car, driving away from the shop, she called 9-1-1 to report a break in.

She needed help and fast. She drove to Ella's house. The bungalow was dark; Ella must have left for the coven meeting. Hettie put the car in gear and drove to Darla's house, the High Priestess of the coven. The windows were ablaze with light. Hettie grabbed her briefcase, jumped out and locked the car.

This would be one meeting none of them would ever forget.

"I'm so thankful to the Goddess you are all here tonight." Hettie stood in the middle of Darla's family room, not knowing where or how to begin.

Darla rose from the small couch and put an arm around her. "Start at the beginning."

Ella patted the seat Darla had vacated. "Come, sit by me. We're your coven. There's not anything you can't share with us."

Mae, the crone of their small group, sat on the recliner.

Young Ivy sat cross-legged on the carpet munching on a bowl of popcorn. Rosalba paced the room a bundle of nervous energy. "Leah, my spiritual guide, came to me earlier today. She told me of dark arts being practiced here in our town, directly related to you, Hettie." She stopped and glared at Hettie. "Are you involved in this evil?"

If looks could kill, Hettie would have been lying on the carpet taking her last breath. Her heart clenched, for she had brought this danger to her friends. Not intentionally, and yet, she felt responsible. Declan was here in the present because of his obsession with her.

"Please, Rosalba, sit down," Hettie said. "I have a story to tell you. I never had amnesia."

"Go on, child," Mae said. She waved her hand in Rosalba's direction. "Sit. Hettie is going to tell us her story. No more interruptions."

Rosalba plopped down on the brown overstuffed chair.

Hettie gathered her courage. "Difficult as it is to believe, I've time traveled from the year sixteen-ninety-two."

A collective gasp filled the air.

"Cool!" Ivy said. "Don't start till I get back." She'd polished off the popcorn and returned the empty bowl to the kitchen.

Darla stood with her spirit staff and then tapped it three times on the floor. "I call our coven to order. I evoked a protection spell on my house earlier. I thought it prudent after Rosalba told me of the black magick. Whatever we hear or say will be kept within these walls. Hettie, you may begin"

"I was born Henrietta Anne Wynn on October first in sixteen-seventy-four." She went on to tell them everything so they would be prepared for the battle to come.

Hettie finished her story by saying, "And Declan showed up at the Crystal Witch this evening. I've got to stop him. He's evil. I have no idea how he got here or if he's going back. I know it's a lot to ask, but I need your help. I can't fight him alone."

Rosalba was the first to reach Hettie, embracing her in a hug. "You poor girl. What you've been through. I'm with you whatever we have to do."

Everyone jumped at a knock on the door. "Probably the pizza I ordered," Darla laughed and went to answer the door.

"Hey, what are you doing here? You know it's our meeting night, cousin."

"Is Hettie here? I've just come from her shop. It looks like a bomb exploded in there." Evan's voice cut through Hettie's thoughts.

"Evan, I'm in here. How did you know where to find me?" Relief flooded through her.

He stood in the living room and removed his scarf and jacket. He only had eyes for Hettie.

"I figured Ella might know, and when she wasn't home I remembered Darla had a meeting tonight, thought Ella would be here." He ran his hands through his hair, "I went by your shop. It was a mess. Soap or something all over the floor, shelves ripped down. The whole shop was a disaster and the front door was off the hinges. What the hell happened?" His eyes blazed like black embers.

Ella got up off the sofa. "Sit, Evan. It's a long story."

Hettie took his hand and led the way to the couch. "It's time to tell you who I really am."

Hettie finished her story and said, "I'll understand, Evan, if you don't want to see me anymore."

"Quit seeing you? When I've just found you?" He pulled Hettie into his embrace. "I'll protect you with everything I've got. I can't lose you."

Hettie's heart filled with joy. Instead of running for the hills, Evan vowed to protect her.

"I am not Waya, but I am descended from the same ancestors. The same blood flows through my veins that flowed through Waya's." Reaching under his shirt collar he brought forth a bone moon on a leather thong. A matching one to the one Waya had given her.

Individually they would be no match for Declan, but with six witches and Evan, they might stand a chance. In a way, she guessed Waya had found her.

It turned out Evan, like his cousin, Darla Blackfeather had some magick powers inherited from their tribal ancestors.

Everyone contributed to the plan to defeat Declan. The ritual would take place on Samhain, four days from now.

Hettie parked her car behind the shop. Evan pulled in behind her, and then Ella's BMW with the other five witches inside. Hettie walked into the shop with the others behind her. She stopped, aghast; the shelves were back up on the walls, the broken items mended and the soaps back on the table in their pretty handmade wrappers. The door creaked, still hanging by one hinge. The rest had been restored to look as it had this morning when she opened up the shop.

"How is this possible?" Hettie looked at the witches.

"While you told Evan about your story, I snuck out and worked a little magick." Ella toyed with her blonde ponytail.

"Thanks, but what about the sheriff?"

"He won't remember the phone call. I didn't think it wise for him to know about Declan." Ella grabbed up the teapot and headed for the sink. "Don't worry, I erased the 9-1-1 call from the on-call dispatcher's memory, and anyone who saw the shop in disarray will not hold the memory of the incident."

"Do you have a toolbox?" Evan shoved his hands in his pockets.

"Yes, in the office on the floor behind the desk." Warmed by Ella's thoughtfulness, she smiled.

Carrying a screw driver he walked over and fixed the door. He shut the door firmly, locked it, and pulled down the shade.

"What are you doing, Ella? It's late. You should all go home." Hettie had to let out a little breath at the happiness in her heart; these were her friends and they cared what happened to her. They had more than proved to be gray witches and willing to join forces with her to fight Declan.

"Hettie's right. You can go home." Evan slipped his arm around Hettie's waist and pulled her close. "I'll be with her tonight."

Hettie felt the surge of energy that followed any contact with Evan.

Darla exchanged a look of "I told you so!" with Ella. "That's fine if you stay with her, but we'll be invoking protection and security spells down here," Darla said. "Declan can't get upstairs unless Hettie invites him. He can create mayhem in the shop, unless we put these in place." She shook her finger at Evan. "There's no changing our minds. Off with the two of you. Being in love, having love and making love are three of the most powerful elements against evil that exist."

Ella gave a shooing motion with her hand. "Off with you!"

Behind them Ivy, Mae and Rosalba chanted a spell in unison three times.

Sleep safe this night, the two of you.
Love surround and protect thee,
Fuse this love that is so new,
So mote it be.

Hettie hesitated with her hand on the doorknob to her apartment. No one had ever entered her sanctuary. She trusted Evan. She felt safe and cared for, and even loved when she was near him. Her sexual awakening was in no small part due to this man. Along with her heightened senses of magick. Since meeting him she had a greater awareness of her strength, her magick powers.

Kitty waited patiently on the landing. Hettie picked him up and stroked the fuzzy orange cat. She spoke the opening charm and entered her room. With a flick of her hand, the Tiffany lamp turned on, the shades closed and soft lovely music of violins played in the background. She set Kitty down on the floor and he jumped up on the rocking chair.

Evan turned her around and touched his forehead to hers. "Hettie, we'll get through this together. I'll sleep on the couch."

She unzipped his jacket, pushed it down his arms. She wanted, needed this man. "No floor for you tonight." She took his hand and led him to the bed.

With another wave of her hand, the lamp clicked off and a dozen candles throughout the room flamed to life. She took off her clothes and stood before him in only her bra and lace panties. Magick and love flowed through her.

He worked fast to strip down, comically hopping on one foot to get his last sock off.

As she reached for her hair clip, Evan caught her wrist. "Let me. I've wanted to take that clip out since the first day I met you." He undid the clip, and finger combed her hair till it hung in curls down her back nearly to her waist. "Beautiful. Your hair, your body, your soul...." He cupped her chin and kissed her sweetly on the lips. He slipped one finger under the strap on her bra followed it to her back and unclasped it. Then he slid her lacey underwear down. The burning in her belly threatened to consume her; she couldn't wait any longer. She pulled him down on the bed with her, kissing him with all the built up passion she had.

"Are you sure this is what you want, Hettie?" He asked, his voice husky with desire.

"I'm sure. Stop talking." She pulled him down on top. Skin to skin didn't cause electric shocks instead their touching made magick. She was vaguely aware of the bed rising off the ground like a wonderful cloud floating in her room. Stars sparkled on the ceiling and the music reached a crescendo each time they climaxed. Evan made love to her three times during the night. Their destiny was sealed. He was hers and she was his. The strongest union between a man and a woman, Gram's tome said, was a bond of love.

Time flew by, and the eve of Samhain arrived. Each time Hettie looked out her window at the woods she felt a dark energy. Declan was near, just biding his time. The protection spells had worked. Tonight Ella and Darla would remove the spells before leaving for the sacred circle. Hettie dressed in her black wool dress, black boots and shawl, the same ones she had worn when she arrived in this time period.

When she entered the shop to see Ella and Darla in their witch's costumes, she had to chuckle. They looked beautiful and deadly at the same time. They were helping her with the shop this evening. Evan was Paul Bunyan, complete with an axe and horn handled knife on his belt. He had told Hettie the knife had been passed down to each Shaman through the ages. At one time Waya had possessed it.

"You all look great," Hettie said.

"Come see the children," Ella gushed. "They are all so darn cute!"

Hettie hurried toward the door, grabbing her witch's hat off the counter.

"Trick or treat!" said a little devil accompanied by a tiny witch and a zombie.

"Oh, blessed be!" Hettie took three little crystal witches and blessed each one before dropping them into the Halloween sacks.

"Thank you," they said in unison.

"Sorry I missed most of the trick-or-treaters," Hettie told her friends. "I was reworking my spell and getting things together for the circle." Mentally she checked off her list: spell, broom, crystal wand, bowl for water, black ribbon, and a sprig of rosemary. Blessed be to the Goddess for giving her the fortitude to start work on the spell last year. The spell to travel into the past would be used tonight to send Declan back.

"Do you think this Declan will show up?" Darla asked.

"He will. He wants me and he wants my power. The hardest part will be convincing him I'll go along." A cold wind blew through the store despite the closed door and windows. "Declan. He's near."

"Evan, can you take Ella and Darla to meet the others, by the old hemlock tree near the sacred circle?" Hettie withdrew her crystal wand and the written spell from her bag of tools and handed her bag to Ella. She had memorized the spell. She put it in her pocket for safekeeping.

Hettie took hold of Ella's free hand and grabbed Darla's hand. "Ella and Darla, sweep the sacred circle, prepare it, and thank you both so much for helping. I... ." For a long moment she looked at Evan. "We couldn't do it without you."

After the others left, Hettie sat waiting. Her mind reviewed all the ways this could go terribly wrong. She shook herself; positive thoughts only. Tired of sitting and tired of waiting, she paced to the front of the store and back, again and again.

Evan would build a fire outside the circle. Fire was a powerful protector and as long as he stayed by it, he should be safe. The fire was important too, because after the incantation was cast, she needed to burn the written spell. The ashes would consummate the spell and seal the incantation. Once burnt, it could never be revoked.

The door to the shop opened. "Hello, Henrietta." Declan's voice was clear and crisp as a frosty morning. He moved toward her with a slow predatory stride.

She could do this, she could do this. She repeated her mantra. "Declan, you came back." Goose bumps scurried across skin so cold even her wool dress failed to warm her.

"How quaint, you kept your dress. But then it is only fitting you go back in time in what you wore when you left." He took her witch hat off her head and tossed it on the table. "My, my, do you have to stoop to playing the part? You are magnificent without this ridiculous hat." He strode to the back of the shop, checking in the storeroom. "No one here just you and me. How delightful!"

She was keenly aware of his scrutiny. He looked her over, circling her, and she stood perfectly still, not moving an inch for fear of his retribution. She prayed to the Goddess Evan and the other witches were at the circle now, preparing for the battle to come; if only she knew they were safe for sure. She needed to stick to the plan and get Declan to the Sacred Circle.

"Aren't you happy to see me?" Declan drew a finger down her cheek across her lip, down her neck, and encircled her neck with his hand. "Are you ready to give yourself to me of your own free will, as promised?" He tightened his hold on her neck and cut off her oxygen. She convulsed in a fit of coughing and he eased up.

Hettie shrugged loose and stepped away, rubbing her sore neck. "Only on my own terms. Only if we go back to Waxing as it was, to Waya, to that night when I left."

Declan chuckled. "Ah-h I suppose you wish to see your Indian lover once more. You know he died trying to save his father. Heroic till the minute my knife stopped his beating heart. It was for the best; he would have died of a broken heart had he lived."

He grabbed her arm in a painful hold, pulling her to within inches of his face. "Kiss me Henrietta, show me you've changed. When we are joined, there'll be no stopping what we can do. Our power will rule the world. Kiss me!"

The plan, she had to stick to the plan. She was drawn to him, a spell he had invoked, surely. Summoning her power, she put up a wall against his bewitchments. She wouldn't kiss him. She pulled away, backing toward the door. "No, 'tis enough I've agreed to go with you."

"I'll taste your treats later. The woods haven't changed much. Some trees fallen and are gone from the landscape, I was pleased to find the old hemlock tree. It's definitely full of magick. It could sense me." He fluttered his fingers. "The needles on the old tree quivered when I walked by." He advanced on her. "And your pathetic excuse for a Sacred Circle. Really, Henrietta, I expected you to create a more powerful circle, not use such a primitive one. However, as it turns out I came through the veil at nearly the same location."

Grabbing her and bending her arm behind her, he aimed her out the back door.

"What's this?" Declan said. "This little gang of witches believes they're going to stop me? Ha!" He pushed Hettie so hard she stumbled. Jerking her back against him, Declan pulled out his ritual knife, and laid the blade against her neck. Warmth oozed a trail down her neck. Declan had nicked her!

Evan's eyes snapped midnight black completely focused on Declan. He clenched his fists. Declan maneuvered Hettie into the center of the circle.

Stick to the plan, Hettie telepathed to Evan. When his eyes locked with hers she knew he heard.

Hettie felt the trickle of warm blood on her neck. Evan wouldn't want to give Declan any reason to slice her deeper. The five witches touched fingertip to fingertip, completing a circle around Declan and Hettie. They moved counter clockwise and lifted their arms skyward.

Ella led the chant as they moved around the circle:

Earth, Air, Fire, Water circle round,
Hold this space, this hallowed ground.

Darla led the next chant:

East, south, west, north,
Goddess, listen to your daughters.
The third time around, all the witches chanted:
Bring power forth!

The circle of witches floated free of the ground. The chanting had changed to the old tongue. Hettie saw Evan slip his Shaman knife from the scabbard.

The magick directed at Declan was so intense he dropped his knife. Now the knife lay in a molten pile of metal. He spun Hettie around to face him and grabbed her wrists. His eyes flashed in anger. "You will come with me!" Declan's voice rose to a devilish pitch as he spoke the ancient words. Binding words.

Hettie prayed to the Goddess.

Would her coven and Evan be enough?

Colored spheres of lights filled the circle, as well as smoke and haze, and through it all, Hettie was aware of Evan. She threw back her head, her face to the sky she shut her eyes, and uttered the words over and over in the language of ancient magick.

She opened her eyes. Evan crouched by the circle, knife ready. Declan's eyes were orbs of red and he chanted faster, and faster.

The other witches spun around her and Declan. The passionate heat from all the magick was powerful.

Hettie locked in an embrace with Declan. They were starting to spin a foot off the ground. She spoke the words, freed her hands and tied the black ribbon around Declan's wrist. She held the other end chanting the final spell:

I tie to your wrist the ribbon of magick;
So Declan you know what I have done.
And when this ribbon touches two;
It's what matters,
When the ribbon is cut in two
The curse is shattered,
Along with you!
So mote it be.

Evan rushed into the circle and sliced through the ribbon. A powerful *whoosh* blew through the circle and the swirling light disappeared.

The witches were back on the ground, encircling Hettie and Evan. Declan had disappeared.

"We did it, it worked! We did it!" Ella laughed. "He's gone."

"That was pure awesomeness!" Ivy declared.

"That was the most powerful ritual I've ever been a part of," Darla said, patting the sweat from her forehead with the hem of her dress. "I thought we were going to be roasted!"

Hettie slowly turned around and captured Evan's eyes. She held the crystal wand, which glowed with charged energy. Blood continued to drip down her neck. "Evan?"

He scooped her up and carried her to a stump. Sitting, he cradled her in his arms. He took his Paul Bunyan kerchief off and dabbed up the blood. "You were fantastic, my crystal witch. What a show, ladies — it was spectacular. Is Declan gone for good?"

"The spell! Quick we must burn it!" Hettie dug in her pocket and produced the piece of paper.

"I'll take that, child," Mae said. She rested heavily on her cane. The crone carried the written spell to the bonfire and set it on fire. She held the paper till only a slip remained and then dropped it into the blaze.

Evan kissed Hettie long and passionately. "No more secrets. Did you send me a telepathic message?"

"I was sure you heard me." Hettie smiled. "You are my true love."

"As you are mine." His voice was low and seductive, and held all the promise of an enchanted life together.

"Yes, always and forever!" Joy bubbled in her laugh.

The End

GHOST OF A CHANCE

by Diana McCollum

Dedication
For Loyd and my children,
for all their love and support.

Acknowledgements

To my critique partners Sarah McDermed and Louise Pelzl thank you for your generous and honest critiques.

To my Beta readers: thank you for taking the time to read this story; because of you it is polished. Beta readers: Lisa Pino, Lisa Daniels, Katie Llamas, Sarah McDermed, Judith Ashley, Louise Pelzl, Leila Schanck, and Andrea McDermed.

And a huge shout-out to my Bend lunch bunch, writers who didn't mind answering all my questions: Marie Harte, Karen Duvall, Linda Berry, Ruth Colter, Paty Jager, Mary Pax, & Vella Munn.

Shelby picked up the key from the realtor and drove to her new house in Bend, Oregon. Not new construction, but new to her. She bought the house after her divorce settlement. She'd had such high hopes of the perfect life with Sean in Portland, Oregon, only he was unfaithful, not once or twice, but over and over again. Six months after the divorce was over she was ready for a new start, in a new location. When the job opportunity arose with St. Charles Hospital in September, she jumped on it.

She turned onto Newport Ave and spotted the "Back-porch Coffee Roasters". Finding an available parking spot in the store's lot, she deemed herself lucky, parked and headed inside. The aromatic smell of roasted beans had her mouth-watering for the rich taste of coffee.

"What would you like today?" The barista gave a final swipe with his towel to the counter top.

"I'll take a large coffee, and which of the sweet rolls do you recommend?" The selection of baked goods was varied and beautiful, mouth-watering beautiful.

"My favorite is the Ocean roll. The cardamom spice is outstanding and literally bursts with flavor when you bite into it." His smile was warm and friendly.

"Toss a couple of the Ocean rolls in a bag and I'll take those too." She edged out of the order line and perused the framed photos of coffee beans on the walls while she waited for her order. The coffee house walls were painted a warm mix of orange-red walls and cream. The polished cement floor and industrial lights added a nice modern ambiance to the place.

"Large coffee and two Ocean rolls to go," announced the barista.

She counted out the correct change and headed outside. This would be the perfect combo to take with her to her new home.

A few minutes later, she turned the key in the ignition. Deader than a door nail. Just her luck. She popped the hood. Pulling on her stocking hat against the stiff breeze she got out of the car. She propped the hood open, and leaned over the engine for a better look. Not knowing what she was looking for didn't help her mood any.

"Crap!" She muttered under her breath.

"What seems to be the problem?"

Shelby jerked up right. "The engine won't turn over." The man had an easy smile.

"Sounds like the battery. Yep," he pointed to the battery connectors encrusted with white crude. "Let me get my tools and I'll clean those up for you. It'll only take a couple of minutes." He pulled his hat down around his ears, unzipped his jacket and laid it on the fender.

After cleaning the connectors, he attached jumper cables and Shelby turned the key in the ignition. The engine jumped to life. She got out of the car, "What do I owe you?"

"Nothing. It's my job to help ladies in distress."

"The least I can do is buy you a cup of coffee." Shelby insisted.

He glanced at his watch. "Okay. I take it black, and I'll need it to go. I have an appointment." He began rolling up the jumper cables.

By the time Shelby got back with the coffee, the man was zipping up his windbreaker. His designer sun glasses reflected the sunshine peeking out from the clouds.

"Thanks for the coffee. Be sure and let the car run for a while when you get home and that should charge the battery up. You might want to stop by a garage tomorrow and have someone check the battery." With a killer smile pasted on his face, he touched his fingers to his head in a salute. "See you around."

Shelby watched as he walked away. There was a slogan on the back of his coat "Ghosts are People too!" What the heck did that mean? He climbed into his black SUV and drove off.

Five minutes later she parked the car in the driveway of the old Victorian with gingerbread trim. Lowering the window half-way, she breathed in the pine scented air emanating from the tall Sugar Pines that lined the drive. There was definitely a hint of fall in the cool crisp September air.

She admired her purchase from inside the car. The peeling green paint would have to be re-done eventually. The screens were missing from the upstairs windows and needed to be replaced. All in all, not bad for a one hundred and fifty-year-old house, she supposed. Her new home appeared to have been fairly well taken care of inside. Most of the work was cosmetic on the outside, and could be done when she had the extra money.

Closing the window, she got out of the car. The front yard consisted of a small grassy area bordered by large unkempt flower beds. With some hard work she would whip the beds into shape for spring planting. She continued up the sidewalk to the stairs, noting that the bottom one needed to be replaced since dry rot had set in.

She turned the key in the lock and entered the hallway. The previous owners had knocked down a few walls and made a great room out of what was once the parlor and library. She liked the spacious feel of the room. Venturing further into the great room, she caressed the oak mantel of the fireplace, admiring the craftsmanship, and the detail on the mantel. The realtor had the cleaning people go through the house one more time before her furniture arrived. All her furniture had been packed, and shipped from Portland, and set up last week by the movers at the direction of the realtor. She tossed her keys on to the small oak desk nestled against the entry way wall.

This was home.

Her cell belted out "I Want You" by Savage Garden. She searched her purse for the phone, finally dumping the contents out on the couch. Grabbing the cell she said, "Hello?"

"Shelby?"

"Anna, what are you up to?" She hadn't expected to hear from her cousin until the weekend. Anna worked for the lumber mill in Klamath Falls, Oregon and only came to Bend on the weekends.

"Hey, I have a couple of days off starting tomorrow and if you would like, I'll drive up and help you get unpacked, get settled."

"Wow, just seeing you would be wonderful! I don't start at St. Charles Hospital until a week from today." Cousin Anna was the ultimate organizer. Shelby had a smile on her face relishing her good luck.

"Great. I should be there around ten."

"Bring an overnight bag and stay, please?" Shelby pleaded. Anna was her cousin, and had been her best friend growing up. Shelby took the job in Portland and they hadn't seen each other often during the past six years. "Say yes. Girl time, I need some, "Shelby pleaded.

"Of course, a sleep over, like old times," Anna laughed. "See you tomorrow."

"Bye, Cuz."

Shelby popped the cork on the bottle of Champagne Anna had brought, grabbed two crystal flutes off the shelf, and was surprised by the twinge of disappointment circling inside her chest. The glasses had been a wedding present. The marriage was over and she was starting a new life. She fought hard against the tears that threatened to spill down her cheeks.

Snap out of it. Really? What better way to toast her new life than with these beautiful flutes. Picking up the bottle of Sparkling wine, she headed into the living room. "Thanks for the Champagne and fruit platter. What a great way to christen my new place." She poured the effervescent liquid into the ornate glass and handed it to Anna.

"Nice crystal." Anna held the flute up so the light from the Tiffany lamp caught in the glass sending sparks of light shimmering around the room.

"Wedding gift," she blinked back tears and took a deep cleansing breath. "Marriage didn't last, but the glassware did." She shrugged her shoulders and sat down.

Anna sat by the fireplace stirring the coals with the poker. The low fire reflected off her long blonde hair. "I'm so glad you moved back, Shelby."

"Me too." Shelby topped off the Champagne in the glasses. "Thanks for all your help today. I can't believe almost all the boxes are unpacked. I can't begin to tell you how relieved I am." Shelby slumped back on the velvet, rust-colored sofa and kicked off her tennis shoes.

Anna took her glass and sat on the overstuffed chair near the fireplace. She pulled the patchwork afghan around her shoulders. "So spill the beans. What happened in Portland, and why have you moved to Bend?"

"Basically, I graduated from college with a nursing degree, got a job, married, bought a house, learned my husband was cheating, got a divorce, sold the house and moved back to my home town." She raised her glass and touched Anna's with a clink. "Here's to renewing old friendships, a new job, a new house and a new beginning."

Anna took a long sip of the bubbly liquid. "Sean Stein wasn't marriage material after all?"

"Hardly. He slept with three other women I know of, and who knows how many I didn't know about." Shelby sipped her drink. "Let's talk about something else. I don't ever want to think about my marriage disaster again. He's out of my life." At least she hoped so. Sean had called her the day she left, begging for another chance. He is an idiot. She could never trust him. She wasn't even sure her bruised heart could trust any man.

Anna dipped a strawberry in whipped cream, popped the berry in her mouth, and chewed. She pointed an index finger at Shelby and said, "I've got an idea. Let's play cards or, better yet, how about a board game?"

"I spotted a Ouija board up in the attic this afternoon. Let's get the game out and ask Mr. Ouija questions about the future." Shelby stood up, "Come on, let's go get it."

"I don't know about playing with the Ouija game." Anna said, biting her lip. "Did I tell you I've been taking a class focusing on psychics, mediums and spirits? According to my professor, Ouija boards can alert malevolent spirits and allow them a portal into this world."

"Don't be a party pooper! Hey, it'll be like old times. We used to have such fun with Mr. Ouija at sleepovers."

"Okay. We'll see what the future holds for you, romance-wise," Anna said, laughing.

"No. No romance for me. My friends, my work, and my house, those are the things I'm concentrating on." Her smile broadened. This would be fun. With a sense of anticipation, she led the way up the two flights of stairs to the attic.

The single dust covered light bulb in the middle of the attic gave off a ghostly light. Shadows crept out from the corners and cobwebs hung from the rafters.

"The game was behind the stack of old magazines there in the corner." Shelby made her way across the creaky floor and retrieved the game. She blew the dust off the top, which sent them both into fits of sneezing and laughter. They hurried back to the warmth of the living room.

This was Shelby's house, no, this was her home. The warmth of ownership, of belonging spread through her, clinging to her and chasing all the bad memories away. She loved the old stone fireplace and the blaze in the hearth added the right touch of coziness the room needed. She sat down on the leather bean bag chair opposite Anna who claimed the couch.

Anna opened the box and set the game up on the rosewood coffee table that stood between them.

"You ask the first question," Shelby insisted.

They both put their finger tips on the planchette. "Are there any spirits present?" Anna asked in a theatrical voice.

The planchette slowly moved to "Yes"

"Anna, are you moving the pointer?"

Anna's eyes widened. "No! Are you?"

"Nope, I guess Mr. Ouija is back."

"Are you male or female?" Anna queried.

The planchette spelled out male.

"Come on, Anna, you're moving the pointer too fast." In the past her cousin would do anything to try and scare Shelby. Even going so far as to insist a spirit was present. "Aren't you going to stick to personal questions about us?"

"I've changed my mind, I want to talk to a real spirit. I know, I know you don't believe in in the psychic unknown stuff, but I sort of do." Anna shifted on the couch. "Remember at Great Aunt Jules' house we asked for a ghost and got O'Henry?"

"I do. I'm sure the footsteps we heard were nothing more than Aunt Jules' dog, Roto, walking up and down the hallway and stairs." Why argue? Let Anna have her fun. Ghosts weren't real. They couldn't be, could they? "Okay, go ahead. Ask your questions, and make them good ones."

"How old are you?"

The planchette spelled "Old, long forgotten."

Satisfied, Anna smiled. "We've got an old spirit."

Shelby rolled her eyes. "Okay, how do we know you are a spirit? Give us a sign."

A frigid cold passed over Shelby. Before she could say anything her keys fell off the hall table with a jangle.

"Wow, we got a sign from the ghost." Anna clapped her hands in delight.

"I tossed my keys on the table when I came home today. They probably were hanging over the side and finally fell." Ghost, spirit, she didn't want to believe in any of them. Anna was starting to scare her with all this ghost talk. "Anna, you can't really believe we've contacted a spirit? This is a parlor game, that's all."

"One more question, then we'll quit for tonight. My professor says those spirits which can be contacted are those who reside on 'the lower astral plane.' These spirits are confused and may have died a violent or sudden death or be scared to cross over for one reason or another." Anna rubbed her hands together. "Ready?"

With their hands on the planchette, Anna asked her final question. "We want to get to know you. Are you in the room with us?"

The planchette began to move slowly this time, and stopped on "yes."

Shelby got up from the beanbag. "I've had enough. This is totally creeping me out. I know you were moving the pointer."

"No, I wasn't. We made contact. This is exciting. We've brought a spirit over from the astral plane." Anna could hardly contain her excitement.

Shelby stared at the board. The planchette had moved off "yes" and now pointed at "h." "*Did* you move the pointer? Tell me, Anna, you did move the pointer, didn't you?" Her pulse raced.

"No, why?" Anna glanced down. A look of horror came over her face as they watched the planchette move from letter to letter spelling out "help."

Shelby moved the pointer to "end," closed the board up and put the game in the box. "Freaky. How could the pointer move by itself?" The champagne had affected her vision, but then Anna had seen the same thing. She carried the box over to the hall table and placed the game there. Kneeling down, she looked around for her keys on the floor. They were gone. She pulled the braided rug back, looked under the oak chair, and behind the drape, no keys.

"Anna, my keys are gone." A chill snaked up her spine. "This is strange."

When Anna didn't answer, she turned around to see her staring at the keys! They lay on the coffee table, spread in a circle with each of the four keys neatly pointing in a different direction, north, south, east and west.

"What the...?" Shelby snatched her keys up and put them in her purse.

"If I hadn't seen with my own eyes, I wouldn't have believed the keys moved to the coffee table." Anna stood and pulled the afghan tighter around her shoulders. "You, my dear, are now host to a ghost. I can't believe we brought a ghost over from the other side."

"Why would the ghost spell out 'help'?"

Anna was shivering. The fire was out. Only a few glowing embers remained, and the room had grown exceptionally cold.

Grabbing a log and kindling, Shelby knelt in front of the fire and stoked the flames to life. Soon the blaze crackled and the room warmed up.

"Maybe he wants to cross over and needs help to do so?" Anna was sitting in the overstuffed chair again with a glazed look in her eyes.

"Guess you'll have a good story to share at your class, won't you?" Shelby couldn't believe how her breathing was steady. The keys didn't travel from under the stand to the coffee table without some help. Anna must be playing a trick on me.

"I didn't truly think we could bring a ghost over. But we did. Now what?" Anna looked pale and lost. "I'm so sorry, Shelby. I didn't mean for this to happen. I didn't think any ghost would cross over."

Shelby plopped down on the couch. Now what, indeed? She didn't believe in ghosts, but her keys had somehow gotten from the hall table, to the floor, to the coffee table.

The sound of glass breaking came from the kitchen. Shelby shrieked and jumped up, with Anna right behind her. They opened the kitchen door to see a glass shattered on the floor. The tails of the red checked curtains blew across the tile counter.

"Do you think the ghost broke the glass?" Anna asked a tremor in her voice.

"Absolutely not. The wind must have blown the glass off the counter." Shelby grabbed the dustpan and broom from the closet and cleaned up the glass. She closed the window and secured it with the lock. "We're too jumpy. I'm tired and I'm sure things will look better in the morning."

"We can have coffee and Ocean rolls tomorrow before you leave, at Backporch Coffee Roasters. You won't believe the rolls. I've never tasted sweet rolls so good." Shelby paused briefly. "Did I tell you my car battery died there? A very nice man helped me get it started. His jacket had the strangest slogan on it: "Ghosts Are People too!" What do you suppose that means?"

"Well, it makes sense ghosts are the essence of humans who've died. But why he'd have that on his jacket, I don't know." Anna stifled a yawn. "Off to bed."

Shelby stood on the front porch waving goodbye to Anna. They'd had a good visit and all her possessions were put away in cupboards, closets and drawers. The garage was another matter.

The ghost, if there was one, hadn't made another appearance. The Ouija board was tucked away in the attic and, as far as she was concerned, the game would never see the light of day again.

In the week that followed Anna's visit, Shelby wasn't accosted by ghosts, but she did notice a change in temperature at times for no apparent reason. Opening the front door, she'd step across the threshold and a wave of the chilly air would wash over her. She'd continue down the hall and the air would warm.

She sighed. If the "ghost" did nothing more than send cold air her way, she could live with the spirit.

Lester Chad Huntley finished his barbell reps. He grabbed the towel off the workout bench and wiped away the sweat meandering down his face and neck. He enjoyed his early morning workouts, especially when he had a late night ghost stakeout the night before. Working out got his motor running, got rid of his stress. He was finding out the boss works as hard as the employee in a two-man operation, but then, he wouldn't have wanted the job any other way. He loved his work.

"Hey, L.C., you ready to hit the road?" Big Jake sauntered over. At six-foot-six Jake towered over L.C. by a good seven inches. Jake had jumped at the chance to work for his best buddy.

"I suppose you want breakfast first?" L.C.'s longtime friend and employee could pretty much eat any time, day or night.

"Hey, wouldn't be right to start the day with no fuel. I'll spring for the grub." Jake hefted his gym bag strap over his shoulder. "I'll wait in the car."

In a matter of minutes, L.C. was behind the wheel driving to Cosmic Creed Control to pick up his new laser grid machine, by way of the coffee shop. Jake the bottomless pit had to have fuel.

The waitress set the coffee carafe on the table and Jake poured coffee into their cups. "Hey, boss, I was thinking I might take a few days off, head over to the coast to see my folks, and maybe do some salmon fishing. Can you spare me for a couple of days?"

"We're not too busy right now. Your leaving for a while shouldn't be a problem." L.C. added cream to his coffee. "I need you to help with the setup on the new laser grid machine before you take off."

"Sure, boss."

"Could you hold off leaving until Tuesday morning? I can cut you a check then and you won't need to be back till after the weekend." He should be able to wrap up the Martin job tonight.

"No problem." Jake took a swig of coffee. "You know, with any luck, I'll be bringing salmon back, boss. You might as well get your smoker out."

L.C. took out his box cutter and opened the large box sitting on his work table. "This is beautiful." He said to Jake. L.C. ran his hand over the cool cover of the machine. He was all but drooling. A laser grid machine had been on his wish list for a long time, and this one was state of the art. "I can't wait to try this bad boy out."

He glanced at the phone, willing it to ring. A new project would help pay for the laser grid machine and give him a chance to try the contraption out. "You know, Jake, we haven't booked anything new in a few weeks."

"I know, man." Jake scratched his blond crew cut. "You think leaflets or an ad in the paper would help scare business our way?"

"Scare being the operative word here. Hauntings, we need ghosts." L.C. ran his hand over the control cover on his new toy. "Since those spirit hunting shows on TV have become popular, most people learn to live with their ghosts. Makes a good subject for conversation, and if the ghosts are hospitable, why get rid of them?" He shrugged.

The phone rang. "Huntley's Spectral Mediator, L.C. here, can I help you?"

"I've a problem with something in my house. Damn ghost, demon, I'm not sure." The man's voice rose an octave with frustration. "I can't sleep with the racket going on at night, things breaking, stairs creaking, and even howling."

L.C. turned and gave Jake the thumbs up sign. "I have free time this afternoon. I could come by and meet with you, would that work?"

"The sooner, the better! Thanks. Nice to know there are business people who will show up the same day you need them." His relief permeated his voice. "And boy, do I need your help."

L.C. took down the man's information then hung up. "Mr. Harper is in dire need of our services. Here's the address." He handed the slip of paper to Jake. "We'll take a ride over after lunch."

Shelby sat straight up in bed. The cold enveloped her, surrounding her like an invisible cloak. She could make out the mist ebbing and flowing in the moon light beaming through the window. Teeth chattering, she got out of bed, padded across the ice cold wood floor, and flipped on the overhead light. The room warmed up immediately.

The clock on the nightstand read 4:00 a.m. She left the light on and crawled back in bed. Dang! Her first day off after four ten-hour days; she'd wanted to lay here a while longer.

For a while, the singing ghost's quiet litany of sing-song, indistinguishable words, and the fleeting patches of cold air that crept into her room had been tolerable. Two nights ago, the air became frigid. And two nights ago one of the vases Aunt Jules had given her flew off the mantle and shattered.

The damn ghost had kept her wide-awake most of last night. She awoke with a start when a couple more knick-knacks crashed to the floor of the living room. The spirit had become more of a nuisance than she was willing to put up with.

Misty, the name she'd given the ghost, wasn't like O'Henry, the jolly ghost who had co-habited with Aunt Jules all those years ago. Shelby and Anna used to set food out for him in hopes of catching a glimpse of the elusive spirit. They never saw the essence of O'Henry, but did manage to converse with him a couple of times through the Ouija board. At night they would sometimes hear his heavy booted footsteps in the hallway upstairs, and his jolly chuckle. Aunt Jules had always re-assured them he was a friendly old sea captain and wouldn't harm them. Shelby didn't think Aunt Jules believed in O'Henry, but the cousins most definitely had when they were younger.

Anna would be arriving this afternoon. Shelby couldn't wait to see the surprise on her face when she learned the ghost had stayed, and was a lady, not a man. They had both been convinced a male ghost had come through. The board had spelled out male. Her nightly visitor was definitely a wom-an, a singing woman.

The novelty of having her own singing ghost had dis-solved with the shattered pottery. The spirit had become more aggressive. Shelby had read in a book about ghosts, specters, and poltergeists, about cases where people were harmed. Many folks were left with unexplained scratches or bruises. Today she would find someone who could help her.

She hadn't been scared of the entity; at least until now. She'd lived with the ghost since moving to Bend two weeks ago. The ghost's increasingly destructive behavior had upped her scare meter to borderline frightened. Enough was enough; she was through with the spirit. She had a demanding job as a nurse in the ICU at the Hospital, and she needed her rest.

"Okay, Misty." Shelby threw back the covers. She got out of bed. "The time has come for you to go. You've over-stayed your welcome."

She put on her bathrobe and pounded down the stairs to the kitchen. The smell of the freshly brewed pot of coffee met her as she rounded the kitchen counter. Sliding a mug over to the automatic coffeepot, she poured the hot, black liq-uid into her cup. After several swallows, she pulled her smart phone out of her purse and started her search.

I wonder if there is a ghost buster in town. What would the number be listed under? Exterminator, Ghostbuster...? Let's see, this looks promising: Huntley's Spectral Mediator.

She punched the number in and waited, counting the rings. Two, three, four and the answering machine picked up.

"You've reached the voice mail for "Huntley's Spectral Mediator," L.C. Huntley speaking. If you have an unwanted entity or ghost, you have dialed the correct number. We work hard at customer satisfaction. You and your ghost both deserve a satisfying resolution. Remember, ghosts are people too. Leave your name, number and a brief description of your unwanted guest. We'll get back to you as soon as possible."

She waited for the tone, and then said, "Hi, this is Shelby Stein, I live over on the west side of Bend. I have a ghost living in my house. Female ghost, she's a singing ghost and no problem up till now, in fact I kind of enjoyed having her, but she has started breaking things and now I'm worried. If you could please call me back at (541) 555-0990 as soon as possible, I'd appreciate hearing from you."

Pouring another cup of steaming coffee, she sipped the brew while she worked her way around the downstairs opening curtains and blinds to let in the early morning light. She disliked having the curtains shut in the daylight. She wanted every ounce of sunlight she could encourage into the old Victorian. The kitchen table with the sun shining through the east window beckoned her. Before starting breakfast, she slid a chair out and sat. Her thoughts turned to the Good Samaritan who helped start her car at Backporch Coffee Roasters; the slogan on his jacket was the same as the phone recording from the ghost buster, "Ghosts Are People Too!"

After breakfast, Shelby got ready for the day. Next she opened up the guest room, dusted, and vacuumed the blue oval braided rug. She opened the window to let the cool morning air chase away the closed up smells. September was one of her favorite months, cool mornings and evenings, warm daytime temps.

The bedroom door slammed shut with a bang and a rattle. Shelby squeaked. The lacey curtains floated down to hang straight as soldiers. The wind must have blown the door shut. She opened the door and slid an old cast iron Basset Hound over for a doorstop. If the door blew shut again, then she would be concerned. She shook her head, feeling silly to have jumped. She guessed she was on edge from lack of sleep.

After eating a home cooked spaghetti dinner, Anna and Shelby sat on the living room couch nursing their glasses of wine. The TV chattered in the background with the local weatherman predicting cooler weather by morning.

"I called a ghost buster." Shelby picked up her wine, twirled the stem in her fingers and sipped. "The ghost has escalated to throwing things."

Anna's eyes grew big and she choked on her wine. "What? I thought you didn't believe we brought a ghost over. What's changed your mind?"

"I don't think, I know there's a ghost in the house." Shelby took another sip from her glass. "I think she came through when we used the Ouija board."

"Wow. But you said this ghost is a woman and the board spelled 'man.'"

"The voice I'm hearing is definitely a woman." Shelby set her glass on the coffee table.

Spooky music emanated from the TV.

Shelby pointed at the television. "That's the company I called."

The announcer gave an irresistibly devastating grin. "Do you have an entity you need to get rid of, or a demon harassing you? Is your house being haunted by a ghost? Call "Huntley's Spectral Mediator" for quick fast service. Ghosts are people too!" The blond Adonis in a black muscle T-shirt turned away from the camera.

Across his back was emblazoned "Ghosts are people too" in fluorescent green.

"That is definitely the same company I called. I had no idea ghost hunting was big business. I mean to afford advertising on TV, I know it costs big bucks."

"Oh, I hope he calls while I'm visiting and maybe he'll stop by, even better. That is one good looking male. Besides, I never met a real ghost buster before." Anna sighed.

"Did he look familiar to you? There's something about him, I don't know what exactly, but I think I've seen him before."

"Well, no, I think I would remember a hot guy like him." Anna got up, grabbed the wine off the counter then added to their glasses.

A door slammed shut upstairs. "Eek," Anna squeaked.

"Don't worry. A door blew shut, that's all. The wind blew one shut earlier too. Come on, I'll show you to your room." Shelby grabbed a heavy book off the bookshelf then hefted the tome up on her shoulder. "This will make a great doorstop."

Halfway up the stairs, another door slammed shut. Shelby stopped and looked at Anna. "Is the wind blowing in all the windows at once?"

"I didn't think it was that windy out. It is the wind, right?"

Shelby wasn't so sure. At the top of the stairs, a breeze lifted her hair off her shoulders, but where did the draft come from? All the doors were shut. Shelby opened the guest room door and the cast iron Basset Hound sat in the middle of the bed. A chill traced up her spine. "This is weird. How did the basset hound get up there? I put Iron Dog in front of the door earlier for a doorstop."

"Come on, Shelby, you are starting to freak me out." Anna's voice shook.

The door slammed shut behind them. They shrieked unison.

"The wind," Shelby insisted. She picked up the Basset Hound, opened the door and put the dog down to hold the door open.

"Shelby, the window is closed." Anna's eyes were round as saucers. "I'm not sleeping in here."

"Okay, okay, you can sleep on the couch in my room." Truth be told, Shelby would feel more secure not being alone.

The morning sun danced through the Sugar Pines, making an ever-changing pattern on the kitchen table. Shelby took two mugs out of the cupboard and filled them with coffee.

She placed one on the table in front of Anna. Cupping her hands around the second for the warmth the cup provided on this chilly morning, she parked herself in the chair across from Anna.

"Did you hear the ghost last night?" Anna said tentatively, and sipped her black coffee.

"No. But she doesn't come every night. In fact, I slept so well with you for a roomie. Guess my subconscious figured you would protect me." Shelby couldn't help but chuckle.

"Yeah, right! As if!"

The phone rang and Shelby picked up. "Hello?"

"Hi, I'm L.C. Huntley, with Huntley's Spectral Mediator. Is this Ms. Stein?"

"Yes. Thanks for calling back." He was on the ball.

"Sounds like your ghost is causing you trouble. I charge by the hour, but if you aren't completely satisfied, I'll refund your money. Including equipment and labor, our rate is forty-five dollars an hour. If you are interested, I have a slot of time this afternoon. I'll need to do an interview with you, and look around the house." He had a nice voice.

"Absolutely, I haven't slept for a few days, except for last night. I want this ghost to be removed."

The doorbell jarred Shelby awake. She sat up on the couch and rubbed the kink in her neck, yawning and stretching. She had only meant to close her eyes for a moment after Anna left on a shopping trip to the Mill District. Anna had called some of the friends they had both known growing up in Bend, and a shopping trip was born. After shopping, Anna would be heading to Klamath Falls.

Outside the window, a small, boxy, neon green Honda Element was parked by the curb. The shrink-wrap advertisement on the side read "Let us put your spirit to rest."

She gave herself the once-over in the hall mirror, patting her hair down and rubbing the sleepy eyes out. She opened the door to reveal a man around her age, twenty-eight, with thick, dark-brown curly hair, designer sunglasses and a black T-shirt with the company slogan "Ghosts are people too!" emblazoned in fluorescent green lettering.

He looked up from his clipboard and did a double take. Sliding his glasses down his nose, he said, "Shelby? Shelby Sawyer?" He gave her a quizzical look with blue-gray eyes.

"Yes...no, I mean I was Shelby Sawyer, but one marriage and divorce later I'm Shelby Stein." Where had she met him? She would have remembered a Ghostbuster, especially a handsome one with all that to-die-for curly hair. "Wait a minute, you helped me with my car a couple of weeks ago. I remember your jacket had the same slogan printed on the back. But how do you know my name?"

He chuckled, slipped his sunglasses off and slid one earpiece over the neck of his T-shirt. "I was in rescue ladies mode when I helped with your car. I have to admit I didn't recognize you at the coffee house. You were in disguise with your shades on and hat. But we went to the same high school. You don't remember your senior prom at Alpine Cascade High School?" He gave an impatient shrug. "I invited you to be my date, and you kept me hanging till the last minute and then turned me down."

"I don't know any L.C. Huntley. Wait, L.C., you aren't Lester Huntley, are you?" Oh, God, this was awkward.

"Lester Huntley at your service." He had a cocky smile plastered on his face and he winked.

Her senior year, her boyfriend Bill broke up with her right before the prom. Lester, the class geek, had stepped up to the plate and asked her to be his date. She put off answering him in hopes Bill would come to his senses, which he eventually did. At the time the last person she wanted to be seen with was the class geek, with his thick glasses and unru-ly curly hair. Back then, in her self-indulgent teens life was all about looks and cliques. She hated her old self for being so shallow.

"Please, come in." They were both adults now. Surely he wouldn't hold the past against her. She was no longer the self-centered, spoiled and shallow girl she'd been ten years ago.

He walked through the open door, grabbed a pen from the top of his clipboard, and began taking notes.

"Tell me about the spirit haunting your house. On a scale of one to ten, ten being the worse possible scenario, where does your ghost land?" He stood straighter, all business now.

"Up until three nights ago I'd have said two. Then the activity escalated to throwing vases and knickknacks. I'd say now the spirit has intensified to an eight."

Lester drew a graph on his paper. "And where has the ghost manifested its self?"

Shelby walked to the stairwell. "She's a mist and glides down the stairs and in front of this wall in the hallway. This an-tique mirror becomes hazy and it is impossible to see my re-flection. When the spirit passes by me the temperature drops about twenty degrees. I can't make out the words, but she's singing. I named her Misty, because the figure is a grayish-white, mist, and her voice has a female quality."

"Sounds like the ghost knows you can hear her or she wouldn't continue singing. Not everyone could. Since you are sensitive to the spirit that could explain why the entity has started to escalate its behavior. She's got unfinished business before she can rest in peace." His forehead puckered. "I'll need to set up my equipment during the time the entity is most active. And that would be…?" He glanced up.

"Between ten p.m. and two a.m., although when Misty was only singing and not breaking things, I sometimes heard her in the early evening too. Yesterday was the first time she might have been active in the daylight." She rubbed the chill creeping up her arms. "Doors were closing, like they were blown shut, but in at least one case the window wasn't open. I used a heavy doorstop to keep the door from closing, and later the door blew shut again and the doorstop was in the middle of the bed." She took a sweater off the coat rack and slipped her arms into it, hugging the sweater close. "Probably the ghost, right?"

"Most likely Misty was making her presence known." His face was a study of concentration as he read over his notes. "I'll tell you straight up, Shelby, the first thing we have to do is find out what type of entity we're dealing with." He tapped the end of his pen on the tablet. "Can you pinpoint a date when the entity first manifested itself?"

"The first week I lived here, about two weeks ago."

"And you've never had a ghost attached to you or your possessions before?" L.C. kept writing and didn't look up.

"Are you kidding? Attached to me or my things?" This was bordering on the insane.

"This is a legitimate question. You could have brought the ghost here. Ghost attachment happens frequently."

"Please sit down," she gestured to the overstuffed chair by the fireplace, settling herself on the couch.

He settled down into the chair. "Nice. Cozy room," he stared at her with the hint of a smile. "Anything else I should know about your entity?"

"I'm not sure if it's important or not. Do you believe ghosts can come over from the other side or wherever through a Ouija board?"

The beginning of a smile slowly disappeared from his face. His expression stilled and grew serious. "It could be a possible. If you invited an unknown entity into this realm through the Ouija board and the entity came through, then we'd know where it came from." He ran his hand through his hair. "First things first, we need to find out exactly what we're dealing with."

"We did. Anna and I used a Ouija board one evening. She wanted to see if we could contact a spirit." A cold knot began to form in her stomach.

L.C.'s unwavering stare gave her a different kind of chill. Flustered under his scrutiny, the heat crept up her neck.

"Considering these episodes with the ghost happened after you played the game, it's safe to assume the entity came over through the board." He stood and paced to the door and back. "In which case, we could be dealing with a demon or poltergeist. Two very nasty creatures."

"You mentioned equipment — what kind were you talking about?" She tilted her head to one side. Lester had definitely changed from the shy, geeky teenager she remembered. He wasn't classically handsome, but good looking in a rugged sort of way. Same curly brown hair growing past his ears, his thick glasses were gone, so he must be wearing contacts, and the skinny kid was now a buffed out man.

"Oh, the usual, tripod, laser-grid machine, temp gauge, and an EMF and EM field output gauge and recorder. We want to get a picture of your ghost if we can and figure out who we're dealing with." He looked directly at her, serious and all business. "Are you available for the next few evenings?"

"Yes, I am. I finished my shift. I work four ten-hour days and then I'm off for three days." A shiver raced up her spine. She wasn't sure if she wanted to confront an angry ghost. "Should I leave the house while you're working?"

"Nope, I'll need you here. If you want to cut costs, you can help me."

"I'll be your assistant?" Her voice sounded tired even to her.

"More or less." He shrugged, matter-of-factly. "In the majority of cases, the ghost is trying to get your attention, not trying to harm you. I'd say the ghost is asking for help. In the spiritual dimension there is a reason the entity can't or won't cross over. The ghost is attached to your house and therefore attached to you. There have been cases where once connected, the spirit follows the host to another location. The spirit knows and uses the energy from a person with mediumistic qualities." He broke into a leisurely smile. "Most spirits have experienced emotional trouble, physical trauma or have unresolved issues here on Earth. Let me do my job, and you won't be bothered anymore, I promise."

"What are you saying? I have mediumistic qualities?" She wasn't even sure what he meant by that. The ghost might be attached to her? Crap. Fear wound inside her chest, sending shivers up her spine.

"Could be you are more sensitive to paranormal activity. I checked into the previous owners, who lived here for fifty years, and no reports on there being a ghost inhabiting this house." He smiled his concern for her. "Put your anxieties aside, I've never lost a client or a ghost."

"Then we have a deal? You'll get rid of the ghost?" She couldn't believe she was hiring Lester, the guy she stood up in high school. He was willing to work for her after she had treated him so poorly. Now she would get a chance to show him how much she had changed. As a matter of fact, she'd make it her mission to show him she'd changed.

"We'll help the ghost move on, you and me, teamwork." He stuck out his hand.

He had a firm handshake. "Do you need a deposit or do I need to sign a contract?"

"I'll draw up the contract. I don't need a deposit till you sign on the dotted line." Pulling his wallet out of his back pocket he flipped it open, "here's my business card."

He held the card out. "If anything happens and you want to talk, call me or text. Day or night, time doesn't matter." He smiled.

Shelby followed him to his company vehicle. "Nice car."

"Gets great gas mileage," he said, patting the roof. "You saw my gas hog when I helped you with your car a couple of weeks ago."

"The black SUV." How could she forget? Her knight rode to the rescue in a shiny new black SUV.

"Yep, that's my baby, bought her brand new last January." His voice warmed with pride.

"Do we start tonight?" Her stomach knotted thinking about another night alone with the ghost.

"Once I get back to the office, I'll check my schedule and give you a call. I have another client in front of you and I'm going to be shorthanded this week."

"Sounds good, I'll be waiting."

"The last person I expected to open the door today was you, Shelby," he said. "Can we start over? As friends?"

Relief flooded through her. "I'd like that." She had a good feeling things would work out. Help was on the way and in a tidy handsome package called Lester.

Ten minutes later Shelby's cell rang. "Hello?"

"Hey, Lester here. Checked with my other client and I should be able to wrap his job up in a couple of days. I'll start yours on your next day off."

"I was hoping you could start tonight." This was disappointing, another night with the ghost.

"You have my card, if anything happens or you're scared, give me a call. I can be there in ten minutes," he said.

"I'm punching your number in my cell now." She did have help now, someone to call. "Thanks, Lester."

The next morning, Lester opened the door to his shop. The cell in his pocket rang. Pitching his keys on the desk, he grabbed his phone. "Hello, L.C. of Huntley's Spectral Mediator. How can I help you?" He crossed the office to a low bookcase where the coffeepot waited.

"Hey, L.C. I'm at the coast," Jake said. "Dad says fishing's been lousy. Thought I'd check in to see how things are there."

"Got two jobs going right now, so things are looking up," Lester replied, measuring coffee into a filter.

"Okay. I'll probably stick around here for a day or two and head back. If you need me sooner, call."

"Thanks, Jake. Enjoy your time off." Lester turned on the faucet and filled the coffee carafe. "Hey, you won't guess who our new client is."

"Female or male?"

"Definitely female."

"Single or married?" Jake quizzed.

"Divorced. Shelbylicious." Lester couldn't help but use the nickname he and Jake had stuck on Shelby in high school.

"Wow, how did you feel coming face to face with a blast from the past?" Jake couldn't keep the disgust out of his voice.

"She's changed. I'm going to ask her out."

"Ah, man, she stomped all over your heart senior year."

"True, she did." Jake had bent over backwards to find him another date, even going so far as to suggest Lester attend with Jake and his girlfriend. In the end, Lester didn't go to the dance. "Don't you think everyone deserves a second chance?"

"I suppose, Jake said. Be careful, dude. I don't want to clean up after another broken heart."

"Not gonna happen. I'm only asking her out. Besides, I haven't asked yet and she hasn't accepted." Lester poured the water in the coffee unit and turned the switch on. He might have a ghost of a chance this time with Shelby.

They hung up and Lester poured his first cup of coffee. He sat at the desk and read the entire manual on the new Laser-grid machine. He took his second cup of coffee into the lab where the Laser-grid machine sat on the work table. He'd need to fine tune the controls before he used this bad boy. Mr. Harper's entity would be the test subject. Mr. Harper had mentioned howling, so there was a good chance he would be getting rid of a demon, not a ghost. With the Laser-grid machine, he'd determine what exactly he was dealing with, and the machine had a demon zapper built in.

Lester toyed with the idea of calling Shelby and asking her out for lunch, but decided on the direct approach. He grabbed his keys, sunglasses and locked the door on his way out.

Lester took in the state of the old Victorian Shelby called home. The peeling paint, missing screens on the upstairs windows, and the front porch stairs in dire need of attention looked like a money pit to him. He got out of his car feeling foolish when he noticed his palms were sweaty. His heart was thumping madly and he lifted the ornate, lion-head knocker. He rapped on the richly carved front door.

Shelby opened the door and Lester didn't think he had ever seen a more beautiful woman. Her flaxen hair was tied up in a blue bandana and she wore gold hoop earrings. Her old torn jeans were topped with a tight pink T-shirt. She had a paint brush in one hand and a puzzled look on her face. "Lester, what are you doing here?"

He cleared his throat. "Would you like to go out for lunch?" He ran his hand through his hair. "Hey, I know I should have called first, but I was in the neighborhood." What the hell, he should have called.

"I was going to take a break now anyway." She looked down at her paint-splattered clothes. "I'm a mess."

"You're hard at work." He smiled. "We won't go anywhere fancy, you don't have to change." Please don't change, he thought, glancing at the tight pink T-shirt. The shirt looked about two sizes too small, which emphasized her figure rather nicely.

"I don't know about going out on a date. I think we should keep this relationship on a business level, not get too personal." Biting her lip she looked away.

He hesitated, measuring her mood for a moment. "Lunch, not a date. I wanted to update you on a few ideas I have for getting rid of the spirit."Coming over here was a mistake. But now he was here, and he definitely wanted to spend time getting to know her. He understood she'd been hurt by the divorce, and was probably still hurting.

"How about we not do lunch, but have an early dinner?" She said. "I'd have time to clean up my mess, shower and look presentable." She tilted her head to the side.

"Great it's a date. Meet you at five o'clock. Does Hola!s at the Mill District sound okay?" His luck was changing. He hadn't had a date in four months and not a serious relationship since Cecelia pulled his heart out and ripped it to shreds three years ago.

"No, not a date," a trace of laughter laced her voice.

"Right, not a date." But absolutely the next best thing to a date. He smiled.

After dinner and conversation lasting well over three hours, Lester was glad Shelby had loosened up. Her laughter was music to his ears, and he didn't want the evening to end.

"This has been nice, Lester. I'm glad we did this. It's been great fun catching up." Shelby sipped on her after-dinner wine. Her eyes sparkled, catching the light from the candle on the table.

"I'm glad you changed your mind and decided to have dinner with me." She had changed a lot. She was funny, smart and a little wounded. "You have any questions you want to ask about ghosts?"

"Sure. Does a ghost haunt a house if no one is home?"Shelby asked one eyebrow arched.

"Kind of like the tree that falls in the forest, does it make a sound if no one is around? The answer is yes. Jake and I set up equipment, photo and sound recorders. We captured images and sounds in a haunted office building while the building was empty at night."

"You take care of commercial hauntings too?" She rested her chin on her hand. "Do you come across commercial type hauntings very often?"

"Oh, yeah, especially if the place was built over an ancient site, burial ground, or Native American site, or a murder was committed on site. Something along those lines." He didn't want the evening to end. Talking to Shelby was so easy. She was so different from the cheerleader he had lusted after in high school. She was a kind, caring person. He'd been pleasantly surprised when she told him about her Peace Corps service after nursing school.

"Several buildings in town are known for being haunted. The Deschutes County Historical Society Building is said to be haunted by George Brosterhous who died there in nineteen-fourteen. Let's see, at the O'Kane Building, people have reported ghostly smoke. Some people have seen weird unexplained lights, footsteps and voices too. Just to name a couple of haunted places in Bend."

"How fascinating. You are really passionate about your job," Shelby said.

"There are many reports of ghostly blue orbs in the cemetery at night, Pilot Butte Cemetery. The orbs have been recorded in photographs." He took a sip of water. "I've yet to see the orbs myself, but one of these days I'm camping out with my camera."

She shivered. "Better you than me."

"We'll have to do this again sometime." Shelby slipped out of the booth. Lester took her jacket from her and held the coat while she slipped her arms in.

"Thanks for dinner." Shelby looked at him with eyes full of promise, or he was hoping they were full of promise. "You're so easy to talk to," she blurted.

He tucked her hand in the crook of his arm. "You'd go on another date with me?"

"This wasn't a date." Laughter lined her voice. "But ask me for a date sometime and I'd love to go, as friends."

Every time her gaze met his, his heart turned over in response. She was giving him the go ahead, and you didn't have to tell this man twice — he'd be calling her for sure.

Four days later, Lester walked Shelby up to her front door. She turned and handed him her house keys. "Would you like to come in for a cup of coffee?"

Puzzlement filled his blue-gray eyes. "Are you sure?" He took her keys, not waiting for her to respond, and opened the door.

Her heart fluttered. She was taking a chance. She flipped on the light. "I make a mean cup of coffee. Come on in." She laughed.

She had a big, honest-to-goodness man in her living room, one she liked and found incredibly nice to be around. The fortress she had around her heart began to crumble. Lester was a gentleman, interesting, and she wanted to get to know him better. If she were being honest with herself, she wanted him to kiss her.

"Should I start a fire?" He gestured in the direction of the cold fireplace.

Her eyes froze on his sensual, full lips.

"Shelby?"

What had he asked her? Oh, the fireplace. "Yes, please, a fire would be nice." He had caught her staring and the heat of a blush crept up her neck. Coffee. She hurried into the kitchen and put a pot on. She was an idiot. *What is wrong with my hormones? Wine?* She didn't want to get involved again.

The nonsensical singing began right before the cold air enveloped her. So cold this time, harsh and frigid like being in the middle of a blizzard, the cold circled round her with icy ropes. Her lips, her hands were frozen and she couldn't move.

"Shelby?" The voice was Lester's but he sounded so far away, like he was in a tunnel. Everything was black; she couldn't see. The sensation reached her of being carried by strong arms, her head against his chest and his heartbeat thumped against her ear.

"Shelby?" Lester shook her gently. "Shelby, come back to me."

She opened her eyes. Her vision was blurred. She blinked a few times and her eyesight cleared. Lester held her in his arms warm, and secure. "What happened?" She relaxed, sinking into his cushioning embrace.

"You went to make coffee in the kitchen. The ghost started singing and I followed you in there. You passed out." He brushed a lock of hair out of her eyes. "What do you remember?"

"I started the coffeemaker, and then Misty began singing. I got so cold. I couldn't move or call out. The pressure on my chest felt like an elephant sitting on me, I could hardly breathe. The next thing I was in your arms." Her voice lowered to a hushed stillness, and she could hardly keep her eyes open.

"Shelby, stay with me. I think Misty tried to take over your body. Ghosts sometimes do. You're okay now. Let's get a cup of hot coffee in you. Help warm you up."

Lester placed her on the couch and tucked the afghan around her. The fire was giving off heat, and she began to warm up.

He handed her a mug of coffee. She positioned both hands around the warm cup, trying to dispel the chill.

"Tomorrow we'll set up the ghost hunting equipment. The other ghost job is over and your ghost is upping the stakes." He leaned toward her, his eyes filled with all kinds of promises. "I don't want anything to happen to you, now I found you again." He smiled with tenderness.

His smile touched her deep inside. Here was a man who cared, who comforted and who would champion her.

"What do you say I sleep here tonight?" He quirked his eyebrow. "The recliner by the fireplace is calling me."

"You would stay? Thank you. I don't want to be alone. Especially tonight, with Misty trying to take over my body, and all our talk about hauntings." She choked back a sob. God, she was frightened. "You won't leave once I'm asleep?" Biting her lip, she looked away.

Lester knelt beside her, his hands resting on the arms of the chair. "Shelby, you can trust me. I'm not going anywhere," he said, in a lower, huskier tone.

The joyful whistling coming from the kitchen woke Shelby early the next morning. She stretched, opened her eyes and inhaled the rich aroma of coffee. She was on the couch with the afghan over her. Why was she on the couch and not in her bedroom? Lester? She moved to the kitchen door. Opening the door a crack to see Lester standing in front of the stove, her only emotion was relief. Relief he was still here, relief Misty hadn't started whistling, and relief the coffee was made. Lester looked darn sexy barefoot and wearing a white T-shirt flipping pancakes.

"Finally up, Sunshine!" he exclaimed, looking at her.

When she opened the door and looked into his eyes, a tingling began in the pit of her stomach.

He crossed the room in two strides till they stood toe to toe. She was aware of his inherent strength, his smell, his heat and the closeness of his lips, lips that brushed lightly over hers leaving behind the smell of fresh mint from the bathroom mouthwash.

Hands pressed against his chest, she took a step backwards. "I'll be back." She murmured and hurried to the bathroom to freshen up.

After breakfast she washed dishes and he dried. Shelby folded the afghan and Lester picked up the bucket of ashes from last night's fire to carry outside.

He stopped in front of her. "I have to go to the office and load up my equipment. I'll be back later this afternoon."

"Thank you for staying last night. I was so frightened." Her hands fell to her sides.

His free hand cupped her neck, gently pulling her toward him for a kiss. She buried her hands in his thick curly hair and kissed him deeply.

That night the kiss still lingered in Lester's heart. He was feeling pretty good, ghost or no ghost. The machines had been set up for four hours. Misty was a no-show. He adjusted the tripod and red grid lines splayed across the wall. When Shelbylious brought him a second cup of coffee, their hands brushed and attraction sizzled between them. The universe was giving him a second chance with her, and this time he was on his game.

"Thanks. Are you up for this?" He took a sip of coffee.

"As ready as I'll ever be. I want this ghost gone," she declared.

Shelby fingered a strand of hair, an escapee of her flaxen ponytail. She hadn't changed much physically, but she wasn't so egotistical and came across as more down to earth. He liked this new Shelby. They had chatted and caught up over the last week.

She grabbed his arm. "Misty's coming!"

An uncanny feeling came over him. Chills ran down his arms and he set the mug down.

"Steady, be quiet," he whispered. He aimed the EMF recorder toward the mist gliding down the stairs and sucked in his breath as the foggy cloud gathered at the bottom. The sing-song voice started and the form drifted over in front of the wall. The grid machine put the mist into a three-D image projected on the wall.

"The ghost's a woman." Shelby whispered in his ear. "Just like I thought."

"This footage will be awesome!" Lester whispered back.

The woman's image shimmered in front of the wall, her slender hands clenching and unclenching worrying the white apron she wore, all the while continuing in her singsong voice. Her attire was from the eighteen hundreds and her hair was pulled back in a severe bun. The image wasn't crystal clear, but the impression from the mist was good.

The cold air engulfed them and he glanced at Shelby in time to see her eyes roll back in her head. He caught her before she hit the floor.

He hit the button on the voice recorder and cradled Shelby up against him.

She started coming around and he lowered her to the wooden chair beside them. Another entity entered the grid lines, a man brandishing a club in a threatening manner. He whacked the woman on the head, and she crumpled to the floor. He yelled something at the crumpled form of the woman. Before leaving, the ghost knocked over Shelby's blue ceramic lamp. With incredible speed, the male entity glided over to Lester and gave a soundless, open mouth scream right in Lester's face. The force of the wind from the scream was merciless, hot, and blew Lester's hair back off his face.

Shelby had jumped when the lamp hit the floor. The episode over, he reached down, pulled her up, gathered her into his embrace. She clutched hold of his shirt, burying her face against his chest. He breathed in the smell of her hair, like a spring day, all warm and flowery. He wondered if she heard the loud drumming of his heart.

His voice husky, he said, "What a show." Slowly he undid her hands from his shirt, and walked over to flip on the light switch.

"The ghosts are gone," he said. We're dealing with two, and a tragedy."

"Misty died a violent death. I'll take the voice recorder back to my lab and let Jake have a listen. He should be able to decipher what she was singing by running the recording through the GVA, Ghost Voice Analysis machine. Knowing what she sings about will give us an idea how to help her." He unplugged the machine and wrapped the cord up. "The second entity, a poltergeist, is the one with violent tendencies."

"Two ghosts?" Shelby's voice went an octave higher. "Can I go with you? I don't want to stay here." Her voice trembled.

"You can come, but I have an assignment for you. Tomorrow afternoon, I want you to go to the library. See what you can find out regarding any residents who lived in this house during the eighteen hundreds."

"I thought you said you researched previous owners?"

"Only the last couple of owners I didn't' think I needed to go back any further, because none of them reported ghostly actions." He shrugged into his leather jacket.

Shelby grabbed her coat off the hanger and he helped her into it. Together they drove to his office where he unloaded his recording machine.

"There's a couch in the next room with a pillow and comforter." He motioned towards an open door. "Sometimes I have to take a catnap before going out on an all-night job. I have some paperwork to take care of. Jake will be here in a couple of hours, seven a.m. Why don't you catch some shut-eye?"

"Okay, and Lester?"

"Yeah?"

"Thanks." She turned to go. He placed a hand on her shoulder and turned her around.

"We'll rid the house of the spirits, both of them." He leaned in and sealed his vow with a kiss.

The next day, Shelby waited anxiously at home for Lester to arrive. She had gotten to know him over the last few days. She had grown to depend on his trustworthiness. And oh, those sweet, seductive kisses! She had definitely grown fond of those.

A car door slammed. She put down the book she was reading, and hurried to open the front door.

He was already leaning on the door frame with a lopsided grin on his face. "What did you find out?"

"I think the woman is Ella Frantz, a servant who had a miscarriage. The child was fathered by the owner of the house. Then he falsely accused Ella of stealing, and later killed her. The wife suspected the baby was her husband's, and his name was — "

"Edward Coultan."

"How — ?"

"After you left, Jake and I ran the tapes through a high-density filter. Ella was singing a song she made up. I think by the time she was murdered she was insane from heartbreak. The song told of Edward forcing himself on her and later kicking her in the stomach when she told him she was carrying his child. When she lost the baby, Ella decided to tell Edward's wife the truth, so he murdered her. When the killing came to light, he accused her of stealing and claimed to have killed her to protect his family. She was buried in a graveyard for paupers and prisoners."

"So how do we make this right?" Shelby said.

"We find her grave and have her remains moved into the church graveyard with the respectable dead." He spoke as if this was an everyday occurrence. "Edward will have no choice but to cross over to hell without Ella here to relive the tragedy with him every night. I will set up the equipment one more time after Ella is moved. If Edward's spirit has stayed on I might have to zap him."

"He deserves a good zapping after murdering Ella," she said with disgust.

A week later, Shelby was relieved Lester had rid the house of the ghosts! Last night had been the best sleep she'd had in a couple of months. He'd be here anytime for his final check, payment for a job well done. This afternoon she baked a pan of brownies for him as a tip. He had told her during one of their late night conversations brownies were his favorite dessert.

The doorbell rang and she pulled the door open. Lester stood there with a bunch of lilies tied with a purple ribbon in one arm, a bouquet of red roses in the other, and a silly look-ing grin on his face.

"Two bouquets?" she asked.

"I was hoping you'd go with me to see Ella's new rest-ing spot. We can put the lilies on her grave." He took a deep breath, and his forehead puckered. "The roses are for you. Will you have dinner with me tonight?"

"Yes, but only if we can come back here for dessert, I baked your favorite." She accepted the roses.

"You bet!" He pulled her close with his free arm and kissed her thoroughly.

Dessert would be more than the pan of warm brownies sitting on the counter.

The End

Thank you *for reading my stories. I hope you enjoyed them
I'd love for you to visit my website at*
www.dianamccollum.weebly.com

.

SARAH'S ANKH

by Judith Ashley

Dedicated to
Michele Lauren
who has been with me
every step of the way on
my publishing journey.

Acknowledgements:

While it is true it was my fingers on the keyboard when writing this story, what is also true is it would not be here for you to read without a village of people. My village for this story are: Michele Lauren, who was instrumental in the creation of this story. While the original idea was mine, she talked plot points and actions over with me. Sarah Raplee, Paty Jager, and Kelly Schaub read and edited Sarah's Ankh so it shines. Of course, all errors are mine.

Sarah Taylor halted in the doorway of the hotel room. "Hey Mimi, what are you doing?" she asked, confusion evident in her tone.

"Packing," Mimi replied as she layered clothing from the dresser drawers into her suitcase.

"Why?" Sarah's scrunched brows amplified the question in her voice.

"Why would I stay when I know my name won't be at the top of the list? I just want to avoid the embarrassment of seeing my name at the bottom," Mimi said in an abrupt tone.

Sarah closed the door and crossed to where her roommate stood, head bent, as she studiously focused on packing. "Hey, I'll miss you." Mimi glanced up and Sarah stared into hazel eyes, bright with unshed tears.

"I'll miss you, too," Mimi said, the words wobbling out.

"Is there anything I can do or say so you'd change your mind?" she asked in a soft voice, her hand resting lightly on Mimi's shoulder.

The response was a shake of the head.

"Then, what can I do to help you finish packing?"

"Double check that I haven't left something in the bathroom or closet."

Sarah quickly checked and found Mimi had been thorough in gathering things up. With nothing to add, Mimi zipped her suitcase and walked to the door.

"Let me come with you to the lobby, okay?" Sarah asked, acutely aware of how close Mimi was to breaking down in tears. At Mimi's nod, she held the door open so her roommate could pass through.

Sarah waited as Mimi checked out, accompanied her outside, and stood next to her as the bellman hailed a taxi. She liked Mimi and knew from their late night talks how hard Mimi had worked to make it to the finals.

"We'll keep in touch, okay?" she asked as the taxi pulled up in front.

Mimi nodded, gave her a quick hug, and said, "Good luck, although I don't expect you need it. You're awesome!"

Sarah remained on the walkway, waving as the taxi pulled away. It paused at the end of the drive before merging with traffic and turning the corner.

"Well, hello there, Sarah," a booming male voice said.

She turned to see Harold Cooper, the president of Relationships First, a top-ranked corporate consultation and training company, descend from the hotel shuttle. She smiled in greeting.

"Sir," she said.

"Harold, Sarah – call me Harold," he strode toward her and gestured for her to precede him into the lobby. "Why aren't you with the others?" he asked once inside.

"I was seeing Mimi off," Sarah said. "She and I were roommates and when she told me she withdrew — well, I wanted to spend a little more time with her."

The open smile on Harold's face faded. "Did she say why she withdrew?"

How do I answer something like that without breaking a confidence? "I'm not comfortable sharing our conversation, Harold. Perhaps she said something in her withdrawal note."

Harold nodded, his gaze sharpened. "Hope I don't have to worry about you withdrawing."

"No sir, I plan on being here for the announcement," she said in a confident voice, maintaining eye contact.

"Good, good to know," he said in his loud voice, his smile back. "Good to know."

Jubilant noise spilled from the bar off the atrium.

"Go and join the others," Harold said and gestured across the lobby. "You've earned a little down time."

"Yes, I think I will join them," Sarah said and started toward the bar. After a few steps, she stopped and turned. "Harold? Thank you for your concern about Mimi." *Another reason to want one of the top slots – he cares about his people.* Swinging around, she continued on.

At the entrance to the lounge, Sarah took in the animated faces and euphoric voices of her co-participants. They'd pulled small square and round tables together and were now crowded around a jumbled rectangle. She noted the four staff sitting among the other ten participants. Less than two hours ago, they'd completed the four grueling days of assessment. It was time to let off steam.

In a few more hours, they'd know who won the three top-level trainer positions. Sarah wanted one of those positions with a dogged determination many others wouldn't understand. Wanted it enough she'd quit her job to make sure she was fully prepared. Why? She had her goals and being top-level staff at a top-level company was one of them. *When I want something, I get it. Other women my age are looking for "Mr. Right," a home, family, babies – not me. I want the top training spot at Relationships First.* Her fingers stroked the ankh dangling from a chain around her neck. *It must be a sign — my spending extra time with Mimi provided an opportunity to talk to Harold. And, he's never been so open and friendly. I'm sure I'm one of the finalists.*

With a bright smile and friendly wave to the others, she stepped into the bar and looked around. Her instincts told her she had the position. But her realistic, pragmatic self knew everything she did and said until the final announcement was critical. An eyebrow rose at the memory of how she'd effectively deflected the unwanted amorous attentions of one of the RF staff. Since high school, she'd worked on how to say "no, I'm not interested" without hurt feelings. *It's one of my strengths.*

Another strength? Her ability to know when someone was being genuine or not and especially how to respond in the latter situation. While the instructor was genuine in his come-on, he wasn't genuine in his interest in her as a person. Not that she'd have acted any differently if he had been really interested in her as a person. Mixing business and pleasure, or engaging in office affairs was not her style.

She'd looked him in the eye and said, "I don't mix business with pleasure, Gary, no exceptions." It was a simple statement. From experience she'd learned they were the best kind because there was no room for ambiguity.

Happy Hour was in full swing and with her group taking up the center of the room, the bar was overflowing. At first glance she saw no room at the cobbled together table. She started to chide herself for spending the time with Mimi and stopped. Mimi had become a friend and friends stood by each other. *Don't forget, it gave you time to talk to Harold.* She smiled to herself. *Synchronicity in action.*

About to wander around the room, chat with people, be seen and heard without sitting down, she heard her name called. She spotted Gary and saw him wave her over to an empty seat beside him…another glance around the table…the only one left. She could stay on her feet and chat with people or she could bite the proverbial bullet and sit down.

This could be challenging. Sarah moved toward the vacant chair but stopped along the way to talk to participants.

"Hey there, beautiful," Gary said, patting the seat and winking.

While his seductive tone and flirtatious manner irritated, Sarah was confident she could manage him. *I can do this. I successfully dealt with one of his propositions. I can do it again. One more time and the position is mine.* She smiled at the rhyme.

"Hey, back, Gary." She slipped into the empty chair while angling her body away from him. "By the way, since you've forgotten, my name is Sarah," she said in a straightforward voice, making eye contact with him.

Half-listening to the animated conversations of the trainees and instructors as they traded stories around the hodgepodge of tables, she remained alert for another pass. *He hasn't apologized or backed off so he'll probably try something again. I've never exchanged sex for special treatment and I won't start now.*

"I like your ankh." A deep male voice penetrated her thoughts.

"Oh, thank you." Sarah's fingers twisted the silver chain around her neck. The silver talisman swayed. The chocolate brown eyes lit with laughter belonged to Sam, another participant, who sat across the small table from her.

"It looks good on you," he said, his mouth tilted in an inviting grin.

"Thanks," she replied, her voice unusually husky. For an instant in her mind's eye, she saw herself lean forward, reach out, and brush the lock of dark hair off his broad forehead. While she knew who Sam was – one of the participants – she'd never been in a small group exercise with him. But that didn't mean she hadn't noticed him across the room because she had. Now he was up-close, only a few feet away.

Black eyebrows arched over intense, almost hypnotic eyes, a largish, almost hawkish nose somehow fit his face. The stubble of beard did nothing to hide his strong jaw. Her gaze focused on his mouth, on his full lips still quirked in a smile before dropping to his hands. Large hands with tapered fingers curved possessively around his glass of beer. Her breath hitched when her mind's eye saw a flash of those hands sliding down her bare leg.

Aware of an energy about him she found mesmerizing, she leaned forward when she answered. "My friend was traveling to Egypt and I asked her to pick out a souvenir for me."

Under the table, Gary's hand squeezed her knee.

Her muscles tensed, the urge to strike him clenched her fist. She firmly grasped his hand and removed it. Turning, she said in a low-pitched voice, "Stop!" Her stare never wavered as she added, "It's not acceptable behavior and you know it."

"I was delighted when she picked out an ankh," she continued turning back to Sam, a relaxed smile on her face.

Gary leaned toward her and insinuated himself into the conversation.

"It draws a man's eyes to your...assets." Gary's gazed skimmed past the pendant and fixated on her breasts.

Sarah's fingers closed protectively around the ancient symbol. What is going on here? She looked at the table and saw one empty glass and a full one in front of him. He had been drinking but not that much. *It's as if he wants to cause a scene.*

Gary reached for the hand that held the ankh, brushing against her arm.

She shifted in time so he missed her "assets."

"Hey, beautiful, let me see it." Gary's hand wrapped around her own, his fingers pulling hers open.

More was at stake here than letting Gary see the piece of jewelry. The game had changed. He wasn't taking "no" for an answer.

"The ankh is the hieroglyph meaning life," Sam said from across the table, now leaning forward.

Sarah kept her eyes fixed on Sam as her mind raced with ways to deal with Gary. Sam no longer grinned, his eyes no longer held laughter. Tension radiated from him. Dark and dangerous came to mind.

Gary's hand stilled.

She grabbed the opportunity to shift away and stood. "Bye, everyone, see you later," Sarah said in a breezy voice. She raised her hand in a wave as she glanced around the table before starting toward the entryway.

"Hey, beautiful." Gary was beside her, gesturing for her to precede him.

She stepped into the atrium, felt Gary follow her. Her stomach churned and her chest tightened, her hands were fisted at her side as she steeled her resolve and whirled to confront him.

"Hey, beautiful...,"

"My name is Sarah, Gary," she said in a no nonsense voice, a slight smile on her face as she made eye contact.

"Hey, Sarah." Gary leaned closer and winked. "Better, beautiful?"

"Not really," Sarah said in a firm voice. The smile gone, she looked him straight in the eye. "What do I need to say, to do, for you to hear that I'm not interested? That I don't mix business with pleasure."

Head cocked to the side, Gary watched her with a considering gaze.

Spine straight, Sarah maintained eye contact and waited for an answer.

Warmth throbbed at the base of her throat. Without breaking eye contact, she raised her hand to the source of the heat – the ankh. As her hand touched the heated silver, other meanings for the symbol crowded her mind: good fortune, the universe, heaven and earth.

Sam appeared at her side. "Sorry to keep you waiting, Sarah," he said, a welcoming smile on his face. "Our table is ready. Are you?"

What should she do? Wait until Gary answered or accept the lifeline Sam offered?

The amulet in her hand pulsed, its heat coursed through her. She gazed at Sam. *The ankh represents good fortune.* The silver pulsed. *Is it telling me to trust my instincts, that my good fortune is connected to him?*

"Yes," she said moving closer to him. Hot energy surged through her and she knew she'd made the right choice. "Yes, I'm ready."

Sam kept his touch light on her elbow as he guided Sarah into the restaurant. His fingers burned from the heat of her skin, his nostrils flared with her cinnamon scent, his peripheral vision expanded taking in the red-gold curls framing her profile. She looked serious or perhaps thoughtful. One of the fallouts from the game she was involved in, a game she didn't know she played.

Within minutes the maître de sat them at the table he'd reserved at noon just in case this opportunity arose. *Don't like this game and never did. It may be effective on some level but there has to be a better way.*

"Thank you, John," Sam said and nodded to the maître de, who handed them menus. *Interesting — I've played it before but it feels different this time. Definitely need to talk to Gary and Harold about it later.*

"Elliott will be your server tonight, Mr. Manetti, Miss." John bowed and left.

Sam turned his attention to Sarah who studied the menu. "What strikes your fancy tonight?" he asked, watching her slender fingertips glide over the offerings.

"I'm not sure. Everything has been excellent." Her head remained bent over the menu. "What have you eaten here?" she asked looking up, her lips slightly parted — waiting.

Anticipation. One of Sarah's strength's was her forthrightness, her being in the present – like now when she leaned slightly forward awaiting his response. There was something heady about someone being so tuned in, concentrating on you, waiting to hear your answer.

"The salmon is excellent."

"Oh yes, it is," she purred drawing out the words.

He felt the stirring of arousal. *Oh yes*, marched through his brain as a vision of them tangled in sheets flashed. Sam wrestled his unruly thoughts and reminded himself that Sarah's seduction was not on tonight's menu.

"I think I'll try the veal parmesan with a baked potato," he said. He took a sip of water and mentally shook himself. *Back to business.*

Setting her menu down, Sarah smiled at the waiter who approached to take their orders. "I'll have the shrimp salad, thousand island dressing on the side, no olives, and an Arnold Palmer," she said.

The seasoned waiter gave her a wink and Sarah's face brightened with a smile.

"Oh," she added, "and please save me a piece of tiramisu. If I don't have room to eat it now, I'll take it to my room for a late night snack."

The tip of her tongue slipped around the edge of her lips as if already savoring the dessert. Sam glanced away and thought of cold showers to steady his voice before he ordered his meal.

Before either had a chance to launch into conversation, a young man with a water pitcher appeared, filling their glasses and the quiet with water and chatter. He was followed by a young woman with a basket of warm bread. The yeasty aroma filtered through the air.

They both reached for the bread, hands touched, and electricity arced. Sam's hand jerked back. Sarah froze, her hand on the bread, her cobalt-blue eyes wide, her rose-red mouth agape.

"What was that?" she asked.

"Static electricity," Sam fibbed. He ran his tingling fingers down the glass of water, picking up slight condensation.

What had sent sparks flying through his body was not static electricity, it was primal sexual attraction.

The service was excellent. Their waiter seemed to know when there was a lull in their conversation because he never intruded when they were involved in a discussion.

And discussions they had.

"What was going on with Gary?" Sam asked.

"I don't know," Sarah replied. "I know he understood I'm not interested in having a fling with him. I was clear and consistent. It seemed he wanted to cause a scene but that doesn't really make sense. He's an RF staff. It just doesn't make sense." Her words drifted off at the end, her gaze drifted off to his left.

Classic posture. She's still trying to figure it out.

A shake of her head and her attention was back at the table. "What do you think is going on?"

"My guess is it has something to do with the selection process," he answered. *I've never seen Gary take it this far, though. I wonder what is going on with him.*

"You're probably right. I just didn't see anything like this going on with any of the other women," she replied. A slight shrug and she added, "I was wondering how long I'd have to stand there toe-to-toe with him waiting for an answer when you stepped in. Thanks."

"Not a problem," Sam said and changed the subject. Over the course of their dinner he learned many things about her and shared a few things about himself.

Her favorite vacation spot was a little B & B along the western coast of Ireland followed closely by an old motel on the Oregon Coast. She loved the former and had fond memories of her one and only visit there but spent at least three and usually four long weekends a year at the latter.

Sam pictured the quaint Irish countryside as she regaled him with stories from her trip — flat tires, sheep, and banks of fuchsias. She had a way of describing her environment that drew him into the time and place. He could smell the salty air with no hint of human habitation and hear the waves crashing on the Oregon Coast rocks. Listening to her talk about places she loved was a kind of aphrodisiac. *What would it be like to experience these places with her?*

As he engaged with her, Sam's brain was sorting, cataloguing, and making assessments. It was intoxicating to have a beautiful woman totally absorbed in conversing with him. The picture of them tangled in sheets flashed again...and he mentally shook it off. *What's going on here? What is it about her that arouses me? I've certainly been around beautiful women before.*

Dinner was long over and still they stayed. He sipped his coffee, she sipped ice water.

She was extraordinary in so many ways. Physically attractive, intelligent, a blend of quick wit and gentle humor and always, when she was "on" (he did recognize that state), she was focused, present, and in tune with whomever she was with. *I know she figured Gary would hit on her when she sat down in the bar. She'd handled everything up to then so well. Why Gary thought he needed to keep pressing her, I sure as hell don't know.*

Internally he shook off his musing and focused on the present. The question he'd been asked to determine was, "What is Sarah like when she isn't on?" The more that question simmered in the back of his mind, the more he thought that wasn't the right question. Sarah wasn't "on" as in working the room right now. She was immersed in the moment, in him, which wasn't the same thing.

He found out what she did when she wasn't working — she read — they shared the love of a good mystery but she favored romance and he favored biographies. She took long walks through her neighborhood surrounding herself with the scents and sounds of Mother Nature. He preferred the routine of a gym workout.

The more he learned about her, the more drawn he was to her; the more intrigued he was by her which made his job more challenging.

Another flash of them tangled in the sheets of a large bed somewhere the ocean roared. The image was so vivid, he heard the pounding waves.

He stood, his napkin discretely held in front of him, when Sarah excused herself to powder her nose. As he settled back into his chair, his thoughts rampant with images of her, of them together, he let them run amok. Sarah glancing over her shoulder at him, her eyes full of laughter as they raced down the beach. Sarah leaning across the dinner table to kiss him softly on the nose. Sarah naked, her arms and legs wrapped around him in welcome.

"Will there be anything else, sir?" Elliott said, interrupting his thoughts.

Sam glanced up and watched Sarah make her way back to the table. "No, the check please."

Elliott turned as Sarah approached. "Don't forget my tiramisu," she said to the waiter as she slid into her chair and reached for her purse.

Seeing her pull her wallet out, Sam reached across the table to stop her movements. "My treat."

Sarah continued to open her wallet, pull out some bills, and put them on the table. "Either I pay for my meal or Elliott will have an enormous tip."

Sam was going to argue when they were approached by three other training participants.

"Hey you two," Marcie said as the group stopped by the table. "Have you seen the notice?"

Sarah snapped to attention. "No, what's it say?"

"There's been a delay in the announcement," Marcie said, exasperation tinting her voice. She stood with one hand on her hip and blew her bangs up with her exhale. "At least they didn't keep us circling the announcement board all night."

"I, for one, appreciate that," Donald said, draping an arm around Marcie's shoulders. "It's been great but a bit stressful waiting to see who's getting the top slots."

Even though he participated with the group, Sam's attention was on Sarah. The slight frown at Marcie's announcement was fleeting and her involvement in the conversation with everyone complete. At one point, when he'd purposefully held back, she'd half-turned to more physically include him in the discussion.

"Was there any indication when the announcement would be made?" Sarah asked.

"We're supposed to meet in the training room at ten a.m.," Donald said. "I figure they'll let us know then. I was sure we'd just read the results on the board. This is really a surprise and not at all what they said would happen when we started."

No, not anything like they were told. Sam watched the exchange, commenting here and there. He stood when the bill was paid and suppressed a smile at the size of the waiter's tip – not as large as it might have been, but generous just the same.

His hand on Sarah's elbow, they followed the others out of the restaurant. The heat from that touch raced through his body and her cinnamon scent made his mouth water.

As a group they walked to the elevator. He was grateful the others were staying on a different floor.

Sam walked her to her room and stood to the side as she unlocked her door. When she turned back, the soft hall lights picked out the gold in her hair. Gold flecks reflected in her azure blue eyes and even the silver ankh was brushed with gold. The scent of cinnamon was an invitation to feast. The urge to lean in and kiss her, to follow her through the open door was strong. But that wasn't his job.

"It was a delightful evening, Sam," Sarah said smiling up at him. "I had a wonderful time." Her smile deepened.

"Me, too." Sam kept his eyes on her face, acutely aware of the waiting bed beyond the open door. His hands fisted as he fought the urge to raise them, to tuck her hair back behind her ears, to skim his fingers down the side of her neck, to tip her chin as he leaned in for a kiss.

Harold was waiting. He had a report to give so decisions could be made.

He steeled himself, nodded and turned away.

10 a.m. – Training Room

Sarah slipped into the first empty seat she saw just as the clock clicked on ten. She heaved a sigh of relief and set her purse under her chair. They were in the same room where the training was held, the round tables scattered throughout with a stage along one end. Absently she ran a hand over her hair and smoothed her jacket. *I'm running on fumes here.*

Once in her hotel room last night, doubts ran rampant. Had she quashed any hopes of gaining a top spot because she handled Gary's passes wrong? That had been the question ... and she mulled it over and over during the long hours until she fell asleep around five. Of course she overslept and what with checking out and leaving her bag with the bell captain had almost been late. *Having dinner with Sam seemed like the right decision last night but....* She fingered the ankh. *I've never let my attraction for someone get in the way of reaching my goals. What was I thinking?*

She settled back in her chair, smiled at Marcie and Donald who sat at the same table. Her eyes scanned the room looking for the man who'd infiltrated her dreams once she'd found sleep. There he was at a front table, an empty seat beside him. When Sam turned, caught her eye, smiled, and gestured to her to join him, she shook her head and pointed at her watch. *I think I still have a chance. Harold has talked to me enough to get his own impressions. Hopefully Gary will be too embarrassed to say too much.* Her tired brain rattled on. *I hope Sam gets one of the spots. It'd be great working with him.*

Harold strode to the front of the room, microphone in hand. "You're a great group of people," he said, gesturing expansively around the room. "Really great which made the selection process very difficult, which is the reason for the delay in this announcement." He started to pace, waving his arms, pointing for emphasis as he talked about Relationships First and his goals for the company.

"As I introduce you, please come and join me," he said to the people seated in front.

"You all know Gary Mains. What you may not know is that his job was to test you on how you dealt with annoying customers. For the women here, that included male customers who put the move on you. While we don't tolerate sexual harassment, it's equally true we're hired when a company's employees don't have good relationship skills. It's important in business to be able to clearly communicate you aren't available while maintaining a positive relationship with the customer.

"You men will remember Gary attempting to draw you into inappropriate conversations about the women. Men need the skills to know how to handle these situations, too."

Gary seemed at ease as he stood next to Harold. Gone was the man with the flirtatious, winking, roving eye. His calm gaze rested on each participant in the room. When he looked at her, she blushed. It had never occurred to her he was testing her. *How did I miss that? I thought it strange that he kept coming on to me. Why didn't I think it might be a test?*

"Come on up, Miriam Walsh." Harold invited Gary's female counterpart up front. As Miriam made her way to the front, Sarah saw Sam turn toward her again. He patted the seat next to him. She shrugged and shook her head. *What is wrong with him?*

She'd known Miriam was staff just as she'd known Gary was. A conversation they'd had replayed in her mind.

"Isn't Ted sexy?" Miriam had leaned close, her voice a throaty whisper.

"I hadn't noticed," Sarah had replied.

Now she wondered if that had been enough. Should she have been more definitive that this wasn't an appropriate conversation?

Oh my, I've really screwed up, haven't I? She resisted the urge to lay her head on the table or get up and leave. *Maybe I haven't screwed up that bad.*

Two other employees were introduced. They were the ones who ran the small groups, role played the clients in various situations, kept track of the time, and the myriad details needed in a fast-paced, well-run training.

"Last but not least, I'd like to introduce my friend, Sam Manetti," Harold said, a grin splitting his face.

Sarah watched in horror as Sam slowly rose and made his way to stand next to Harold.

"Sam here is my secret weapon, aren't you?" He grabbed Sam's hand, pumped it twice, and slapped him on the back.

Stunned, Sarah watched Sam search for her, watched him catch her eye, and watched him turn away. *His secret weapon?* The bitter taste of betrayal bit the back of her throat. *What is happening here?*

"And now for the moment you've all been waiting for!" Harold said. He strode across the room and back. "It wasn't an easy decision to pick three from this stellar group," he said, his serious voice lowered, "but we believe we got it right."

Sarah examined Sam's face for any sign she'd hear her name called. He didn't look at her, he didn't smile, he looked ill – no that couldn't be right. Something else she had wrong. Her hand fumbled with the chain holding her ankh. No heat, no energy – just cool metal. "Marcie Davidson, Donald Wright, and Pearlann Barton, come on up," Harold bellowed.

What? Bile rose in her throat. *How could I have been so wrong, missed so much?* Tears threatened. *I really screwed up when I misinterpreted the energy from my ankh and accepted Sam's invitation to dinner. I know now what Mimi wanted to avoid...the pain of humiliation.*

Marcie and Donald rose. Sarah enveloped them in fierce hugs. They deserved this chance. "Congratulations, you two. I know you've worked hard and earned these spots."

She grabbed her purse and started for the door congratulating Pearlann, who sat at the table behind her, on her way out. She trotted into the hotel lobby. *I've failed. I've failed. I've failed.* Her hand clutched the ankh. No energy emanated from the sacred symbol. Not even soothing energy. Pain, only pain, pain from the furrows marking her palm as she held on tight. Tears of anger and humiliation burned her eyes as she got her bag from the bell captain and headed out the door. In less than five minutes from the announcement she was in a taxi and headed to the airport.

Three days later, Sarah was at her special place on the coast. Blinding sunlight glittered off water and fractious waves crashed on rocks. She sat on the promontory, knees pulled to her chest, and surveyed the never-ending march of white caps to their destruction. *How could I have been so wrong?* She asked herself for the thousandth if not millionth time.

Burying herself in a book, she'd kept tears at bay on the flight home. Busying herself with unpacking and the mundane details of her daily life had kept the flood contained. Buying herself time at her favorite spot at the beach had unleashed the torrent.

She wore her dark glasses. And while they hid her red, puffy eyes, they did not hide her red and runny nose or her red and blotchy face. Crying did nothing to enhance her looks, her feelings, or change anything. But between the reality of her failure and the strong sense of Sam's betrayal, the tears wouldn't stop. Thank goodness she booked a room for two weeks. Heaven knew one week wasn't going to be enough.

The waves continued on their self-destructive path to the shore. She saw the similarities in her self-pity, self-recriminations, self-doubt. *I must stop asking myself "why" or "how."* Exhaling from deep within, she drew in a breath of the fresh, ion-laden air. *I've got to get a grip, get my footing.* She wriggled her toes. The sparkling polish twinkled in the light. It isn't the end of the world. The waves continued on their journey. Some crashed on the rocks, some sank into oblivion before they reached shore, and some seemed to have a second life rebounding off the rocks only to hurl themselves at the lava flow once more. *I've crashed on the rocks but I'm going to pick myself up and try again. Just because I won't reach my career goal by the time I'm thirty doesn't mean I won't ever reach it. When one door closes, another opens. I've just got to find that door because I'll never be someone who sinks into oblivion — who stops trying.*

A hunched lone figure sat silhouetted against the bright sun – Sarah. Sam had used her vivid descriptions of her favorite spot when he'd asked around about places to just sit and watch the waves. He'd checked two others out before he found her sitting on this point of land looking out at the vast ocean.

Bands of sorrow constricted his chest. He cared about her. How that happened in four days, most of which was spent across the room, he didn't know. But care about her he did. He squinted against the relentless glare of the sun. She hadn't moved. He'd found her and in comparison to the next step in his plan, that was the easy part. Sam rocked back on his heels, his mind examining his strategy. The element of surprise was his – or was it? Sarah's predictability wasn't, well, predictable.

Case in point: he'd expected her to be early for what he now thought of as "the disastrous meeting." She wasn't. He'd expected to have time to tell her who he was. He didn't. He'd expected to have time to prepare her for who had won the coveted positions and what else Harold had planned for her. Obviously, that didn't happen. When the commotion surrounding the winners had died down, Harold was ready to make the other announcement, the announcement concerning Sarah, but she wasn't there.

Frantic to see her, to go to her, to assure her everything was going to be more than fine, he had scanned the room, searching for any sign of her. He didn't find her. At that moment he was grateful for his strong friendship with Harold who ended the meeting at his request. Harold may have complied, but he was not pleased Sarah had up and left. In the privacy of Sam's hotel room he ranted about Sarah's lack of maturity and how glad he was they'd seen her true colors before it was too late. Clearly she wasn't mature enough for the position and it was a good thing they'd found this out now were his main points. Sam had kept his thoughts to himself and let his friend vent.

Whenever he remembered those panicked minutes, minutes when he couldn't find her, tightness still constricted his chest. He rubbed his chest and idly wondered if his shirt now had a hole in it. Did his heart? *How can it when I haven't known her that long.* He rubbed his chest in a futile effort to ease the pain. *I don't believe in love at first sight or even love in first week.* He rubbed his chest hoping it would help, knowing it wouldn't.

Sweat beaded his upper lip and soaked his armpits. Here he was at the beginning of the path that led to the promontory where Sarah stood looking out to sea. She hadn't seen him yet so he could turn and leave and she'd never know he'd found her. His heartbeat matched the churning sea. He could wait until she did turn and see him – wait to see if she came to him. Or, he could be a man – and go to her. His feet were striding down the path, before the thought fully registered in his mind.

Sam was still a few yards from Sarah when she turned away from the ocean and, head bowed, started down the path.

"Sarah," he said.

She looked up and froze.

It was the old cliché of time standing still. But it did. Or perhaps it was the contrast of the rolling waves, the grasses dancing in the wind, the seagulls swooping in the sky, the clouds gliding overhead – all that movement except for the two of them.

Her red-gold curls swirled around her face. Her azure-blue eyes were concealed by dark glasses. Her rosy lips pursed in an angry pinch. Like a sucker punch in the gut, her pain slammed into him.

Something else was wrong, something beyond the stark angle of her chin, the taut skin around her mouth. Something was missing. Before he could figure out what, Sarah surged past him at a dead run.

"Sarah," he called as he pursued her. "Sarah, wait!" He sprinted past her, wheeled and stopped, blocking her exit. "Sarah, please." It was humbling to see her so desperate to avoid him.

"I've nothing to say to you and you've nothing to say that I want to hear," she shouted. She shoved him, started past but he caught her arm.

"Please, Sarah, please let me explain." He wanted to hold her, to assure her everything would be okay, to wipe away the pain etched on her face.

Sarah exploded. "How could you?" She stomped on his foot. He dropped her arm. "What kind of deceitful, manipulative, exploitive man are you? No, don't tell me. I don't want to hear your lies." Shaking, her arms clutched her body. She turned back to the ocean.

Sam caught her shoulders. She shook off his hands and stalked away several steps before turning back. "You deceived me. You deceived the others. You are worse than Gary ever was. He at least was obvious. Smarmy. But you, I thought you were different, that you were one of us," she yelled, her fist pounding her heart. She swallowed before continuing. "I–I thought we had a connection, I thought you cared." Tears leaked out below her glasses. She swiped them away with the back of her hand.

They did have a connection, a strong one. He did care. Why? It was hard to put into words. He'd known her such a short time. That spot on his chest burned. His heart pounded, his head ached, and he didn't have a clue what to do next.

The tears stopped. Sarah drew her shoulders back, her hands anchored on her hips. "I don't know what's wrong with me. I've prided myself on seeing what's beneath the surface, beneath the mask people show to each other. Evidently I'm not as good as I thought because I didn't see what was really going on with Gary or Miriam much less you," her quiet voice was laced with pain.

"I'm sorry," Sam said, "I never meant to — "

"Don't," she interrupted. "Just don't. I don't want to hear your apology. I don't want to hear your explanation. I don't want to even see you again." Her voice broke on the last few words and she turned away.

"We both know we're not done here, Sarah," he said. He turned on his heel and walked away.

Sam didn't change his plane reservations after his confrontation with Sarah choosing instead to spend some time in the area he knew she loved, choosing to stay close but also choosing to avoid her. He knew now what was missing. How to help her get it back – that was the question and his task.

To complete any task, one needs a plan. Sam's plan commenced three days later when he strode into the office of the President of Relationship First. "Thanks for seeing me, Harold."

"You said it was urgent. Not really like you, Sam." Harold stood and reached across the expanse of wood to shake hands.

"I've come to ask a favor of a friend," Sam said, stepping back from the desk.

"In that case, let's move over there." Harold pointed to the comfortable dark green leather-clad club chairs in a corner of the room. "What about something to drink?"

"Water will do," Sam said and walked over to the chairs and sat down.

"What's this all about?" Harold retrieved two bottles of water from the small fridge next to his desk.

"I want you to call and talk to Sarah Taylor," Sam stated in a straightforward manner.

"Sam, you know I won't hire her," Harold said, his voice firm.

"I'm not asking you to hire her. I'm asking you to explain why she wasn't picked for one of the top three slots. I never got a chance to talk to her or even slip her a note that morning. Even though I've tried to explain, she won't listen to me. I think she'll listen to you."

"What do you mean, you never talked to her? And why am I only hearing about this now?" Harold popped out of his chair and started to pace. "What the hell happened?"

"I don't exactly know. I got there at nine-thirty and waited. She slipped in at the last minute and sat at another table. Several times I motioned her to come sit by me but she didn't. Under the circumstances, it didn't seem appropriate for me to get up and go get her." Sam shook his head staring at the floor. "What a mess!"

"I still have major reservations about hiring her," Harold said.

"I know. And I don't expect you to change them. Before this training I was approached by Worldwide Business Seminars for help in putting together a series of open seminars targeting the special issues of women in the workplace. They asked me for ideas of who to check out as their lead trainer. As soon as I saw Sarah, I knew she'd be a perfect fit with them."

Sam hurried on, Harold was sitting forward, leaning toward him, listening. "I also know you and I've talked at different times about adding this feature to the in-house trainings Relationships First already does." He hurried on as he saw Harold lean back in preparation to argue. "I appreciate you don't want to spread the company too thin and you don't want to dilute the brand you've worked so hard to establish. I actually agree with you on these points."

He resisted the urge to get up and pace, kept his voice calm, and continued, "I don't think the project Wordwide Business Seminars has in mind would be in conflict with RF. We've been friends a long time, Harold. I hope you know you can trust me. I've already mentioned you to the WBS folks who, you'll be pleased to know, are impressed with the work you do. I doubt there would be a problem to refer clients to RF whose issues are too big for a two or three day seminar."

Sam waited. By the time he'd finished, his friend was up and pacing. He knew from experience Harold liked to move around when he was sorting things through.

"So you aren't asking me to hire her?" Harold stopped pacing and plunked himself down in the chair.

"No, I really don't want you to hire her," Sam said, a chuckle escaping. The heaviness weighing him down lifted. "I want you to talk to her, explain there was more going on, and that if the timing had been different, she'd have known there was more. Will you do that for me?"

Three days after the scene with Sam, Sarah sat on the balcony outside her room looking with unseeing eyes into the distance.

Her cell phone rang. She ignored it.

Glancing up at the morning sky she saw the moon still visible in the sun light. *I've heard stories about Grandmother Moon and Grandfather Sun. I can't imagine passing each other day after day, night after night seldom spending time together, basking in each other's light. It isn't what I want in a relationship.* She wrapped her arms around her middle, curled her legs under her and sighed. *That's not something I need to worry about.* Unshed tears brightened her eyes. *I wish….*

Shortly after noon, her cell phone rang again and then just before five. She didn't immediately answer it nor did she listen to voice mail messages. The afternoon of the second day, she knew in her heart the phone would ring again just before five. Not that today was any different and she wanted to talk to anyone, but she had decided to answer the phone the next time it rang. *I can't hide forever.*

"This is Sarah Taylor," she said, answering on the fifth ring.

"Sarah, Harold Cooper, Relationships First. Hope you have a few minutes to talk."

His booming voice pounded over the line. She held the phone away from her ear. "I don't really...."

"Two minutes, Sarah. All I want is two minutes. Surely you can squeeze me in for two minutes."

She sighed. "Two minutes, Harold."

"Things didn't end too well last week. I want you to know I'm sorry for that. And, I want to explain what happened. The truth is you were so much better qualified than everyone else; we were going to offer you a staff position. You would have worked alongside Gary and Miriam. Sam was tasked with talking to you before the training so you wouldn't be blind-sided. Unfortunately, he never got the chance."

"Wha...," she stuttered, her hand clenching the phone.

"Thanks for listening to me, Sarah."

The dial tone buzzing in her ear registered. The phone slipped from her hands and fell with a clunk on the counter. *I misunderstood everything. They wanted me on staff. Sam recommended me to be on staff.*

In a numb daze, she wandered out on the deck off her room, leaned on the railing, and faced the sea. Out of habit, her hand reached for the ankh. It wasn't there. She hadn't worn it since that dark day and wasn't sure where it was. *They wanted me on staff.* The darkness surrounding her from the profound sense of betrayal lightened. The bruises on her pride faded. They wanted me on staff. Her eyes squinted against the sun's reflection off the water. *Wanted. Obviously they don't want me now. And I can understand why.* She sighed. The pain ebbed replaced by a memory of Sam gesturing her to come sit by him, mouthing words she didn't understand and to be honest, ignored. He had looked ill. *Because he knew what was coming and knew I didn't.*

Pride goeth before a fall. She shook her head in dismay. *I don't usually think in Biblical quotes.* A wry chuckle escaped. *I'm not even sure how accurately I'm remembering this one.* However there was something about it that rang true. When she thought of how confident she was of getting one of the top slots, how confident she was of her skills, it fit. And when Sam tried to explain? Her cheeks flamed with the memory of how her deep sense of betrayal and hurt pride had turned her into an arrogant and righteous shrew.

She glanced at her watch. It'd been fifteen minutes since Harold called and her world had shifted. *Where is my ankh?* She needed her talisman. A sense of urgency infused her movements as she searched her jewelry roll and purse.

What was I wearing that day? Remembering the dark blue pantsuit, she groaned. *I didn't bring that with me.* Going back to her purse, she dumped the contents on the dining table. Not there. She pulled her jewelry roll out and went through every pocket again. Not there. The cobalt blue jacket she'd worn on the drive down hung on a peg by the front door. She found it in the small inside pocket.

Holding the pendant in her hands, she closed her eyes and prayed for a way to undo the harm, to make things right with Sam. Her skin warmed where the silver touched. *Energy. I can feel the ankh's energy.* She watched herself in the mirror as she fastened the clasp and turned the chain so the ankh rested at the base of her throat. Calm invaded her, joy flowed through her. *I don't know what's to come but I do know I'll be all right. Something else, something that is meant to be is in my future.* The energy from the charm heated her skin and beat in synchronicity with her heart. *Something special is coming my way.*

Sarah turned away from the mirror, the ankh enclosed in her hand, and retreated to the deck. A few minutes later she heard the knock on her door. Energy pulsed through her. Her step quickened as she crossed the room. She paused at the door, a moment of doubt assailing the confidence. *So soon? Nothing can happen so soon.*

A moment more of hesitation.

Another knock.

Throwing caution aside, she opened the door. Her feet stuck to the floor, her lungs seized, and her heart stuttered.

Sam.

"May I come in?" His deep voice reverberated down her spine. His dark chocolate eyes revealed the hope in his words.

Her breath caught, blood pounded in her veins, her stomach churned. Sarah nodded and stood aside, too overcome for words. He was here.

Sam walked through her room and out on the deck. Turning, he leaned back against the rail and observed her come toward him. It wasn't a dispassionate, calm, much less cool observation but more of an intense scrutinizing one. She looked tired and drawn but much better than she had when he'd last seen her on the path by the ocean. *She let you in. Don't blow it.*

"How did you find me?" she whispered.

"Dinner," he responded. "You talked about this place when we had dinner. If you hadn't been here, I'd have gone to Ireland."

"Oh...."

"I'm asking you to hear me out," Sam started. "I'll be upfront and tell you straight out I'm nervous."

Sarah moved next to him and leaned on the rail to face the sea. "I'm listening."

Sam glanced at her profile. She was here, in this moment in time, with him. The sun reflected off the silver ankh now hanging away from her body. His racing heart calmed and he relaxed. "Harold and I have been friends since high school. We were roommates in college and have always supported each other. He asked me to help select the people who'd be in the top spots and I agreed because we are friends and because I've been involved in training and consulting businesses myself. After you and I had dinner, there was no question that you were the top pick."

Sarah swung towards him, her mouth open to reply.

Sam held up his hand. "I'll answer questions when I'm done, okay?" He smiled and waited for her nod.

"You were so good your talents would have been wasted in one of the top slots. Harold and I talked about what your role could be and he decided to create a third staff position. He was going to announce that you would be joining Gary and Miriam. When you left, I stopped him. It wouldn't look good for Relationships First, for Harold or...." His intense gaze locked with hers, "Or, for you."

"I- I- I didn't know," Sarah stammered. "Not until Harold called. I just saw all the things I'd missed as Harold was talking about the company and figured I'd flunked out."

"Not at all. The plan was that I'd talk to you in the morning so you'd know what was going to happen. That part got all screwed up...."

"Because I came in late...," she interrupted, stepping back so she faced him.

He shook his head and shifted so he also stood away from the railing. "Partly that but partly because our plan didn't take into consideration that you might not be there early. You aren't the only one to blame for screwing up here."

Her head high, Sarah said, "Thanks for coming and explaining things to me. I'm sorry I didn't give you a chance to explain the other day." She started inside. Sam's hand on her arm stopped her. "What?"

"There's more," he said. "You know there's much more between us, Sarah." His touch was gentle as he tugged on her arm.

She turned back and faced him, arms across her chest. She nodded. "I'm still listening," she said in a voice that shook.

"Good, because I've a few more things to say, starting with an apology." He reached out but let his hand drop to his side. "I'm sorry. If you feel I betrayed you I understand. It was never my intention but — " He stood before her, watched tears slip down her cheeks, dribble off her chin, and catch in her ankh, the sign of eternity, of eternal life.

"I let you down. I could have and should have come to you and talked to you when I first saw you at the meeting. In hindsight that would have been for the best but, in the moment, all I could think about is how inappropriate it would look given some of the others saw us have dinner and you being hired as staff and my being Harold's 'secret weapon'."

She opened her mouth to comment. He gestured for another minute.

"I'd notice you from the first day, been drawn to you, had an attraction I struggled not to act on. I wanted you to see me as someone you wanted to get to know, to see if the attraction is more than ephemeral, to know I'm not another Gary."

Sarah's smile was shaky and she swiped at the free-flowing tears with the back of her hands.

"Can you forgive me?" Sam asked, his voice mirroring his serious expression.

Sarah nodded.

Relief flooded through him. His shoulders relaxed, his knees unlocked, and his breath whooshed from his lungs. "One more thing," Sam said stopping himself from stepping closer. "I've a job opportunity I'd like to tell you about."

At her quizzical look, he continued. "I've been approached by Worldwide Business Seminars. They want to start a series of open seminars on the issues women face in the workplace. While it would be open to anyone, the focus would be on teaching women how to handle difficult situations, how to document sexual harassment, how to act in order to be taken more seriously if that is a problem. They've asked me for the names of women I thought would fit. With your permission I'll give them yours. Unless you have something else you're considering – well, even if you do, I hope you'll consider them."

"You'd do that after all that's happened?" Sarah asked in an incredulous tone.

"I will," Sam said. "And, in the interest of full disclosure, I'm telling you up front, I want to explore the attraction that exists between us and I hope you feel the same."

Prayers can be answered in an instant. Sarah drew in his scent, his heat. She saw the question on his face and hope in his eyes. The ankh throbbed like it had on the day they'd met. Its heat burned her skin. Energy zigzagged through the air connecting her to him. The answer welled from deep within her.

"Yes," she said and stepped closer. "Yes, yes, yes, yes, yes."

"Yes to Worldwide?" Sam asked.

"Yes to it all," Sarah replied. "Yes, to it all."

The End

I hope you enjoyed my story! I'd love for you to visit my website at

www.judithashleyromance.com .

Grandmother Moon

by Judith Ashley

Dedicated to Judith Hobbs
for her unfailing encouragement and support.

Acknowledgements

While my fingers are the ones tapping out this story on my computer keyboard. Every story takes a village to get it from inspiration to publication. My village for this story: Paty Jager and Sarah Raplee for initial editing. Kelly Schaub for final editing. Michele Lauren and Jean Rubel for Beta Reading.

Inspiration for this story popped into my head one day. Initially the old standard "Blue Moon" played in my mind as I wrote the different sections. (A blue moon is the second full moon in a month or the fourth full moon in three months. Since it is also known as a "traitor" or "betrayer" moon, it didn't fit. In my tradition Grandmother Moon and Mother Earth along with Grandfather Sun and Father Sky are sacred. Add to that I'd been reading Linda Lael Miller and Paty Jager books, so western themes were certainly on my mind.

May, 1998
Faribault, Oregon

Emaline Forester propped herself in the corner of the sofa and tugged the dark blue blanket tighter around her legs. From this position all the windows along the south side of her house were visible. Anticipation over what was to come later this evening curled through her like the steam from the hot cup of tea on the low coffee table. Two pieces of chocolate and a sliced apple were arranged on a plate next to her tea. Heat radiated through the glass doors of her fireplace where a cheery fire burned. Her book, a romance novel, was face down on her lap, splayed open to where she'd last been read-ing.

Em picked up the book recalling where the story was now. The hero, Trey Hardesty, had met prickly Maude Bartell, undoubtedly the woman who would become his love interest. Maude was the oldest of four children and was applying for a job as housekeeper/cook at Hardesty's big ranch. She was desperate to get this job; the alternative was unthinkable. The main barrier to her getting the job? She wasn't much of a cook, but the gutsy nineteen-year-old was not letting that small fact deter her. Her plan was to fix the one meal she knew by heart if asked to prove her skills in the kitchen.

A quick glance out the furthest window at the dark sky told Em she still had plenty of time to see where the story went. Turning back to her book, she finished the chapter, pleased that Hardesty had given Maude the job and a small cabin not far from the pig sty. Although the location may not be ideal, Maude, her sister, and two younger brothers would have a roof over their heads and protection from the Eastern Oregon high desert winter that would be upon them soon.

OMG! Maude's lack of skill in the kitchen became evident all too quickly, at the beginning of the next chapter, when she burned not only Hardesty and the ranch hands' dinner but also her own hand. Painfully.

Afraid she'd be fired on the spot, she ran out the back door and into the night with Trey hard on her heels. "Fool woman," he'd growled when he caught up to her.

The book fell back into Em's lap. Tears glistened in her eyes as a gruff male voice echoed in her head. Instead of "Fool woman!" she heard "What the hell is wrong with you?" Her upper arm had been imprinted with the viselike grip of a man's work-hardened fingers as he jerked her back from the canyon rim.

What is wrong with you? The words rang in Em's memory, reminding her of times past when that very question had battered her unmercifully. She battled them back, reminding herself she was building a new life, a good life for herself here in the little town of Faribault.

But the words still echoed and the memory of her afternoon run-in with her highhanded neighbor flared. A hard grip, a hard chest, and hard words assaulted her in her cozy, snug little fortress. The sensation of being safe, of being protected, of being cared about was threatened by the hard memory.

Had she been going to jump? No.

Was she too close to the edge of the rim? Probably.

Her "rescuer" wasn't a ranger from the nearby national park. That might have made a difference. Instead he was a nosy neighbor busybody who thought he knew more about things than she did.

The flash of anger in his green eyes, his wind tossed sandy hair, the scent of cloves and soap on the clean fresh air — it was all so real it was as if she was back on the canyon rim held tight against his strong, lean frame. Her body roused to the thought of being close to him as it had when she'd clung to him, startled at being grabbed and hauled back. Betrayed again.

What is wrong with me? Em reached for the cup of tea, glad it was in a thick china mug and still hot. Her hands were cold, and she took a moment to warm them before taking a sip. She wiggled deeper into the cushions, taking comfort in the wraparound sense of protection of her oversized sofa.

Em resisted the temptation to jump to the last five pages of the book. She knew Maude and Trey overcame their challenges, faced their demons and their story ended with a Happily-Ever-After or HEA. But she didn't know the exact words they said to each other or how they would resolve all their problems. *One of the best things about reading romance is I know the hero and heroine always get their HEA.*

Another sip of tea, nibble of chocolate, and glance at the farthest window. Em picked up her book and kept reading — from where she left off.

By the light of the kerosene lamp in the kitchen, Trey inspected Maude's burned hand, smeared ointment over the reddened skin, and wrapped it in a clean towel. He bid her a good night and went out to check the stock before going to his own bed.

Maude held her bandaged hand protectively to her chest as she walked to the cabin. How was she going to manage with this injury which throbbed like the devil? Her distress bordered on panic. If she lost this job, her only other option would mean a life of misery in a most unsavory profession. Her younger sister had already been approached by the bartender at Miss Lansdowne's place. What was she going to do?

What was she going to do? The words rang true for Em as well. What was she going to do? She was cozy and warm in her little house outside Faribault. The settlement from her polite divorce eight years ago, which she had wisely invested, had allowed her to pay cash for the property. Five years after her divorce, she'd quit her job and established a consulting business where she assisted small businesses grow by find ways to work with some of the biggest corporations in the world. Finally she'd realized her dream of living in rural Oregon while working with her clients by phone, internet, and scheduled trips to the city for meetings. Someone looking at her life from the outside would think everything was going well for her. However, she was looking at her life from the inside and worried about being welcomed into the small tight-knit community, making friends — being accepted.

Like a broken record, this afternoon's scene on the canyon rim replayed in her memory.

Em sucked the whole second piece of chocolate into her mouth, let the creamy richness melt, let the dark flavor coat her tongue and slide down her throat. This piece had a hint of mint, the other a hint of chili.

Her eyes focused briefly on the apple slices turning a little brown around the edges. *I really should eat those instead.* As quickly as the thought formed Em dismissed it. Tonight was a chocolate night.

The far windows framed a faint glow. Em sat up straighter, knowing what was coming, what fed the anticipation which was once again stirring.

Back to her book — an anthology of short stories set in the Oregon high desert where she lived now. Even though it was a romance, it was helping her learn about the history of the area.

The author knew how to build sexual tension and Em's own body reacted to the attraction between Maude and Trey. She enjoyed how the author developed Trey's awareness of Maude's situation: first he noticed how thin she was; how smooth her hands were and how protective she was of her siblings. He knew very well she needed this job. If she didn't have a respectable job, she would end up a working girl. Miss Lansdowne's place always had room for a pretty young girl.

Em also liked the authenticity of the setting and the fact the author had done her homework. It was 1893 in Maude and Trey's story. In that day, people had to cook on wood stoves, draw water from a well, grow their own food, and take care of livestock and equipment including horses and buggies for transportation. In general they had to be independent and self-sufficient.

Maude's parents had died of typhoid a year ago. She had worked valiantly to keep the children together by managing their small farm and keeping the house. Her sister, Tess, had done the cooking, and the boys had tended the two cows and the horse. They also kept the wood box filled. They had managed until the fire burned their small house to the ground.

Had the boys been lax about embers, or had someone set it? Maude would never know.

On their small farm, the four of them had worked together to stay together. Now, as the oldest, she was responsible to make sure they stayed together. She wanted her brothers to get some schooling, and she wanted Tess to go back East to get a teaching certificate. If she had a profession, she could earn a living and would never be vulnerable to the predators who frequented Miss Lansdowne's establishment.

Em saw the answer. Tess could cook and Maude could keep house. Together they'd make Trey's house all he could ask for and more. As she read on, she saw Maude's stubborn pride "I have to do this", "it's up to me". Why couldn't she see that doing it all herself wasn't how they'd initially survived? What kept her from being more open to other ways?

A tiny voice in her head turned the question back on Em: Why can't you see how things could work if you asked other people for help? If you let them help? Why can't you be more open to other ways to get what you need?

The shimmering light had spread and now streamed in through the windows she could see in the room to her left. *Just a little farther.*

If she was honest with herself, she did need help to take care of this place. While she was capable of taking care of the house and outbuildings, there was more to taking care of the land than she'd realized. The real estate agent told her she needed to start weatherization in late September at the latest and mentioned it might be wise, her being new to the area and all, to move into town for the worst months.

She'd had an offer of help, from Carter Montague, the nosy busybody who owned the place next to hers. This afternoon, when he'd stepped back, releasing her from his embrace, he'd introduced himself, jerking his thumb over his right shoulder indicating his property line. Both their properties butted up to the national park where a pretty red rock canyon wound across the otherwise flat desert. He'd asked where she was from. The surprise and dismay on his face when she'd pointed to her own property line had stung like a slap to her face. She was not welcomed.

When he'd offered to help her "any time," pulled out a scrap of a notepad and scrawled his phone number and shoved it in her hand, she was tempted to throw it over the canyon rim. To do that would only gain her a moment of pleasure as she watched him scowl; maybe try and grab the slip before the draft caught it and it twirled out of sight.

The memory faded and she sighed. Never would she knowingly litter or vandalize a sacred place — and the red rock canyon was certainly a sacred place. The energy she'd felt standing on the rim drew her closer and closer. Never did it occur to her that energy would allow her to fall.

How could that man live in this special place, be so close to the land, and not feel the mystical energy? Em's brow scrunched in puzzlement as she tried to understand. *I'll never know,* she finally admitted to herself. By then, Carter Montague had mounted his horse, tipped his hat, whistled to his dog, and ridden off. He'd never even looked back. *So much for his wanting to help!*

Em's focus returned to the room and the glowing pearlescent light streaming in the windows in the other room. She still had time to read more about Maude and Trey as they circled each other, dismissing the attraction between them, he trying to help her and her pushing him away.

When Maude decided she'd fix a couple of shingles on the tool shed that had come loose in the recent wind storm,

Em knew something bad was going to happen. Climbing up the ladder, nails in her pocket, hammer tucked into the waistband of her skirt, Maude went to work. Finished, she started to go back down the ladder and realized it was easier coming up and onto the roof than going down. She shifted trying to see how she might step onto the ladder without falling. Trey's shout startled her.

Arms flailing, skirts flying, legs twisted around each other, she landed with a thump, unable to breathe. Stunned and unable to speak, she realized her right arm was bent at an awkward angle. Pain seared through her, so sharp she couldn't cry or scream.

Trey had first bellowed for help and then hollered at her — called her a ninny. The ground under Maude had trembled as ranch hands came running. Trey's touch was as gentle and soothing as his voice was gruff and rough.

Em resisted the urge to skim. One of the hands was sent for the doctor, at least three hours away; Trey carried Maude into the main house to his room, laying her on his bed, Tess and her brothers crowded around, worry etched on their faces.

Trey liberally dosed Maude's cup of strong tea with whiskey but it was Tess who helped Maude lift her head enough to drink. It was also Tess who eased her sister out of the filthy skirt and cut the blouse away from her broken arm, washed the dirt from her face, and brushed the dust from her hair. Using one of Trey's shirts, Tess slipped her good arm in the opposing sleeve and pulled the body of the shirt across Maude's chest gently tucking it around her injured arm.

Hours later, the doctor came, set the arm, gave her something stronger than whiskey for the pain. When Maude next woke, the smell of bacon, eggs, bread, and coffee filled the air and her brother's happy voices filtered into the room. Opening her eyes, Maude saw Trey standing in the doorway, a cup of coffee in his hand. He was watching her with brilliant green eyes, his tousled sandy hair....

Em gasped. Trey Hardesty had turned into Carter Montague. She looked at the cover and realized since it was an anthology, no one character was portrayed on it. She skimmed through the first chapters when Maude and Trey met trying in vain to find a description of him. She'd been sure he had dark hair and brown eyes but no trace of that man existed.

Because she'd read so many romance stories before, she knew the ending. Tess would cook. Trey and Maude would marry. As the ranch prospered, her sister and brothers would get that education. And all would be well. She slipped a page marker in the book and put it aside before turning off the light.

The window next to the fireplace was illuminated by a sliver of shining light.

It was time.

Em shrugged off the blanket and stretched. Rising, she crossed the room, picked up her horsehide drum, and waited for the moment the moon came into view. Curbing her eagerness to see the full moon for the first time from this house, she radiated expectancy in her stillness. *In the city Grandmother Moon's light is dimmed. Here I can feel the strength of her light.*

There *She* was! Full, bright, shimmering pale yellow ringed with a silvery circle. She started a slow beat mesmerized as the orb crossed the pane. As the moon slipped out of sight, Em increased the beat and moved outside to her deck where she stood, head up and shoulders back. The thrumming of the drum beat reverberated down her spine, through her legs, into her feet and on downward — through the wood of the decking and into the ground. *I am so blessed to live in this house, on this land, in this country; so blessed to have the space to drum outside without bothering my neighbors; so blessed to release my feelings in this primal way.*

Em held her drum high so it covered the moon and continued to strike the hide, seeing the light of the moon seep around the edges. Standing tall, she continued to drum. The light from Grandmother Moon flowed around her, encasing her in its muted glow as the round orb traced an ancient path across the starlit sky.

Carter Montague heard the primitive sound of drumming carried on the winds. Following it, he knew even before he approached the little house who he'd find. He stopped his horse in the copse of trees twenty-five yards from the house and motioned his dog to sit.

She was magnificent. Her long silvery blond hair traced down her back, lifting and swaying with her movements and the wind. A hunger to know her, to taste her, to claim her roared through him. Swinging down from his horse, he stood reins in hand and watched as she ceased drumming, laid the instrument aside, and raised her arms to the sky.

Her words drifted through the charged night air. "Grandmother Moon, watch over, guide and protect me. Light my path so I may know each step takes me to my destiny."

Carter started to take a step forward, towards her — away from the safety in the shadows of the trees. A cloud skittered over the moon and all was darkness. He knew he hadn't moved, but when the cloud passed they were both illuminated by the full moon's light. He heard her indrawn breath, saw her breasts rise, and knew the instant she realized it was him. He fought the urge to fade back, get on his horse, call his dog, and go home.

He'd been out checking the wild mustangs that grazed on part of his land when time got away from him. The steady beat of a drum carried on the air. No need to lie to himself. He knew who was drumming, knew how she felt in his arms, knew she hadn't a clue what it took to make it on the land. *Hell, we even get freak storms with freezing temperatures and snow this time of year.* He'd lived here all his life and had developed an awareness of what was going on around him. That's what you needed to make it. *Can't always count on those forecasters.*

His hand curled as if holding her slim arm. He'd grabbed her — foolish woman that she was — before she fell off the canyon rim. He'd pulled her hard against him. He'd thrust her away as soon as it registered how right it felt to have her in his arms. *She belongs here* had whispered through his mind. Just the thought of holding her tight against him had his body warming.

Too bad he'd sworn off women. Going over to the next county and picking up some willing woman in the casino's bar had no appeal. It wasn't that he didn't have physical needs, he was human — but he no longer got the satisfaction from a one-night stand that he did ten — fifteen years ago.

Charlene had cured him of that. He shook his head to clear her out of his mind and took a step forward. *What the hell am I doing?*

He was in full view of the house. No turning back now. His next step was a shuffle but that didn't work for him. He wasn't going to shuffle up to the house, hat in hand, aw-shucks ma'aming. Carter stood a little taller and strode to the porch. He felt Jacks brush against his leg, heard the jingle of Joker's tack and felt the thud of his horse's hooves in the earth following him.

"Ms. Forester," he said and tipped his hat. "Heard your drumming and wanted to make sure you were okay."

"Mr. Montague," Emaline said standing her ground. "I didn't realize our places were so close that my drumming would bother you."

Carter chuckled. "Don't worry none. I was out checking on a herd of mustangs and started back a little later than I should've. Sound travels in the night. That's why I heard you."

Joker nudged his back and Carter stumbled forward tripping on the bottom step of the deck. *Blasted horse!* Jacks dashed forward, his tail waving a friendly welcome.

"Stop that," he ordered, jigging to recover his balance. "Infernal horse," he muttered as he stepped to the side. When he looked up, his traitor dog was nuzzling Emaline's hand, his way of asking for attention. "Jacks, come." With a small whine, Jacks returned to his side and sat.

The house was dark behind her. The light from the moon caressed her. Her silvery hair sparkled as if the night sky had sprinkled stars in it. He willed himself not to stand and stare, or shuffle his feet, or hem and haw. He cleared his throat.

"All settled in are you?"

"Yes, I'm unpacked and the pantry is stocked," Emaline answered.

"Offer still stands," he said. "You need anything, just holler."

She nodded.

He turned and swung up on his horse. Gathering the reins in one hand, he tipped his hat. "Evening, Ms. Forester." He guided Joker with his knees and rode off toward the trees whistling for Jacks to follow. *Hell and damnation. That went about as well as....*

Carter paid attention, albeit from a distance, to what was happening when it came to Emaline Forester. He knew when Emaline went into Faribault, that she was friendly with Mrs. Cooper at the Library, that she'd stopped by the high school when Janey Smith was sick and volunteered in the office until Janey came back. She even brought Jacks, that traitor dog, back one afternoon. Damn dog hadn't been off chasing rabbits, he'd been off visiting with her. She was making a place for herself in the tightknit community and truth be told, he wasn't sure he liked that. What was worse, he couldn't rightly say why.

The full moon, he knew from seeing her, meant she'd be drumming full out. Paying attention, even from a distance, garnered him some information about what she did on different phases of the moon. On the new moon she told Mrs. Cooper she used a deer hide drum. Looked like she was trying to find other people who wanted to drum and do that woo-woo stuff. Her poster inviting anyone interested to join her was up at the Library and the Mercantile.

His buddy, Nate Beacham told him she'd asked permission to go rock hounding in his small sunstone mine and she'd pulled out some cash to pay him. *Yep, she was into the rocks and energy woowoo stuff.* It wasn't that he didn't believe in the energy of the land. *I might've been raised different but, hell, I live and work on it.* It was just that... he scrubbed the back of his neck with his hand. It was just that... he scuffed his boot toe in the dirt. *There's just something about her.* He kicked a small rock, watched it skip a few feet away. Three months later, when thoughts of her popped into his mind, he could feel her in his arms, the scent of apples in the air, the warmth of her body pressed to his.

Carter pulled into an empty parking spot outside the Grange Hall. He waved a greeting to other folks coming to the Fall Harvest Dance which was held the weekend before Halloween. The whole town turned out because, if winter was bad, they wouldn't see much of each other until the spring thaw.

The wide-open door to the Grange Hall framed the dancers. The beat of the bass guitar kept feet tapping and hands clapping. From the looks of it, The Hoe Down Boys were in fine fettle.

He spotted Emaline before he was all the way through the door. There was something about her, something that dulled the pain of Charlene's betrayal, something that spoke to that hidden place he'd boarded up when he'd found her in the back of a truck with some passing-through-cowboy.

Emaline was dancing the two-step with Nate. A frown furrowed his brow and a pang stabbed his heart. He stopped before he charged onto the dance floor and pulled her away. He had no right, no call, to interfere. She wouldn't appreciate anything he did right now so he did nothing.

Callie Brown sashayed up to him, leaned in, and brushed her breasts against his arm. He was not tempted in the least.

"Dance with me, Carter," Callie said, smiling up at him.

He took her elbow and led her onto the floor, swung her into the Cotton-eyed Joe and kept as much space between them as the dance allowed. He'd seen the invitation to dance and more in her eyes. Now, he avoided eye contact and pretended he didn't hear her talking to him. It wasn't his proudest moment, but he knew Callie and knew she loved drama. The last thing he needed was her pouting and stomping her foot because he refused to dance with her.

His evening dragged on and on as he danced with first one woman and then another — anything to avoid another run-in with Callie. It was obvious she was on the prowl tonight. *Must have broken up with that guy in Coldwater.*

The band signaled last dance. He looked around and realized he'd done his part and partnered with just about every toe-tapping female in sight except one.

He spotted Emaline with a circle of men around her. She smiled and nodded as different ones spoke but he sensed something else going on. To him she looked tense and about ready to bolt.

Carter walked into the circle surrounding her, clasped her elbow, and steered her onto the dance floor. Words would have been nice, but if he'd asked her to dance, she could have said "no." In that moment he knew he had to have her in his arms tonight — later he'd think about why.

The Hoe Down Boys always played a slow one at the end of the night and tonight was no exception. Carter gathered Emaline close, one arm around her waist with his splayed hand covering her lower back where her hips flared, the other hand held hers close to his chest. He pulled her closer and she fit just right. As the music played, she relaxed, her head nestled against his shoulder, her feet shifted between his, her leg brushing his thigh, his leg brushing hers. He'd noticed her full breasts and reveled in the feel of them gently crushed against his chest. The scent of apples swirled around them as they danced.

He did his part dancing with the single ladies and a few of the married ones when the community had a dance. Other than that, dancing wasn't something he did or thought about. Tonight with Emaline in his arms and a slow song with a deep beat pounding in his veins, he imagined winter nights and another kind of dance — one where they were naked, tangled in sheets, consumed by a passion that melted the icicles hanging from the eaves.

"Hey, Carter," Nate called out.

Carter heard the music in his blood and kept shifting and swaying down the floor.

"Hey, Montague! The band stopped playing."

The hoots and hollers finally registered, and he stepped back keeping Emaline in his arms.

A bemused look in her turquoise blue eyes, a soft smile on her rosy lips, she shook her head and started to step back.

He held on.

The formal, rigid Emaline Forester emerged. Her eyes lost the bemused dreamy look, her lips firmed into a thin line, her body stiffened and she pulled away. Gone was the soft, warm woman.

"Thank you for the dance, Mr. Montague," she said in a starch-laced voice.

"My pleasure, ma'am," he said with a nod. His hand slipped from her waist to her elbow. "I'll escort you to your car."

"That isn't necessary," she said.

"It's what we do here, Ms. Emaline. We don't let the women-folk wander off on their own. Never can tell what might happen." *Women-folk? Where is this crap coming from!*

"I'm sure I can make it from the Grange Hall to my car without incident." She tugged her elbow from his grasp.

"I'm sure you can," he said, matching his steps with hers.

Carter stood in the parking lot watching the brake lights on Emaline's car flash on as she stopped before pulling out onto the road. He jumped when a hand landed on his shoulder.

"Lost in thought?" Nate asked. "She's a hard worker, kind, compassionate, intelligent, and doing her best to fit in. Someone hurt her bad, I think."

"Why do you think that?"

"She's skitterish. You know, like a hungry, stray dog that don't trust you won't hurt her if she comes too close."

"Didn't know you'd spent that much time with her." Carter hoped his voice was nonchalant because those feelings stirred, the ones he noticed when he saw Emaline with another man.

"She comes out to the mine every now and again. Persistent little thing. She's got an idea of what she's looking for and will keep searchin' until she finds it."

"You mean she's not found any sunstone on your place?"

"Nope, she's found a bunch. Gives 'em all to me 'cause they aren't what she sees in her mind's eye, she says. I suggested maybe what she was looking for wasn't on my place but she told me it was there — she says she just hadn't found it yet."

The two men walked in companionable silence to their trucks parked within a few spots of each other. Carter waited. He'd been friends with Nate since childhood and was familiar with his disjointed way of telling a story.

"Interesting, she doesn't seem discouraged or upset, just more determined — quoted some guy who said something about you don't fail, just take another step toward what you want, or something like that."

As Carter went along to his vehicle, Nate called out, "You sure got tongues wagging with that last dance! Bet you find Callie sitting on your porch when you get home. The fling with that dude is long over and she's on the hunt. Has you in her sights." Nate's chuckle rang through the night as he climbed into his rig.

Driving toward his ranch, Carter let his mind wander. Winter was coming and while in some ways he had less to do, it was harder because he was alone. He'd be well-stocked, so running out of food and fuel wouldn't happen if they a blizzard blew in, but that meant lonely days and long dark nights with only his sorry self and his traitor dog for company.

He'd already moved his cattle closer to the ranch house, had stockpiles of hay scattered in shelters near the herd, and his snowmobile had been serviced. He hated using the dang thing because it was so noisy, but when the snow was deep, it got him out to feed the cows and wild horses better than anything else he knew of.

Charlene's face appeared like an apparition in the windshield. The anger and sense of betrayal was still there but a weaker version of its former self ... even a couple of weeks ago it was stronger. Callie's obvious interest in him didn't even stir a hormone in his body. He'd changed. And recently. When?

Carter pulled into the attached garage, relieved to see no other vehicles in his drive. Jacks greeted him at the door and scampered out into the night — obviously grateful he was home. He flipped on the kitchen light on his way to his study. The desk lamp bathed the room in a warm glow. He poured himself two fingers of whiskey and slouched in his chair, feet on his well-worn desk.

He sipped the fiery liquid, mentally tracing it down his throat to his belly. He had a good life here on his ranch. It was profitable enough he was comfortable if not wealthy. He could donate land for the wild mustangs. He was looked up to in the community — if he did say so himself.

What was he missing? He had everything he worked for.

But — his gut told him something was missing. And, he'd gotten where he was by paying attention to it.

Emaline Forester's face floated in the darkness. *Guess tonight's one of those meant for seeing things.* Confusion furrowed his brow. He sipped his whiskey. *It'd never work between us.* His hand fisted around his glass, Carter's feet thudded on the floor as he stood and began to pace. Somehow she'd gotten to him. Ever since that day on the canyon rim, she'd been in the back of his mind. Ever since that night he watched her drumming under the full moon, she'd come to him in dreams. Ever since tonight, when he held her in his arms, he felt the rightness of her.

Charlene and Callie's faces floated through his mind's eye, replaced by Emaline's. He shook his head but her face didn't fade. He closed his eyes, but she was still there. The faint scent of apples....

He opened his eyes, finished his whiskey, and put his glass in the kitchen sink.

I thought I'd found 'the one' in Charlene and look how that turned out. Another restless night awaited him but what else was he to do? He made sure Jacks had fresh water and filled his food dish before letting him in and closing the garage door. As he trudged up the stairs to his room, Nate's words echoed. *"She's skitterish. You know, like a hungry stray dog that don't trust you won't hurt her if she comes too close."*

Emaline stood in front of the large picture window, looking out at the postcard perfect winter scene. Snow was everywhere, piling against the fence, drifting along the bushes, growing deeper and deeper. The stark pattern of tree limbs against the silvery white was muted by the wind-whipped snow. She shivered, pulled her thick dark-grey cable-knit wool sweater closed, and wrapped her arms around her middle.

Leftovers from Thanksgiving dinner just two days past meant she had food in her refrigerator to last a week. And if the power went out, it was cold enough outside — *Don't think like that.*

She tossed another log in the fireplace and stood with her back to the flames. *Am I really cold or just anxious? It's my first storm since I moved to Faribault, after all.*

Checking the fireplace screen was in place; she then crossed the great room to the kitchen, ran water into the tea-kettle, and set it on the stove to heat. She pulled down her favorite mug decorated with a soaring red tailed hawk from the shelf under the cupboard and got out the peach mango tea she loved.

The wind whistled around the corners, singing a lonely song of loss. *Now you're being fanciful. I wonder what else your fertile mind will come up with during this storm.*

Shrilling announced the water was boiling. Emaline made a cup of tea before fixing a full pot. She got out a tray for the teapot, now covered with a tea cozy, and her cup. Setting the tray on the fireplace hearth, she tossed another log on the fire the better to keep the pot warm. Snuggling down on the couch, she tugged a dark blue throw with dancing snowmen over her legs. The lights flickered but remained on. *Wish I'd tried the generator I bought before this storm hit.*

Curled up on the couch, watching the flames' wild dance, she fought the sense of impending doom. If only she wasn't alone. Someone to talk to would help ease her nervousness. If only she'd learned to operate the generator. Trying it out once in the store didn't really count. If only she'd accepted her new friend Meredith's invitation to rent a room from her for the winter. *If only —*

The cup gripped in her hands, Emaline distracted herself with memories from her first Thanksgiving in her new home. She'd met so many people since moving to Faribault last spring and had plenty of invitations to join other families. It would have been easy to accept an invitation, bake a pie, and spend time somewhere else. But this was her first Thanksgiving in her new home and that wasn't how she'd wanted to celebrate. So she'd invited Meredith and three other single women to share the holiday meal with her.

I'm so glad I did that. We had a wonderful time! By the end of the evening, they'd made a plan to get together every month — well, every month depending on the weather. *I think we may have the foundation for a sacred women's circle. How wonderful to celebrate the turning of the wheel here where I feel so close to the Mother.*

Music sounded — the tune the old hit, *Blue Moon* — her cell phone was ringing. Emaline tossed back the throw and dashed for her home office.

"Hi, Em." Meredith's cheery voice was dimmed by the static. "Just wanted to check on you. Still got power?"

"I do have power and food. Plus I've a stacked wood-pile outside and enough by the fireplace to easily get me through 'til morning if I need it."

"Talk to you later," Meredith said and hung up.

A log shifted on the fire. Emaline put her phone down and rushed back to the living room to make sure everything was okay. *So many things to keep track of. Gas in the car, wood stockpiled, food in the pantry. I even have a hand-crank can opener just in case the electricity is out and I can't use my electric one. Whew!* She blew a puff of air as the ever growing list formed in her mind. *I may even need to trade my car in for a four-wheel-drive vehicle. So many decisions still ahead. But one thing I know for certain — moving here was the right one for me.*

Night came early at the end of November. By six o'clock, it was pitch black outside, the snow still falling. Emaline guessed she had a good two feet on the ground and a lot more in the drifts. She'd gone out every couple of hours and shoveled and swept keeping the porch and steps clear as well as a path to the wood pile. As she looked out the window once again, she sighed. *All that work and it will be covered again by morning.*

A thump at her front door caught her attention. She peered out the window attempting to see who was there, but in the dark saw nothing. Another thump and a noise.

A bark?

Emaline opened her front door and Jacks jumped up, front paws on the storm door's glass.

"What are you doing here, Jacks?" Emaline opened the door and the dog and a blast of bitter cold air streaked into the house. She shivered and shut the door. Jacks raced around her, barking. She reached for his collar. He dodged and her hand grasped thin air. "Jacks, sit." She ordered in a voice she thought mirrored Carter's in firmness.

The dog sat squirming at her feet, looking over his shoulder at the door every few seconds.

"Where's Carter?" she asked the whining dog. "Does he know where you are? He must be worried sick about you." She strode to the kitchen and picked up the landline phone — dead.

"Not a good sign," she said on her way to her cell phone. She dialed the number she had for Carter and listened while the phone rang and rang and rang. With each ring her worry meter ratcheted up a notch. After several minutes and with no answering machine or voice mail coming on, she hung up.

Jacks continued to race from wherever she was to the front door and back again. He was back at the front door, scratching to be let out. She opened the door and he dashed out but stopped at the edge of the porch, looked back at her, and barked. Just the one bark, but it was obvious to her he expected her to follow. Her worry meter exploded. Stomach churning with nerves, shoulders locked tight, head pounding,

Emaline knew deep inside her something bad had happened to Carter.

What am I to do? I have a parka and warm boots and gloves, but what if I can't find him? What if I get lost in the snow?

Jacks came back to her and nudged her hand before trotting to the edge of the porch. He held one paw up as if he were in a bird dog stance and faced out into the snow.

"Come, Jacks," Emaline ordered, patting her thigh. As soon as the dog was inside, she shut the door. Shivering from the cold and a good dose of anxiety laced with fear, Emaline half-trotted through the house to the mudroom off the back. She pulled on her sweat pants, snow boots, a warm sweat-shirt, her parka and grabbed her gloves. *Lights.* Turning on all the lights in the house as well as the ones attached to the gar-age and outbuildings, she hoped they'd be enough so she wouldn't get lost. She debated about taking her cell phone. It was almost dead and reception was scattered at best. At the last minute, she stuffed it in her pocket, opened the back door and stepped out.

"Let's go," she said, and motioned for Jacks to lead the way. The first steps into the biting cold took her breath away. Even though the wind had eased, snow still fell in heavy flakes. She stopped to get her emergency kit out of the car — two emergency blankets, a small first aid kit, a flashlight and a whistle — and stuffed them into one of her coat pockets. She ducked into the toolshed. Inside, she hauled two long exten-sion cords and a rope off the shelving and looped them around her shoulders. *I hope this works.* Em remembered in the story she'd read about Trey Hardesty and Maude, in the winter they strung ropes from the house to the barn so they could get out to check on the horses and milk cows.

"I'm coming, Jacks," Emaline said, when Jacks whined at the door of the toolshed. The dog dashed off but was soon back, his anxiousness telegraphed to her through his whimpers and yips. She fought the panic when she saw snow had erased her shallow tracks. *Will I have to trudge through the deeper snow in order to leave footprints?* She banished that thought from her mind.

She struggled to keep up with Jacks, castigating herself for loading herself up with so much equipment. *I know Carter is in trouble but I don't know where he is.* Every few feet she turned to look back at the house. *As long as I see the lights I can find my way home.* The air was bitter cold, seeping through every buttonhole and seam, whisking down her neck. Even in her snow boots, her toes were getting numbed. She tugged the neck of her parka up to cover the lower half of her face, tipping her head down to protect her nose.

"Jacks, come," she called. A glance back showed her how far away from the house she'd gone. The lights in the distance were dim. Finding a tree, bush, or fencepost in the dark snowy night wasn't easy with only a small flashlight, but she persevered. She tied one of the extension cords to a post and forged on. One hundred feet later, she connected the second cord to the first. When she looked back, all she saw was white snow. Her lungs burned from the cold. Her eyes teared, the wetness freezing on her lashes. Even her eyeballs felt chilled. Reaching the end of the second extension cord, she fumbled to tie the stiff rope to the cold rubber line. Her gloves made her fingers clumsy. She took them off, tucking them under her arm as she completed the task. When she put her gloves back on, her hands ached from the cold.

Her muscles burned; the biting cold stung her cheeks. She stumbled, nearly falling more than once as her legs screamed against the harsh use. The idea of giving up and turning back lured. Only the idea of Carter out here somewhere and Jacks' dogged determination for her to follow him kept her moving forward. The dog shepherded her onward through the barest areas, between drifts as high as her waist or higher. Emaline concentrated on putting one foot in front of the other and keeping the dog in sight. The weight of the rope lightened until ... the end.

She held the end of the rope in one hand, stretched her other hand ahead into the softly falling snow. *Now what?* Her body trembled from fatigue, her mind balked at the decision she must make. Drop the rope and trudge into the darkness or admit failure and turn around. The inevitability of her decision mocked her. It wasn't about admitting failure — it was about leaving Carter out here.

Calmness settled and her pounding heart and laboring lungs eased. The worst thing would be she failed in finding Carter and lost her own life. No, that wasn't right. The worst would be not finding Carter and surviving. He'd held her in his arms twice and the rightness of it swept away all doubts. She must prevail.

Jacks bounded ahead, out of sight, his barking more frantic.

The dog rushed back, barking then raced a circle around her before streaking off into the night. He was obviously distressed. Darting here, dashing there, the constant barking interrupted by his pathetic whine.

She'd stood still long enough that the exhaustion was taking its toll. If she just rested for a bit — *I need to move* — *staying here means my death.*

One more look over her shoulder, another glance around in an attempt to pick out any landmarks to help her find the rope again. Nothing.

All is as it should be. I am where I am to be. I am doing what I am supposed to be doing. The familiar words, words that in times of trouble brought her to a place of peace, floated through her tired mind. Emaline dropped the rope in the snow and followed Jacks into the darkness.

A cold nose nudged Carter's hand. A rough tongue rasped his cheek. In one part of his mind, he knew Jacks was there, heard his yips, felt Joker nuzzle his ribs. The other part of his icy mind worked at the speed of a glacier.

"Carter? Carter, is that you?" Emaline's voice? *I must be hallucinating.*

Hands brushed snow off, roved over his head, his face, his back accompanied by constant feminine chatter. Fingers gripped his shoulder through his jacket, attempting to roll him onto his back. He'd help if he could figure out how to make his arms and legs work. She pulled on his shoulders and shoved his legs, maneuvering him so he wasn't as face down in the snow.

The rustling sound of a package being opened, something metallic being moved about and then the whispering air as that "something" settled over him.

"I'm covering you with an emergency blanket, Carter. Jacks, come!"

The blanket moved and Jacks curled up next to him, licking his face. Cocooned with his dog, eau de wet Jacks permeated the warming air. Every few minutes, Emaline made an opening and asked a question.

What was his full name? Where was he? Who was she? What was he doing out in a storm like this? The last question was asked in a testy tone of voice.

Jacks licked his face and nudged him with his nose. He recognized the message. Move. With considerable effort he shifted onto his back. Eyes closed he waited until the worst of the pain subsided. The blanket moved and his face was uncovered. Opening his eyes, a vision? Nope, Emaline, — a silver foil emergency blanket wrapped around her shoulders, frowning at him.

"Can you stand with my help?"

"Don't know." With her staring at him, her toes probably tapping in her boots, he figured he needed to try. Besides, if he didn't he'd finish freezing to death, her too.

"I'm not sure how to help you," she admitted. "What are your ideas?"

Carter knew she'd asked a question. His brain was working on an answer, but it was slow going.

Emaline bent over, flashed a blinding light as she peered in his eyes. "You've got a concussion," she announced.

"Probly." His head hurt. Matter of fact, he hurt all over, all over except for where he was numb. How to get up and back home?

"If I help you stand, maybe you can get back on Joker and I can lead him home."

That was a reasonable plan, dependent only on him being able to stand up. She pulled his blanket off and scooted behind him.

What the hell is she doing?

"Try to sit up."

He clenched his stomach muscles but nothing happened. "Can't."

"Okay, we'll think of something else."

He could practically hear the wheels whirring in her brain.

"Can you move your arms and legs?"

Pain shot through his left arm and ankle.

"Where?" she asked, slipping to his side. "Where does it hurt?"

"Where doesn't it hurt," he ground out.

"Okay, where does it hurt the most?"

"Left side."

She scooted away and stood up. Grasping Joker's reins, she led the horse around to Carter's left side. "Now, I'm going to get under your right side and help you up. You'll need to lean on Joker instead of your leg."

"Won't work."

"Why?"

"Cause I can't lean against him. My elbow's bad."

The weight of the world seemed to settle onto Emaline's shoulders. Quiet reigned in the snowy stillness. Joker shifted his weight, Jacks whined.

Emaline had wrapped the second blanket back around Carter's legs. She shivered. How was she going to get them out of this mess?

"Get these blankets off me," Carter said in a pain drenched voice. "I'm going to try something."

Emaline complied, folding the blankets up and stuffing them into her pocket. *What is he doing?*

Carter turned back onto his side and then shifted onto his stomach.

Is he out of his mind? Her curiosity won out. "What are you doing?"

"Getting up."

Fascinated, Emaline watched Carter shift and sway, lurch and lean until he was on his hands and knees, his weight toward his right side. Jacks scooted under Carter's belly. She moved Joker to his right side and then wedged her shoulder under his arm.

"On the count of three," she said.

It took four tries before Carter was upright, leaning heavily against her. She was squished between the man and his horse. Her idea was to slip out from under him and have Joker take his weight. There was no way he could walk to her place, no way she could carry him, no way she could leave him here until she could get some help.

"Here's the plan," she said in her most authoritarian voice. "Joker is right beside me, less than twelve inches from you. I want you to raise your right hand and grasp the saddle. I'll move away and guide Joker closer, so you can get a better hold. Once we've got that accomplished, we'll figure out how to get you up on him."

"Rope."

"My rope is somewhere back there," she said pointing, she thought, in the direction she'd come from.

"Horse."

She reached up and found the rope. Emaline knew he was weakening by the moment and time was running out. His answers were back to one word. Rope in hand, she turned and raised Carter's arm toward the saddle. "Hang on."

Emaline ignored the sharp intakes of breath as Carter struggled to help her get him onto Joker. She could only imagine the pain he was in. At last, he hung over the saddle, head on one side, feet on the other.

"Tie me." The order came out on a groan of misery.

She followed his directions and looped the rope round the saddle horn and around him praying all the while it held and he didn't fall off. If it didn't and he fell, he'd be in worse shape than he was now, and now was pretty bad.

With Jacks jumping around, Joker stomping around and her own tramping around, there was no way to see what direction she'd come from or which direction to go. The half-moon was out, the snow had stopped, but the wind was still a factor. The wind chill was clearly below zero.

How far were they away from the house? Which way did they need to go? Back the way they'd come....

"Jacks, home," she said and waved her arm. She stumbled with relief as Jacks bounded off. Reins in hand, she moved forward, elated when Joker followed.

When the lights of her home shone in the distance, Emaline fought back tears. She'd kept up a steady stream of chatter as they slowly made their way through the snow. There were times when she thought Carter lost consciousness. If he knew how worried she was, it wouldn't help so she kept her voice light, the chatter inconsequential.

Glad for the peak over the front steps, she led Joker up onto the porch. An old pair of crutches and an office chair with wheels were commandeered from her storeroom and office. It still took ten minutes to get him off Joker and onto the office chair she'd anchored to the porch rail. Jigging the chair over the doorsill and into the house, Emaline wheeled Carter into the house and helped him onto the couch.

"What about Joker?" she asked. "He can't stay outside all night. Can I put him in the garage, out of the weather?"

"Water, blanket," he mumbled.

Emaline filled her biggest kettle with water and put it on the stove to heat. Then, leaving Jacks on guard, she retrieved Joker and led him into her garage. She found a large bucket and filled it with pails of water from the kitchen. She found a quilt in her trunk and tossed it and one of the emergency blankets over the horse, using twine to tie it all together under his belly.

"That will have to do for now," she said. She patted his strong neck and stroked his nose. Living here in Faribault she'd certainly seen lots of horses but never up close like this. She took a few minutes to explore finding the hair on his hide coarse with an underlay of softness. Joker snuffled and nuzzled her. "You were magnificent," she told the horse with a final pat. Joker tossed his head as if in agreement and then drank from the bucket.

To be on the safe side, she returned to the kitchen for more water making sure the bucket was full. She debated about whether to leave the lights on finally deciding to turn them off. At least she knew horses slept standing up and she didn't have to figure out how to make a bed for him.

Back in the house, she pulled off her gloves and parka, hanging them on hooks in the mudroom. Next she took off her snow boots and slipped her icy feet into wool-lined slippers. She peeled off her wet sweat pants and pulled on a pair of jeans she kept in the mudroom. Sharp, needle-like pain stabbed her toes and she rubbed her legs to warm them.

Em poured the hot water from the kettle into a pan. From the closet she got towels and a couple of elastic bandages. Depositing her wares on the coffee table beside the first aid kit, she took a good hard look at her patient.

Her land line still down, her cell phone now dead, there was no way to call for help. Whether Carter liked it or not, she was going to take care of him.

Unzipping his coat, she gently pulled his right arm free before easing the sleeve off his left arm. He groaned and his face turned a greyish color as she probed around his elbow with her fingers.

With scissors she cut the material of his flannel shirt so she could examine his injuries. The bruised, swollen flesh brought tears to her eyes. *How did he do so much to help me get him here?*

Next she tugged off his boots and watched with horror as his left ankle swelled. His jeans had been covered by a pair of chaps and had been somewhat protected as had his flannel shirt. *First things first.* She got a pair of wool socks for his feet.

"I've ice packs for your elbow and ankle as well as elastic bandages to help stabilize them until I can get you to the hospital."

"Whiskey."

"The only alcohol I have is port." She knew he had a concussion so really didn't want to give him any alcohol, but she also knew he was in considerable pain. Would a shot glass full really hurt?

"Kay," he said, the word slurred. His eyes closed. He had a serious concussion. If he went to sleep, would he wake up?

No alcohol. He needs a stimulant!

A brilliant light flashed in the distance. Darkness!

Her power was out.

The light from the fireplace illuminated the great room. Em gathered up flashlights, giving one to Carter, putting one on the kitchen counter, and one next to her bed. She lit a lantern and placed it on the coffee table next to the couch. A second one she set on the hall table. Emergency candles and matches went on the mantle.

Lighting two candles and putting them in a bowl, she got out her jar of instant coffee and made a strong cup. Returning to the living room, she perched on the edge of the couch and put the cup to Carter's lips.

He sipped, sputtered, and swung, barely missing the cup and Emaline. "What the hell!" Carter's words were strong but his voice wasn't. "Where's the wine?"

"You have a concussion. You have to stay awake. You need coffee."

"Tastes like dishwater."

"It's the best I've got. I only drink tea or hot chocolate."

"Chocolate, then."

Emaline stomped into the kitchen area of the great room, her patience with her patient at the breaking point. She was tired, no — make that exhausted. She was cold — well, actually warming up. She'd been so scared — still was scared. How was she going to manage until she could get help? She added marshmallows to the hot chocolate, hoping that would satisfy the man.

A few minutes later, he was sipping the drink when she returned to the couch with a tray. She carried a turkey sandwich and piece of pumpkin pie for him, and a bowl of water and some cut-up turkey mixed in with kibble for Jacks. *I'm glad I bought the small bag of kibble last month when I realized Jacks was going to be a regular visitor.*

After handing Carter the sandwich and pie, she made a bed with an old blanket in front of the fire for Jacks and set the bowls of food and water on the hearth. She added another log to the fire while the dog gobbled his meal. Then she stood aside, smiling, as Jacks turned around three times before settling down with a doggie sigh.

"What about you?" Carter asked, gesturing towards his now empty plate.

"Not hungry," she replied, her voice soft with relief. He was aware of what was happening around him.

"You need to keep your strength up," he added.

"You need to rest."

"Nope, I need to pee."

Emaline considered offering him a bottle or can but thought before speaking. Before using the wheeled chair and crutches for the trip to the bathroom, she went ahead with the lantern leaving it on the counter for Carter. In her bedroom she lit candles and turned back the covers. When he signaled he was ready, she helped him from the bathroom to her bedroom and into bed.

"Don't go." Carter's hand clasped hers. "Stay."

His vulnerability showed in the dark circles around his leaf-green eyes now dulled with pain and the discomfort etched on his face. *What must he have thought about lying there in the snow, slowly freezing to death?*

"I'll be right back," Emaline said. She detoured back through the house making sure the lantern and candles were out, the doors on the fireplace closed, before heading into the bathroom. Her old pair of sweats hung on the back of bathroom door. She shrugged out of the jeans and into comfort. Padding back into the bedroom, she pulled on thick wool socks before climbing in on the opposite side and snuggling down.

Grandmother Moon's pale light shone through the window at the end of the bed creating shadows on the covers and phantoms on the walls.

"What happened out there?" she asked as curiosity and the need to keep him awake coincided.

"A branch came flying out and struck me on the head. Must have knocked me off Joker or else knocked me out so I fell off."

Emaline scooted closer and began a thorough search of his scalp. "Ahh, here it is," she said finding a lump and feeling him wince. "I can get some ice for it."

"No ice. Still trying to get warm."

"Another blanket?"

"Better idea," he said his voice soft with a husky note. His arm around her shoulders, he drew her near. "This works."

Goose bumps popped. She shivered. His scent of fresh air and cloves tickled her nose. She glanced up. "What were you doing out on a night like this?"

His eyes were closed but he wasn't asleep. There was an alertness about him. She waited. He took a deep breath and winced before replying.

His intense, leaf-green eyes scanned her face. "Coming to check on you."

His head dipped, his lips brushed hers. Emaline's toes curled. For the first time in a long time, she was exactly where she needed and wanted to be.

The End

Thank you for reading my story. I hope you enjoyed it as much as I enjoyed writing it! For more information about my books, please stop by my website, www.judithashleyromance.com .

New Release Mailing List:

You have just finished *Love & Magick – Mystical Stories of Romance*. Be the first to learn about future releases, any pre-release pricing or sales and special events by signing up for our mailing list at http://eepurl.com/NWglH.

We share our list with our publisher, Windtree Press.

For More Information about the Authors:
www.judithashleyromance.com
www.sarahraplee.com
www.dianamccollum.weebly.com

A Request from the Authors:

    If you enjoyed Love & Magick, please tell your friends and family and write a reader review on Amazon, Goodreads and/or Barnes and Noble. Goodreads reviews are important because Kobo and other places use them to help their readers find books they'll love.

ABOUT THE AUTHORS

Sarah Raplee

Sarah Raplee honed her love of adventure growing up on a tropical island. After high school, Sarah married her firefighter-cum-Coast Guardsman True Love, who is the inspiration for all her heroes.

Paranormal experiences run in Sarah's family. She's had her own brushes with telepathy, prophetic dreams, a poltergeist and ghosts, so naturally she writes paranormal romance stories.

Sarah writes paranormal romance stories that examine difficult issues with humor and insight. She writes to entertain, educate and uplift her readers. Plus, writing is more fun than most of the alternatives!

She's always up for trying something new, such as exploring urban undergrounds, hacking osprey chicks for the conservation department, or sailing into the Graveyard of the Pacific.

Sarah and her husband have settled near Portland, Oregon, with a cat who loves to fetch, a German Shorthair who doesn't and a feline phantom who ignores them both.

You can reach Sarah Raplee at www.SarahRaplee.com

Diana McCollum

Diana McCollum retired from her job working for MCM Construction, Inc. in Sacramento, California, and moved with her husband to the Pacific Northwest. They reside in Central Oregon in view of Mt. Bachelor. A lifetime avid reader, Diana loves creating worlds where anything is possible. She can't help but include an element of the paranormal in her stories, and always a happily-ever-after.

When she isn't reading or writing, she enjoys fishing, hiking, tole-painting and volunteering at the local hospital.

Diana is a member of Romance Writers of America, Rose City Romance Writers RWA, Sacramento Valley Rose RWA, Central Oregon Writers Guild, and Bend writer's lunch bunch!

This summer she will be releasing the second short story about one of the witches from the Costal Coven series. There are five witches to choose from Ella, Ivy, Darla, Mae or Rosabal. If you have a preference, let Diana know via the blog or Facebook.

Coming this fall, her first novella will be released, "The Rose Witch". It is a story set in the year twelve-eleven. This historical, paranormal has romance, murder and a mystery.

You can reach Diana McCollum at:
www.dianamccollum.weebly.com

Judith Ashley

In her real life Judith has been a part of sacred women's circles for over twenty years and knows first-hand how important spirituality is when dealing with life's challenges.

Her imagination has always been active taking her into the books she's read. Through books Judith has been a princess rescued from the tower by the handsome knight, a missionary in India, an explorer in the Amazon jungle, a priestess of the Goddess, and a nun. She has lived with people from all walks of life including different tribes of indigenous people on five continents in tents, wood cabins, igloos, castles, mansions, high-rise apartments, penthouses, dungeons, basements, and cottages.

Then one day in Judith's real life, the stories that make up The Sacred Women's Circle series flooded through her in daydreams, lucid dreams, and conversations so real at times she wondered about her own sanity. It was a compelling experience! An experience that was a catalyst to starting her journey to tell these stories and see them published.

Judith's Prayer for you:
Each and every day of your life may you find joy, may you see beauty, may you experience wonder, and may you know you are unconditionally loved.

You can reach Judith Ashley at
www.judithashleyromance.com

For more fiction and non-fiction books from the heart please visit **Windtree Press**.

http://WindtreePress.com

Windtree
Press